"WE HAVE BEEN COMPROMISED ON A MAJOR LEVEL, AND BY A PROFESSIONAL."

The President raised a hand to massage his temple. "As of this moment, our unknown thief owns a billion dollars' worth of American technology."

"Orders, sir?" Brognola asked grimly.

"Search the wreckage and find out who stole the Chameleon—or if nobody did. Maybe this is all a gigantic coincidence. They do happen sometimes."

"If it is not a coincidence, sir?"

The President leaned closer to the screen. "Then get the Chameleon back at any cost. Get it back, Hal. And if that proves impossible, then destroy the prototype."

"Sir?" Brognola said, putting a world of questions into the single word.

"You heard me. I'll eat that billion dollars, and another billion on top, if that's what it takes to keep the U.S. safe. The Chameleon is dangerous enough in our hands. But at least we have checks and balances in our government. However, under the control of a terrorist group, or rogue nation, we'd never even know what was happ̶e̶n̶i̶n̶g̶ ̶u̶n̶t̶i̶l̶ Manhattan, L.A. or even D.C. was blow̶n̶ ̶u̶p̶ ̶w̶i̶t̶h̶ millions dead."

Other titles in this series:

STONY MAN VIII	#41 SILENT INVADER
#9 STRIKEPOINT	#42 EDGE OF NIGHT
#10 SECRET ARSENAL	#43 ZERO HOUR
#11 TARGET AMERICA	#44 THIRST FOR POWER
#12 BLIND EAGLE	#45 STAR VENTURE
#13 WARHEAD	#46 HOSTILE INSTINCT
#14 DEADLY AGENT	#47 COMMAND FORCE
#15 BLOOD DEBT	#48 CONFLICT IMPERATIVE
#16 DEEP ALERT	#49 DRAGON FIRE
#17 VORTEX	#50 JUDGMENT IN BLOOD
#18 STINGER	#51 DOOMSDAY DIRECTIVE
#19 NUCLEAR NIGHTMARE	#52 TACTICAL RESPONSE
#20 TERMS OF SURVIVAL	#53 COUNTDOWN TO TERROR
#21 SATAN'S THRUST	#54 VECTOR THREE
#22 SUNFLASH	#55 EXTREME MEASURES
#23 THE PERISHING GAME	#56 STATE OF AGGRESSION
#24 BIRD OF PREY	#57 SKY KILLERS
#25 SKYLANCE	#58 CONDITION HOSTILE
#26 FLASHBACK	#59 PRELUDE TO WAR
#27 ASIAN STORM	#60 DEFENSIVE ACTION
#28 BLOOD STAR	#61 ROGUE STATE
#29 EYE OF THE RUBY	#62 DEEP RAMPAGE
#30 VIRTUAL PERIL	#63 FREEDOM WATCH
#31 NIGHT OF THE JAGUAR	#64 ROOTS OF TERROR
#32 LAW OF LAST RESORT	#65 THE THIRD PROTOCOL
#33 PUNITIVE MEASURES	#66 AXIS OF CONFLICT
#34 REPRISAL	#67 ECHOES OF WAR
#35 MESSAGE TO AMERICA	#68 OUTBREAK
#36 STRANGLEHOLD	#69 DAY OF DECISION
#37 TRIPLE STRIKE	#70 RAMROD INTERCEPT
#38 ENEMY WITHIN	#71 TERMS OF CONTROL
#39 BREACH OF TRUST	#72 ROLLING THUNDER
#40 BETRAYAL	#73 COLD OBJECTIVE

DON PENDLETON'S

STONY

AMERICA'S ULTRA-COVERT INTELLIGENCE AGENCY

MAN®

THE
CHAMELEON
FACTOR

A GOLD EAGLE BOOK FROM
WORLDWIDE®

TORONTO • NEW YORK • LONDON
AMSTERDAM • PARIS • SYDNEY • HAMBURG
STOCKHOLM • ATHENS • TOKYO • MILAN
MADRID • WARSAW • BUDAPEST • AUCKLAND

To all of the brave men and women
who do not go gently into that good night.

First edition December 2004

ISBN 0-373-61958-8

THE CHAMELEON FACTOR

Special thanks and acknowledgment to
Nick Pollotta for his contribution to this work.

Printed in U.S.A.

THE
CHAMELEON
FACTOR

DEDICATION

To all of the brave men and women, who do not go gently into that good night.

"It is the soldier, not the reporter, who has given us the freedom of the press. It is the soldier, not the poet, who has given us the freedom of speech. It is the soldier, not the campus organizer, who gives us the freedom to demonstrate. It is the soldier who salutes the flag, who serves beneath the flag and whose coffin is draped by the flag, who allows the protester to burn the flag."
—Sergeant Dennis O'Brien, USMC

"Freedom favors the strong and the wise. May God grant that we stay both."
—Carl Lyons, leader Able Team

PROLOGUE

Military Target Range, western Alaska

The guard went stiff as the knife blade slid into his head.

Mouthing a silent scream, the U.S. Army guard dropped his weapon as Professor Torge Johnson shoved the blade in deeper, exactly behind the right ear where there was a small opening into the brain, a slim passage known to many as Death's Doorway.

Gurgling, the guard began to claw at his side for the semiautomatic pistol in his shiny black holster. Frowning at the man's resilience, Johnson savagely twisted the blade to sever the brain stem. The guard went limp, his body turned off like a light switch, his rapidly dying brain only a few moments behind.

Easing the corpse to the grass, Johnson yanked out the bloody blade just as a tremendous explosion sounded in the distance. As the professor wiped the murder weapon clean on the guard's uniform, cheers sounded from the grandstand above.

Sliding the blade up his sleeve, Johnson checked the

cheap watch on his wrist. Good. Everything was precisely on schedule. Taking a cigarette pack from his jacket pocket, he carefully peeled off the back to expose a thin layer of adhesive. Reaching up, he just managed to press the pack to the bottom of the wooden seats of the grandstand overhead. As his hand came away, the pack stayed in place and there was an audible click of the electronic device arming itself.

Glancing briefly at the bright rectangle of light that marked the only door to the space under the grandstand, Johnson stepped over the cooling body of the guard and weaved his way through the maze of struts and support beams to reach the middle section. Attaching another cigarette pack there, he continued the process slowly, emptying every pocket of the deadly cargo until reaching the opposite side. Glancing back just once to check his lethal handiwork, the professor allowed himself a brief smile of satisfaction, then set his expression into neutral and stepped through the open doorway and into the bright sunlight.

Taking a real cigarette from the pocket of his old suit, Johnson lit it with a butane lighter and drew the smoke in deep, savoring the building excitement. Soon now, very soon.

Walking out of the bushes that blocked the entrance of the doorway, the man pulled up his fly and tried to look embarrassed as if he had been inappropriately relieving himself in the greenery.

An elderly U.S. congressman sitting at the edge of the grandstand happened to catch the gesture and chuckled in sympathy.

"Don't blame you." He grinned. "Hell of a day, isn't it, Professor?"

Johnson pressed a finger to his lips and hushed the plump politician. Although he looked exactly like the professor, his voice didn't match in the least. The impostor's heart was pounding as he fingered the second butane lighter in his pants pocket. The device was actually a pneumatic dart gun of considerable power, the flesh-colored darts coated with a neurotoxin that paralyzed instantly, and death came in foaming agony a few seconds later. Come on fool, go back to the show and enjoy the last few seconds of your life. The reaction of the darts closely resembled a heart attack, especially in older people, but the trick lighter carried only three darts: two for victims and the third for himself to prevent capture. The Americans disliked torture, but in his case their military intelligence and CIA would happily have made an exception. Being captured alive wasn't an option in his mission.

Touching two fingers to his brow in a mock salute, the congressman winked at the professor and turned back to the display on the target range below. Johnson relaxed slightly and exhaled a long stream of smoke. Good.

The grandstand, filled with politicians and high-ranking military personnel, was situated directly behind a tall barrier of wire mesh as protection from any stray shrapnel. Fifty feet below was a wide field that stretched to the distant ice-capped Baird Mountains. The target range was pitted with huge craters of assorted sizes from the wide variety of missiles used this day. The green tundra was beginning to resemble the surface of the moon, a few of them still smoking. Standing untouched in the midst of the destruction and desolation was a small concrete bunker with a slim radio antenna raised high enough to sway slightly in the warm breeze.

"Look there!" somebody cried, standing to point.

Johnson gave no reaction as two Harpoon-class missiles rose over the horizon, their fiery exhausts as bright as newborn stars. The politicians and generals in the review stand cheered at the sight. Unable to tear himself away for a moment, Johnson stayed to watch as the missiles rose sharply, then rotated about their long axis to sharply angle downward toward the ruined field. Flashing forward at nearly Mach speed, the Harpoons raced for the bunker and then incredibly went on by, their wake churning up clouds of dust and scorched earth.

The crowd roared its approval as the deadly missiles continued onward to slam into the pitted side of a hill a mile away.

"Son of a bitch, the bloody thing works!" a colonel shouted while applauding. "It really works! The missiles couldn't see the bunker!"

"So that's what this is, a radar jammer?" a senator grumbled with a scowl. "Big deal. We've had those for decades."

"Not like this!" a general stated proudly. "There's never been anything like this thing!"

"Well, we certainly spent enough on the damn program!" a senator yelled over the crowd noises.

Turning away from the jubilation, Johnson started for the gravel walk that led to the parking lot when he noticed a Marine guard looking in the bushes.

"Lose something, Corporal?" the professor asked in a friendly manner.

The Marine looked hard in return, and Johnson felt the hairs on the back of his neck start to rise. This man wasn't like the rest, he realized. Everything looked fine, but he felt that something was wrong. That combat-sense thing soldiers were always talking about. Part instinct, part training.

"Just routine," the corporal said, straightening the strap of the M-16 assault rifle slung over his shoulder.

But Johnson could see that the bolt had been worked on the weapon, making it ready for firing. No! There was no time for this! Seconds counted. He had to move fast or die with the rest!

"I know what you're looking for," Johnson whispered. "Come on, he's over here."

Leading the soldier to the open doorway below the grandstand, Johnson stopped at the entrance. "It's darker than shit in there. Got a flashlight?"

The soldier shook his head, and Johnson pulled out his cigarette lighter.

"This'll do," he said, and pressed the hidden stud.

There was a soft hiss. The soldier grabbed his throat as the tiny dart went deep into his flesh. Suddenly, his eyes began to roll about in panic as he stiffened, unable to move a finger.

Taking the Marine guard by the collar, Johnson half dragged the dying man back into the shadows under the grandstand and flicked his left wrist. A blade dropped out his sleeve, and he pulled back the Marine's throat to finish the job with a single clean stroke. The neurotoxin was fast, but not instantaneous like a blade. However, there was no time to enjoy the kill; the numbers were falling. He had to move fast.

Moving quickly away from the grandstand, Johnson proceeded along the gravel path until reaching a wooden kiosk. An armed guard raised a hand, but Johnson simply pointed at the photo ID on his lapel. The guard nodded and waved him by.

Past a wire fence woven with plastic strips to block the sight of the curious, Johnson moved onto the parking lot, forcing himself to not walk too fast. That would raise suspicion, and he might be detained for questioning, which would mean death in about ninety seconds from now. However, there were more armed guards lining the edge of the parking lot, U.S. Marines, Army and even some Navy intelligence. Incredibly expensive, Chameleon was a multiservice project. At opposite ends of the lot sat two Apache gunships, their blades at rest, but with a full crew inside, the wing pods bristling with weaponry, 35 mm minirocket pods and Sidewinder missiles in case of an aerial attack. The Alaskan test zone was a military hardsite, armed and armored to withstand any imaginable attack. Chameleon was all-important. The theoretical-danger team at the Pentagon had thought of everything, except him.

Reaching his car, Johnson pressed the fob on his key ring to unlock the door. The EM signal unlocked the door and also silently activated the packages hidden in the trunks of two other cars. Now the die was cast, and there was no turning back.

Starting the engine, Johnson pulled away slowly,

keeping a careful eye on his watch. Exactly at the proper moment, he pulled the cigarette lighter halfway out of the dashboard and then plunged it back in hard. There was a click as it locked into position.

Trying to hide a smile, Johnson wheeled for the exit, waving goodbye at the Marine guards standing alongside the entrance to the isolated valley.

DOWN IN THE TARGET range, inside the concrete bunker, the real Professor Torge Johnson lowered a pair of binoculars and turned. "Cut the field," he ordered briskly.

"Yes, sir," the technician said, and pivoting in a chair, he flipped several switches on a complex control board. On a stout wooden table in the middle of the bunker, a small gray box stopped humming and went still.

Squinting out the slit in the thick concrete wall, Johnson patiently watched as two more stars rose into the sky over the horizon and started coming his way.

Trying to control his excitement, the professor inhaled deeply and let it out slowly. This was it, the last test. These were two of the new breed of Delta Four missiles, equipped with the very cutting edge of radar guidance, satellite-assisted navigational system, and proximity warheads, all supported by an onboard computer more powerful than anything else in the world. Three waves of Delta Four missiles. If the Chameleon could stop those titans, there would be no question that his project was a complete and total success.

"Power up," Johnson instructed.

"Power is good for go, sir," the technician replied

crisply, checking some dials on the board. "We are on-line and ready."

"Good. Engage the field," the professor said calmly, raising the binoculars and adjusting the focus. Although a man of science, he did enjoy watching the missiles fly by stone blind, their wonderful radar eyes dead from the jamming field of his Chameleon.

"Ah, sir, I did, but nothing happened," the technician said, flipping the switches again. The man pressed buttons and twirled knobs with frantic speed, but the dials stayed inert. "And I'm getting no response from the override!"

Spinning, the professor clutched the binoculars to his chest as if for protection. "But the missiles are on the way!" he gasped, felling his belly tighten with fear. "Wait, use the backup unit!"

Lurching from his chair, the technician flipped open the top of a second gray box and reached inside, then froze.

"What in hell are you waiting for?" Johnson yelled, almost beside himself. "Turn on the Chameleon!"

"I can't," the pale technician said softly, turning to look at the professor. "The second unit isn't here. The box is empty."

Empty? The world seemed to reel at the word. The elderly professor went pale and clawed for the emergency radio clipped to his belt. "USS *Fairfax,* this is Johnson!" he yelled into the transponder. "Abort the missiles! Repeat, abort the missiles!"

But there was only the crackle of static in reply. Johnson checked the frequencies and tried again twice more before the answer punched his soul. Jammed. The radio

broadcast was being blocked from outside. But how...
who...?

"It's a trap!" Johnson threw the radio aside and charged
for the armored door. "We have to get out of here!"

A sudden light filled the slits of the bunker with hellish intensity.

"Too late!" the technician screamed, throwing an
arm before his face.

"MOTHER OF GOD," a general whispered, recoiling
slightly as the two Delta Four missiles slammed directly into the fortified bunker and violently detonated.
Broken slabs of concrete and steel beams blew into the
sky as the twin fireballs washed over the target range in
searing fury.

As a mushroom cloud of dark smoke rose into the
blue sky, it exposed a gaping hole in the ground. Muttering curses and prayers at the terrible sight, the crowd
of dignitaries remained in their seats, unable to move
from the horror unfolding below.

"We've got to help them!" a lieutenant cried out,
standing. Pushing his way through the stupefied throng,
the lieutenant tried to reach the stairs leading to the
ground. Then somebody grabbed his arm.

"Don't be a fool, man! They're beyond help," a general snapped. "The professor is already dead. Nobody
could have survived that first salvo."

Scowling darkly, the lieutenant yanked his arm free
and stared at the decimated target range once more. The
fortified bunker was reduced to a mere handful of
cracked pieces and rubble, ringing a blackened crater.

"Sorry, sir," the lieutenant muttered, clenching his fist in frustration. Then a motion in the sky caught his attention, and the Army officer turned to see the next set of Delta Four missiles lift over the horizon and angle over to start for the destroyed bunker.

Then they abruptly changed course and swung directly for the grandstand.

"Hello, give me the White House," a congresswoman said into a cell phone. "There's been a disaster at—"

"Incoming!" the lieutenant bellowed.

At the incredible sight, men and women both began to scream in terror, and the crowd became a mob fighting to reach the stairs. A handful of military personnel pulled out their dress side arms to empty the weapons at the approaching Delta Fours. If the subsonic lead had any effect on the ultrasonic missiles, it wasn't noticed as the Deltas smashed directly into the grandstand. Hundreds of bodies blew apart from the triphammer blasts, the rolling waves of chemical fire obliterating the grandstand, and the homing beacons glued to the underside of the wooden seats.

A death wave of splinters and boards blew across the parking lot, killing everybody in their path. A heartbeat later, the hidden charges in the car trunks went off, adding their thermite charges to the assorted destruction. Melting cars flipped into the air, gas tanks exploding like firecrackers. The startled pilots of the two Apaches had no time to react before the shock wave and shrapnel arrived, throwing the gunships sideways. Their blades snapped off as the helicopters tumbled over and over along the ground until they erupted into flames.

Shrieking insanely, the pilots burned alive in the wreckage until their cargo of rockets and missiles ignited.

WATCHING FROM the side of a road on a hilltop, the man disguised as Professor Johnson looked up from the destruction of the target range just as the last two Delta Four missiles climbed into view. As they reached azimuth, he looked to the east, down into a rugged arroyo filled with a small complex of buildings surrounded by lush greenery. Pulling out a fountain pen, Johnson aimed the disguised transmitter at the complex and pressed the side hard. The pen gave an answering beep as its signal was received and the next set of homing beacons was activated.

Climbing back into the car, Johnson saw the Delta Fours streak past, heading for the office buildings. Looking up, he saw the missiles angle about and streak past the test site to head for the office buildings. Done and done—the Chameleon now belonged to him.

Starting the engine, the man turned the car and headed south toward the Kobuk River. There was a speedboat waiting for him there, and after that...

Following a gentle curve in the road, the nameless spy glanced in the rearview mirror and saw writhing tongues of orange flame reach for the sky, then an outcropping blocked his view and they were gone. Now there was only open road stretching between him and freedom.

CHAPTER ONE

Virginia

With its rotors beating steadily, the U.S. Army Black Hawk helicopter moved through the crisp morning air. Reclining in the jump seat in the rear of the massive gunship, Hal Brognola looked out the port window and watched the lush Virginia countryside endlessly flow by, the dense forests melding into sprawling towns of tree-lined streets and green parks. A hundred years or so ago, all of this land was torn and bloody as brother fought brother in the Civil War.

"Did you know that more Americans died in the Civil War than in World War II?" the blacksuit pilot said over a shoulder.

Roused from his thoughts, Brognola turned from the window. "Yeah, I did. History buff?"

The pilot flashed a smile. "I am in the military, sir."

The big Fed waited for the pilot to also mention his skin color, but apparently it was not relevant to the discussion. White and blacks both died in the war, each fighting on both sides. Hell of a thing.

Harold Brognola wasn't a soldier in the traditional sense, but he had certainly seen more than his share of warfare. As a high-level official in the Justice Department, Brognola was one of the top cops in the nation, answerable only to the President. Chief of the ultracovert Sensitive Operations Group, based at Stony Man Farm in Virginia, Brognola was returning to Washington from a quick visit to the Farm, hidden in the depths of Shenandoah National Park. Recent defensive renovations included a newly installed antimissile system. Upgrades to weapons systems were ongoing, and every once in a while Brognola would drop by the Farm to check things out. Any excuse to escape the frenetic pace of Washington, D.C., was acceptable.

The pilot touched the side of his helmet. "Sir, I have an urgent call for you from Dover," he reported crisply.

Brognola frowned. Dover. As in the white cliffs of Dover. That was this month's code name for the White House.

"I'll take it back here."

"Yes, sir!"

The big Fed pulled a briefcase onto his lap when his cell phone chirped.

Deactivating the locking mechanism in the briefcase, Brognola lifted the lid and the compact computer inside automatically cycled on. Typing a few passwords onto the miniature keyboard, the big Fed watched as the plasma screen scrolled identification signatures and countersigns as the machine dutifully checked and then double-checked to confirm it was receiving an authenticity signal on a secure frequency.

Exercising patience, Brognola waited. The man was aware that the White House had its own private communication satellites, and that the President had access to several that nobody else even knew existed. But it never hurt to make sure.

The gibberish on the screen melted into a familiar face at a well-known desk.

"Good morning, sir," Brognola said.

"Good to see you, Hal," the President replied. "We have a situation."

"So I gathered, sir. Can it wait until I arrive? I'm already en route to D.C. ETA, twenty minutes."

"Sorry," the President said, frowning. "This cannot wait, and you have to turn back."

Return to the Farm? "This relay is secure, sir," Brognola reminded him respectfully.

"For now, yes."

The President reclined in his chair and lifted a sheet of paper edged with red stripes. Even as he held it, the paper turned brownish where his fingers rested. Brognola scowled at that. A level-ten report, for the President only. This was big.

"It's called Chameleon," the President said, putting the paper down, "a brand-new kind of jamming field that blocks or interferes with about ninety-five percent of all modulated electromagnetism."

Brognola raised an eyebrow at that but said nothing. Ninety-five percent? That would scramble cell phones, and even landline phones, and make radar absolutely dead. Doppler or focused radar, even proximity fuses on warheads might not work. It would be the ultimate stealth shield. Tanks, planes, hell, even aircraft carriers would become as close to invisible as modern science would allow. In the hands of terrorists, they could fly cargo planes of troops or bombs anywhere and America would never know until it was far too late.

Lifting a cup of coffee into view, the President took a sip and waited while Brognola worked out the details.

"How close are they to completion?" the big Fed demanded.

"This morning was the final test."

"And what went wrong?"

"Everything, my friend," the Man said honestly. "The missiles being fired from a U.S. Navy corvette in the bay first took out the control bunker, killing the inventor, a Professor Torge Johnson, and destroying every working prototype of the device."

Brognola bit back a curse.

The President leaned closer. "We received a piece of a phone call from Congresswoman Margaret Anders at the sight, then she went off the air. A recon flight from Fairbanks confirmed that the second wave of Delta Four missiles hit the grandstand, killing a couple of hundred people, mostly politicians and high-ranking soldiers."

"Could still just be an accident," Brognola said slowly, then he noticed the hard expression in the other man's face. "There's more."

"Unfortunately, yes. The third wave of Delta Four missiles went straight past the firing range and curved around a mountain to strike and destroy the laboratory where the Chameleon had been invented."

Brognola opened his mouth to say "Impossible," then

closed it with a snap. "So we have a traitor who planted homing beacons for the missiles."

"That is also the opinion of the Joint Chiefs."

"What was the breakage?" Brognola asked, frowning.

The President drummed his fingers on the desk. "Total. The plans are gone, the working prototypes are gone, everything is gone, and everybody involved with the project is dead."

"What about the off-site backup files?" Brognola demanded gruffly.

"Unknown," the President replied, hunching his shoulders. "Everybody who knew their location is now dead."

"Everybody?"

"Yes."

"Shit."

"Agreed. We have been compromised on a major level, and by a professional. As of this moment, our unknown thief owns a billion dollars' worth of American technology."

"And there's no way to re-create the work?"

"Over time, of course. Eight months, maybe a year. But by then…"

Brognola felt a gnawing sensation in his stomach. A year from now the world could be in total chaos, or worse, total warfare. Unlimited smuggling, unstoppable hijackers, it was a nightmare!

"What are the various agencies doing so far?"

"Nothing. This is a White Project. Level Ten personnel only. As far as the FBI and the media are concerned, there was a gas explosion at a military warehouse in Alaska."

"Orders, sir?" Brognola asked grimly.

"Search the wreckage, find out who stole the Chameleon, or if nobody did and this is all a gigantic coincidence. They do happen sometimes."

Yeah, right. "If it isn't a coincidence, sir?"

The President leaned closer to the screen. "Then get the Chameleon back at any cost. Get it back, Hal. And if that proves impossible, then destroy the prototype."

"Sir?"

"You heard me. I'll eat that billion dollars, and another billion on top, if that is what it takes to keep the U.S. safe. The Chameleon is dangerous enough in our hands. But at least we have checks and balances in our government. However, under the control of a terrorist group, or rogue nation, we'd never even know what was happening until Manhattan, L.A. or even D.C. was blown off the face of the map with millions dead."

"Understood, sir," Hal said in a strained voice, and then bluntly added, "What a shitstorm!"

The President gave a strained smile. "You took the words right out of my mouth, my friend."

A light flashed on the briefcase computer.

"You should have the full files and aerial reconnaissance photos by now," the President announced, doing something off-screen.

"Just arrived, sir. Standard decoding?"

"Yes. Move fast on this one, Hal. We're completely in the dark so far, and that light at the end of the tunnel isn't daylight, but a goddamn express train coming down our throats."

With a swirl of colors, the link was broken and the screen returned to its neutral silver sheen.

Closing the briefcase, Brognola cupped a hand to his mouth and loudly shouted, "Hey, pilot!"

In the wide cockpit, the blacksuit glanced over a shoulder. "Yes, sir!"

"Turn around. We're going back."

The man arched an eyebrow in surprise, but said nothing and tilted the stick in his grip. The pitch of the blades overhead changed, and the Black Hawk started to swing around in the sky.

As the sun reappeared on the other side of the gunship, Brognola opened his briefcase once more and started to access a secret satellite.

Within a few minutes, the screen cleared to show a blond-haired woman leaning forward on a desk. She was dressed in a simple blue workshirt, with no jewelry.

"Forget your wallet, Hal?" asked Barbara Price, mission controller at Stony Man Farm.

"Wish I had. Call them back," Brognola ordered. "Both teams. Call everybody back. We've got trouble."

CHAPTER TWO

Cassatt Federal Penitentiary, South Carolina

Soft and low, the mournful call of a freight train moved through the night as armed guards in the high watchtowers closely scrutinized the arrival of an armored bus at the front gate of the Cassatt Federal Penitentiary.

The first line of guards checked the driver's ID and did an EM scan of the vehicle, then finally passed it through the outer, thirty-foot-tall fence. Once the bus was trapped between the first and second fences, more guards arrived with dogs to sniff for explosives or narcotics before the transport rolled through the inner, electric fence and finally onto a featureless parking lot. There were no concrete bumpers or ornamental bushes for anyone to take cover behind. Just a flat expanse of bare asphalt studded with tiny reflecting squares set into the tar and gravel, range finders to assist the sharpshooters in the watchtowers.

In an ocean of bright lights, there came the sound of pumping hydraulic, and the huge ferruled doors on the

Cassatt Federal Penitentiary began to ponderously cycle open.

With the close of Alcatraz so many years ago, there had been an urgent need for new prisons to hold the worst of the worst, the mad-dog killers and terrorists that the courts had condemned to death. With nothing to lose, the prisoners would use any opportunity to escape, and since a person could be executed only once, taking another human life meant less than nothing to the cold-blooded psychopaths. Hence the creation of the Bureau of Prisons' supermax facilities.

Cassatt had been the first supermaximum prison created in the country, level six, absolute security. Yet there had proved to be men that even this ultralockdown couldn't contain, and so there was forged the prison within a prison, the violent-control ward. Boxcar-style doors permitted no communication to other prisoners, video surveillance was twenty-four hours and there were no windows. Each prisoner had his own private cell. There was no mixing with other prisoners for his entire stay. Guards in the lotus-style control room could electronically open the cell door, and the unescorted prisoner would walk down empty corridors for his shower three times a week. There was no human contact with these violent repeat offenders. Ever.

Yet the ingenuity of the criminals was incredible. Staples were attached to the tips of Q-Tips and blown through tubes made of rolled paper to strike passing guards. Dozens of makeshift weapons were created out of seemingly innocuous items, and more than one guard lost an eye, or worse, to the ingenious prisoners until full-coverage body armor and goggles became standard dress uniform.

Cassatt supermax, and its fellow penitentiaries, weren't ICCs, correctional institutes trying to correct the career of the professional criminal. The supermax was the end of the line, the edge of the world, and damn few who ever went in ever came out again, except in a black body bag.

Security was tighter here to keep the prisoners in than it was at Cheyenne Mountain, where the purpose was to keep invading enemy armies out. The land beyond the perimeter of the second fence was barren and dead, a former uranium milling dumpsite that the EPA was still trying to clean after forty years. There was no grass to hide in, no weeds in the muddy creek, no trees whose branches could be used as a club. Additional sentry posts stood between the deadlands around the penitentiary and the city of Cassatt, forcing any escapee into the slag heaps of the toxic waste dump. A hundred men had tried to escape from Cassatt supermax over the years. Ten made it to the gate alive.

Six got over the first fence, and two got over the second fence only to be blown apart by the radio-controlled land mines.

The infamous Ossing of New York and Leavenworth of Kansas were considered luxurious country clubs compared to Cassatt supermax. But there were even more secure facilities now: Pelican, Logan and the infamous Florence in Colorado. Many of the inmates were insane, but no asylum ever built could hold the killers, and the violent-control ward of a supermax was the only chance of containing these enemies of civilization.

Many people believed it would be much more humane to simply kill the prisoners than send them to the steel-caged hell of Cassatt. Every prisoner and guard of the supermax penitentiary agreed, except for four special inmates.

As the final lock on the armored front gate was released with a hydraulic hiss, additional lights glowed into blinding brilliance, illuminating the parking lot and the grounds beyond for more than a mile. On the stone walls, searchlights swept the sky looking for small planes or helicopters. It was unknown who would want these four men free, but the list of people who wanted them dead at any cost was a mile long. Although they would be executed some day by the state, that wasn't the right of any individual, and as much as they hated the idea the Cassatt guards were ready to die in order to protect the criminals from any vigilante justice, no more how much it was deserved.

Ten guards in full combat gear stepped from the armored bus and waited while twenty men in full riot gear walked four prisoners through the doorway of the penitentiary. The inmates were dressed in bright orange prison jumpsuits, heavy shackles on their legs, handcuffs on their wrists, and a black box encased their hands and forearms to forestall any attempt to pick the lock on the cuffs. The cadre of guards was fully armed, and carried military-grade stun guns and bulletproof plastic shields studded with electric probes. One touch and a bull gorilla would drop unconscious from the terrible pain.

"Hold it right there," an amplified voice called from

above, and everybody waited a few moments for the wall guards to decide that the area was safe for everybody to continue.

"Okay, move along," the voice commanded.

Circling widely past the four men, a guard lifted his face mask and passed over a sheaf of papers to the colonel from the waiting bus. Blue smoke puffed from the double tailpipes under the chassis and the two additional exhaust vents on the roof, every opening covered with a steel grille to prevent the insertion of an item to clog the exhaust and choke the engine. The windows were double sheets of Plexiglas separated by a lattice of steel bars, and the only door was three inches thick.

"Here are their papers," the lieutenant said, offering a file folder. "Transport orders for prisoners 49724, 97841 and 66782."

The USP colonel holding a clipboard scowled at the four men standing quietly in the evening chill. The cool night wind was ruffling the thin cloth of their loose jumpsuits. In the clear overhead lights, the four were haggard and thin faced. Heavy scarring marred their faces from constant fighting in the yard of their previous prison. Their long hair was slicked down, their pointy beards oily with liquid soap. The bright lights seemed to be bothering their eyes, but then they may not have seen sunlight for months.

Then one of them looked the colonel in the face and he felt a chill run down his spine. If the rumors were even half-true, these guys were actually too dangerous to let loose in the general population of even a level-five-security penitentiary. The transfer papers on his clipboard said that in their previous place of incarceration they had beaten another prisoner to death and eaten parts of the corpse before the guards could get into their cell. They had jimmied the lock somehow to give them enough time. Some bleeding-heart liberal lawyers wanted them sent to an insane asylum for treatment, which was exactly what they'd been hoping for. But these men would blow out of any hospital in about an hour, leaving a trail of dead doctors and nurses behind. Thank God somebody in the Justice Department was paying attention for once and was moving these psychopaths to the new supermax in Florence, Colorado, the brand-new level-seven facility. A prisoner escaping from that underground facility would face a fifty-mile trek through scored earth and bare rock with helicopter gunships on him every step of the way. It was as close to being thrown off the planet as anybody would ever get. The new Devil's Island, and these bastards would be the reigning devils once they arrived.

"So this is them, huh?" he said in disdain. "So this is the last remaining members of the terrible Black Vipers. Big deal."

The Cassatt lieutenant stared at the shivering men in frank hatred. "Don't be fooled, pal. Give them an inch and you die. It's that fucking simple. You know that movie about the cannibal guy who escapes wearing a guard's face as a mask?"

"Sure. Good flick."

He gave a thumb jerk. "It was based on these men."

"Yeah? Well, Manson looked tougher," the colonel muttered, checking over the paperwork.

Suddenly the first prisoner started to slump to the ground, and the lieutenant jumped away just in time as the fourth prisoner swung his boxed hands at the guard's head. The steel trap passed by so close he felt the breeze of its passage and knew that he missed having his skull crushed by a fraction of a second. Christ, they were fast!

Without pause, the guards converged on the men with the stun shields and rib-spreader batons, the electric sparks crackling over the terrorists as they were driven to the ground into submission. Nobody made any move to stop the beating.

"Been wanting to do that for quite a while," a guard snarled, panting from the exertion.

A man alongside hawked juicily and then spit on the sprawled bodies. "Damn Feds should have blown their heads off when they were captured. Keeping these ass-holes alive is like sticking your dick in a working blender."

"The chair ain't good enough for them," another snarled. "I got a brother in the Navy. Ya know how many of our guys these bastards aced with their trick bombs?"

"Don't let the warden hear you say that," another warned, glancing at the wall guards hidden behind their bright lights and stone walls. "Or you're out on your ass. This state doesn't execute prisoners anymore. It's not cost effective."

"Cost effective? And what about justice?"

The smaller man shrugged. "So move to Texas."

"Check the shackles before removing the black boxes," the lieutenant directed.

"And you," he added to the colonel, "constantly keep your weapons on these prisoners. If they make another move, kill them."

Loosening the flap covering his holstered 10 mm Falcon, the colonel nodded.

Weakened by the stun shields, the prisoners didn't make a second try for freedom and submitted meekly to being herded onto the armored transport and chained in place. This fooled nobody, and the bus guards were dripping sweat from the tension until the four were shackled into different chairs of bare steel bolted and welded directly to the armored floor of the transport vehicle.

"Good luck," the lieutenant said as the armored door closed.

The colonel flipped the prison guard a salute as the armored door cycled shut and locked tight.

"And good riddance," another prison guard muttered softly, removing his protective helmet. "I hope the bus crashes and the prisoners burn alive."

"Wishful thinking," the lieutenant said coldly. "Damn the politicians and lawyers. Men like that should just be hung. Cost effective or not, it sure as hell makes it hard for them to kill again once their neck is stretched."

"Amen to that, chief," another man agreed.

"I wonder why the government kept them alive," another muttered. "It's not like they could be used for anything."

Throwing back his head, the lieutenant laughed for the first time in days. "And who the hell would have enough balls to try and use the goddamn Black Vipers for anything?"

"Come on," a corporal said on a sigh, running a gloved across his sweaty face. "Let's get out of this gear and go have a beer."

Turning to face the prison, the guards tested their equipment once more to make sure everything was in proper working condition, then marched back into the sterilized confines of Cassatt Federal Penitentiary. High on the walls overhead, the unseen guards watched their every move purely out of habit. The rifle marksmen watched everything and trusted nobody. That was the job, and they were damn good at it.

OVER TWO MILES away, far outside the circle of light around the supermax facility, three men with Starlite scopes stood alongside a battered gray SUV, the license plates obscured with mud permanently glued into place.

In unison, Able Team tracked the progress of the USP transport along Highway 37 as it headed due south away from the supermax facility. The man in front was blond, with a crew cut and ice-blue eyes. The next was stocky with wavy salt-and-pepper hair, and the third had dark brown hair and a full mustache. Swaying slightly in the evening breeze so that they wouldn't stand out from the rustling forest, all three of the men were wearing camouflage-colored jumpsuits designed for urban warfare.

"Stony One to Stone Two," Carl "Ironman" Lyons said into his throat mike, Starlite still pressed to his face. "We are in position. Copy?"

"Roger that, Stony One," a gruff voice replied in the earphone. "We rendezvous at Point Charlie in one hour. Over."

"Ten-four," Lyons replied. "See you there. Over and out."

"Don't be late," Rosario "The Politician" Blancanales said in the background.

Climbing into the SUV, Hermann "Gadgets" Schwarz grimly added, "If they are, then we're dead, chum."

AFTER AN HOUR of driving, the countryside of South Carolina began to change from gray grassland into a plush forest of tall trees and countless small brooks. Shackled to their metal seats, the four members of the Black Vipers sneered at the beauty of nature as if they preferred the concrete corridors of the federal jail.

Glancing about to see if anybody was watching, the largest and most heavily muscled of the Vipers jerked hard on the chain holding his wrists to the bolt in the floor, and instantly a gas vent hidden in the ceiling sprayed him with Mace. The terrorist flopped in his seat fighting for breath, his eyes and tongue almost popping from his flushed face.

"That's warning number one," the colonel said from the front of the bus, a wall of thick bars separating the two sections of the vehicle. "Warning number two is a lot worse. So behave, convict, or else."

"I am a political prisoner of the American government," the tallest member of the four said. "Once more I beg for asylum from the overlords of Washington."

"Oh, shut up," a younger guard said, jacking the slide of the sleek black Neostead shotgun.

Designed by the new democratic government of South Africa, the high-tech alleysweeper had two tubular magazines and could be switched from one to the other by the flick of a selector switch. For this journey, the guard had the first magazine filled with stun bags, the other mag filled with fléchette rounds that could reduce a man into hamburger in under a heartbeat.

The terrorist opened his mouth to speak again, then decided against it and leaned back in his hard chair, his thoughts seething with revenge.

"What the hell?" the guard riding alongside the driver said with a puzzled expression. Frantically, he began to work the controls of the built-in radio switching frequencies.

"Something's wrong," he said swiftly over a shoulder. "We've lost contact with USP HQ, and every channel is filled with hash."

"Jamming?" the colonel demanded, releasing the flap over his side arm. The ivory handle of a Colt .45 pistol was revealed, a line of deep gouges in the grip appearing to be hand-carved notches.

The guard in the front passenger seat looked up with a pale face. "Confirmed, I can't get a bounce signal off a repeater tower. The airwaves are being jammed," he replied succinctly. "But whether or not it's for us, or some natural phenomenon, I have no idea."

The guards were silent as the armored bus jounced slightly onto a picturesque stone bridge.

"Sir, if this is an escape attempt..." the younger guard started to say, flicking the switch to the second magazine of fléchette rounds.

"Don't kill them yet, Corporal," the colonel said, pulling the Colt and jacking the slide.

Going to the front windshield, he looked out into the starry night. "Maybe this is just another weird solar storm like last year that knocked out all of the satellites for a day. Could be anything, or nothing. I'm not going to ace these men just because we're not sure."

In tense silence, the armored bus rolled off the bridge and onto the paved roadway once more. A split second later the night was split apart by a violent thunderclap. Fiery light blossomed from behind the transport, and rocks began pounding the bus in a deafening rain of debris.

"Son of a bitch!" the driver cried as the flaming shrapnel washed over the armored transport, breaking out the rear windows. "The bridge is gone! Completely gone!"

"That bomb missed us by a heartbeat," the colonel growled. "Get us the hell out of here, man!"

The driver slammed onto the gas, and the big Detroit engine roared with power for only a single moment. Then the vehicle crashed hard, to a halt the front windows exploding out of the frame. Every loose item went flying, the prisoners were thrown forward in their seats, setting off more Mace, and the guards tumbled to the floor in a loose pile of bodies.

It took a few minutes for the pinned driver to regain his composure and pull a knife from his belt to stab the airbag pinning him tightly into place. As the metallic cushion deflated, the USP guard gasped at the sight of a smashed pile of fallen trees blocking the forest road, the trunks painted black to render the barricade invisible. Damn! The bridge had to have been blown just to make them go faster and slam hard enough into the barrier and cripple the bus. That was a trap!

There was nothing moving in the darkness outside the broken windows, but the driver knew trouble was coming, and soon. Frantically, he tried to get the engine to turn over and only got a clicking sound. The battery wires had to have ripped loose in the crash. Shit! Pulling an M-16 assault rifle from a boot alongside his seat, the driver pulled the arming bolt and started over the jumbled forms of the groaning guards sprawled on the floor to shoot the prisoners when he suddenly felt very warm and relaxed.

As his thoughts became muddy, it became difficult to stand and he slumped to the floor, losing his weapon. Fighting to stay conscious, the driver vaguely understood this was a gas attack. Summoning his last vestige of strength, the USP guard tried to slap the emergency alarm button on the dashboard that would send off a flare and radio signal, plus detonate a series of explosive bolts to lock down the entire transport, rendering it impossible for anybody to enter without using a cutting torch. The Black Vipers couldn't be set free! The feeling had left most of his body and the man could only mentally order his arm to hit the switch. But the warm embrace of the gas filled his universe and everything went pleasantly dark.

SLUGGISHLY, THE FOUR members of the Black Vipers came awake in a field of damp grass, the moonlight overhead bathing them in silvery light.

"By God!" one of the terrorists exclaimed, lifting both hands to stare in wonder at his bare wrists. The handcuffs were gone.

"We are free," the giant rumbled, holding his head. "How is this possible?"

The skinny leader rose and raised his arms high, savoring the sensation of unfettered movement.

"I do not care, my brothers," he said in Arabic, just in case there were listeners in the woods. Years of confinement with guards always monitoring had made the men paranoid, even worse than when they first went into prison. "Let us take this gift and leave."

"But which way?" the third man said in a nasal whine, his strength returning with every breath.

He turned about in every direction, and there was nothing in sight but trees. Maybe they had been thrown from the crash into the Cassatt Forest Preserve? But if so, what had happened to their shackles and cuffs? The terrorist sensed danger of some kind but couldn't readily identify what it was. His first impulse was to stay exactly where he stood and let the police capture him again. Then his anger flared at the very idea that the Americans had beaten fear into his soul and sapped the strength from his will.

Just then, a fiery explosion rose in the distance, illuminating the nighttime.

"This way." The leader pointed and took off in the opposite direction at a stumbling run.

The grassy field was empty and smooth, but it took the men a few moments to get past the wall of their cell. Eight feet was as far as any of them had walked without chains for years since their incarceration. That ninth step felt like bursting out of a bubble of glue. Suddenly, the killers were laughing as they ran, put-

ting on speed and tearing off the hated prison jumpsuits. Naked, they raced through the night. Somewhere
they would find new clothing to wear. A laundry line,
a closed store or from the bodies of murdered
strangers.

"The Americans must not capture us again, my brothers," the leader panted, leaping over a shallow ravine.
"They will slay us on sight and claim we fought back."

In silent agreement, the others dashed into the forest
dodging trees and running for their very lives. None of
them spoke or stopped for miles before reaching a small
creek. The smell of the fresh, clean water was overpowering, and the parched men dropped to their bellies to
lap at the creek like thirsty animals.

"The Yankees shall pay for our years of imprison-
ment," the thin man growled, rising to his knees after a
while. "No, their families shall pay. I have been design-
ing new bombs in my mind. Ones perfect for children.
There shall be a slaughter like America has never seen."

"Revenge shall be ours!" the third cried, wiping the
water from his mouth with a hairy forearm. "By the
blood of the prophet, this I do swear. America will pay
for its crimes against us in the red blood of its children!"

"Not this time, freak," a voice of stone said from the
darkness.

The Black Vipers leaped to their feet as three armed
men stepped out of the nearby shadows. Incredibly, the
newcomers weren't prison guards or police officers, but
soldiers, their camouflaged jumpsuits covered with
weapons.

"What is this, some sort of trick?" the leader demanded, lifting a rock from the mud of the creek. "By the blood of God!"

"God. You do everything for God, right? You ever actually read the Koran, asshole?" Lyons demanded, leveling an Atchisson assault shotgun. "It's a book of peace, not war."

The big prisoner snarled, lifting a piece of fallen fence post from the creek. The wood was old, a poor weapon, but better than nothing.

"Want a weapon? Try these instead," Schwarz said, tossing a canvas sack onto the ground. The bag landed with a heavy metallic rattle.

"That's filled with guns," Blancanales stated in a hard voice. "More than enough to fight your way to freedom. Money, too. Small, nonsequential, unmarked bills. Clothing and passports. Food, medicine, the works."

The terrorists stood there in the chilly night, looking at the freedom given to them in a canvas sack.

"Why would you do this?" the leader asked suspiciously. "Do you support our holy cause? Who are you?"

"Your cause is full of holes, not holy," Lyons said, flicking the safety on the Atchisson and tossing it aside. "As to who we are, we're your sworn enemies and want nothing more than to see you bastards buried in the ground."

The terrorists stood in confusion, the gift and the words together not making any sense.

Blancanales clicked the safety on the M-16/M-203 assault rifle combo he carried and lowered his own weapon. "We knew that there were two more members of your hate group still running around loose in the world. So we arranged for your transfer in the hope they would try to come to your rescue."

"And they did," Schwarz muttered, his hands holding a 9 mm Beretta pistol.

"So they are now captives of the American secret police?" the leader snarled hatefully.

Softly in the distance came the chatter of several MP-5 submachine guns all firing in unison.

"Not anymore," Lyons stated without emotion. "You have friends, and so do we. But I'm betting that our guys just sent yours to hell."

Fighting a shiver from the cool breeze, the leader of the Black Vipers muttered something in Arabic to the others.

"Not quite," Blancanales answered in English. The former Black Beret only knew a few words of Arabic, but as a master of psychological warfare he could guess what the other man had said. "If we wanted you dead, we would have slit your throats when you were unconscious instead of taking off your shackles. But we're offering something you never gave any of your victims. A fighting chance for life."

The terrorists stood in silence, thinking hard, their scared bodies poised for flight, but uncertain.

"Surrender and go back to prison," Schwarz said, using a thumb to click on the safety and tossing away his Beretta. "Or go for the guns. Your choice."

Flexing his hands, Lyons lowered into a combat crouch. "But you'll have to get past us first to reach the guns."

"With snipers hidden in the bushes?" The leader laughed, glancing around nervously. Only shrubbery and more trees were in sight. "Why should we give you an excuse to gun us down?"

"You did that already," Lyons said in a guttural voice. "When you bombed that civilian hospital. Now choose, or we choose for you."

"And even if there were snipers," Blancanales stated in harsh logic, "do you have a better offer?"

The leader waved that aside and said something softly to the other members. "We want nothing of this charade," he said in resignation. "We surrender." Then he whipped his arm around and threw the stone he had been palming while the others charged in a group.

Expecting the betrayal, Lyons ducked out of the way of the rock, then launched a side kick into the belly of the first terrorist, the force of the blow driving the man to his knees. But from there, he lunged forward and snapped his teeth at Lyons's groin. The Able Team leader raised his thigh just in time and drove a rock-hard fist into the other man's exposed neck. The bones snapped with an audible crunch, and the terrorist fell to the ground twitching into death.

Two of the Black Vipers converged on Blancanales, while the leader went for Schwarz. Although an expert with explosives and electronic surveillance, the former U.S. Army soldier had done more than his fair share of unarmed combat and simply stood motionless until the very last second. Then Schwarz twisted his fingers together in an odd way and thrust both hands into the face of the terrorist. Screaming in pain, the man froze motionless to claw at his ruined eyes.

Unexpectedly, the terrorist lashed out a kick, and

Schwarz just swayed out of the way in time to avoid having his throat crushed. Darting forward, he grabbed the snarling man's neck in a complex hold and spun him fast. Still fighting to get free, the prisoner contorted in an odd angle, there was a crack and the leader of the Black Vipers slumped lifeless into the creek with a loud splash.

Moving fast, Blancanales ducked under the hands of the first terrorist and kicked the second in the knee. The joint broke and the man dropped, only to throw dirt into his adversary's face. Blinded for a second, he backed away quickly and felt the oversize hands of the giant terrorist close around his neck. His air was instantly cut off, and Blancanales forced himself to go calm, which used less oxygen, and fingered the other man's arms until sightlessly finding the nerve complex in the wrist. Savagely, he buried his thumbnails into the tattoo-covered skin at just the right angle. The giant screamed in pain and let him go.

Instantly, Blancanales launched into a karate kata, a set sequence of movements normally used to fight your way out of a large crowd of opponents but also served well if you were blind. His hands and legs flashing, he hit nothing again and again, simply protecting himself while his watery eyes slowly cleared away the dirt.

When at last he could see, the Able Team commando dropped into a defense posture just as Schwarz smashed the temple of the small terrorist with a back-kick and Lyons released the giant from a bear hug, blood dribbling from the slack mouth of the last member of the dreaded Black Vipers as the killer started on his journey into hell.

Their chests heaving, Able Team stood for a moment amid the dead prisoners, pulling in the cool air. Often they had terminated the mad-dog killers of society, but usually it was at gunpoint and rarely was justice so satisfying.

"I swore to that dying Marine we would get these scumbags," Lyons said softly, "face-to-face. It took a long time, but the bill has finally been paid in full."

"Those two were supposed to be mine," Blancanales said, wiping his cheeks dry with the back of a hand.

"Aw, but you were having so much fun punching the empty air," Schwarz said with a weak grin, rubbing his oddly lumpy shoulder. "We didn't want to disturb you."

"I'm not a ninja like John Trent," Blancanales replied, linking as his vision cleared. "But I make do. Hey, what's wrong with your arm?"

"Dunno. Hurts like a bastard, but I don't think it's broken."

Going around a corpse, Lyons walked over to the electronics expert and touched the shoulder. Schwarz winced slightly.

"It's dislocated," Lyons said as a warning.

Schwarz nodded, knowing what was coming.

Blancanales took his friend's arm by the wrist, then placed the sole of his foot in the other man's armpit.

"On the count of three," Blancanales said, gently putting some tension on the arm.

Bracing his legs against the ground, Lyons held Schwarz tight by the waist, and instantly their teammate yanked hard on the arm, twisting it just slightly along the radius. Schwarz went white as the arm snapped back into the socket.

"Wh-hat th-the hell happened to three, you bastard?" he demanded, inhaling sharply though his nose.

They both released the man.

Blancanales gestured in apology. "I didn't want you tensing up," he explained. "That only makes the pain worse."

"Worse?" Schwarz gasped, gently massaging his throbbing shoulder. "How is that possible?"

"Trust me," Lyons said in a serious manner. "I've been there. It can get worse."

"Damn."

Just then a woodlark called from the darkness. Lyons spun about at the noise, and waited for it to come again before answering. A few seconds later, Phoenix Force strode into view from the midnight shadows beneath the thick cover of oak trees.

"The prison guards okay?" Lyons asked.

"Bruised, but alive," David McCarter said, easing the tension on his Barnett military crossbow. In the hands of the former British SAS officer, the silent-kill weapon struck like divine justice, leaving only cooling corpses who left this world with a puzzled expression of how it had happened to them.

"Although they'll have a hell of a headache when they finally wake up," the Briton added, slinging the bow over a shoulder. "Without the antidote you gave the Black Vipers, that bleeding sleep gas has nasty side effects."

"But it is fast," Rafael Encizo stated, the compact Starlite goggles distorting his face as he scanned the night for any danger, or worse, any witnesses. "And that's what counted tonight." Heavily muscled, the soldier moved with catlike reflexes that spoke of endless years of combat in the field.

"We took a big chance on this," Hawkins said, nudging one of the dead men. "Not that I disagree, but it was a hell of a chance. I'm surprised that Brognola gave this mission an okay. Pleased, but surprised."

His actual name was Thomas Jefferson Hawkins, but everybody who saw him in combat quickly accepted the nickname of T.J. Trained by the elite Delta Force, Hawkins was relentless and brutal to the enemies of freedom.

Lyons rubbed a palm across his blood-smeared cheek. "Hal understands that there are some crimes," he said softly, "for which a simple bullet in the head is not enough payment. Now the books are balanced."

"Starting to sound more and more like Bolan all the time," Gary Manning said, canting his silenced MP-5 submachine gun against his hip.

"Thanks for the compliment," Lyons growled, almost smiling.

"Incoming call," Calvin James said, touching the radio receiver in his ear. Tall and lean, the night-camouflage paint only took the reflective quality off the man's dark skin.

"We've been recalled," he stated, looking at the others. "Barbara wants us to report in person ASAP."

"The SUV is this way," Lyons said, starting into the bushes. If the farm was calling during a mission, something serious was brewing.

CHAPTER THREE

Nome, Alaska

Death stalked the crowd.

A calm voice called an announcement over the PA system of the airport. Excited children ran ahead of their weary parents. An old couple walked stiffly along the carpeted corridor, holding hands and talking softly. An anxious young man clutched a bouquet of flowers and watched each arriving plane with painfully obvious impatience.

As he stood in line at the airport scanner, the weight of the gun felt heavy inside the blouse of the disguised man. His wig itched, and his lower back ached from the weight strapped to his belly, along with the padded bra and the—

"Next, please!" the guard called out.

His disguise of Professor Johnson long ago removed, Davis Harrison, aka the Chameleon, waddled forward from the yellow line on the floor and placed his lady's handbag on the conveyor belt, then paused and removed a plain gold wedding ring from his pinkie and put it in a little plastic tray. His long nails were manicured and freshly painted, his sneakers worn at the heels and his white support stockings had a small run artistically placed near the ankle, where most runs occurred in stockings. He knew his disguise was perfect, but there was still a small knot of tension in his stomach. After 9/11, the Americans had become exceptionally good at uncovering smugglers—whether it was drugs, money or weapons. He was carrying all three. Plus his technological namesake, the prototype jamming unit.

Armed guards stood in the far corners of the airport, loaded M-16 assault rifles cradled in their arms, hard eyes sweeping the crowds steadily. Briefly, Harrison had a flashback to the armed guards walking the elevated catwalks of the Berlin airport before the Wall came down. Hard times to make a living.

However, as the Transportation Security Administration guards glanced his way, they shifted their attention away from his face to the bulging belly, and those with wedding rings smiled. Posing as a pregnant woman was a favorite ruse of smugglers, but this one seemed to be okay. She was wearing support stockings and her ankles were slightly swollen, her wedding ring didn't fit the correct finger anymore from the water weight gain, her ears were pierced, but she wasn't wearing earrings, there was no scarf to cover an Adam's apple, no razor burn on the cheeks and so on. Satisfied for the moment, their attention moved to more likely suspects.

An Inuit woman in a neatly pressed TSA uniform at the scanner held up a restraining hand as Harrison waddled toward the scanner.

"Your glasses, ma'am," she said, holding out a hand.

"Sorry, I forget they were there," Harrison said as he passed over the glasses.

The guard nodded in sympathy and waved him on.

Holding his bulging stomach protectively, he squeezed through the scanner and it remained silent. It worked! Elation filled the man, but he kept his expression weary. He was pregnant now, and it was exhausting work. Remember that, fool!

Once on the other side, the now smiling guard returned his glasses, ring and handbag, and waved for the next passenger.

Awkwardly shuffling away, Harrison paused for a moment to glance into a convenient wall mirror as he put on the ring and glasses, and fixed his hair. Then he pretended to burp and frantically covered his mouth in embarrassment.

ON THE OTHER SIDE of the mirror, the security guards drinking coffee watched with dull interest as the pregnant woman primped for a moment. A lot of smugglers were caught by the mirror trick. They remained icy cool at the scanner, then smirked in satisfaction at their cleverness in the reflection in the "conveniently placed" mirror.

"Poor thing," a soldier said. "When my sister was preggers with her twins, she belched like a sailor day and night."

Another man laughed. "Well, that explains a lot about you."

"Stuff it," the first guard snarled, the threat softened by a half smile. "Now, your sister, whew! Let me tell you…"

WADDLING AWAY, Harrison joined the short line heading to the China Air counter. His ticket was for New Delhi, a city closely watched for smuggling things out, but not well monitored for smuggling things into. The nation was poor. Why would anybody smuggle something into India? Harrison kept his face pensive, but smiled inside his mind. Why indeed?

As the line to board the plane moved slowly forward, he started shifting his weight from foot to foot, and began breathing a little heavily.

An alert flight attendant noticed the action and briskly walked over.

"Come on, dear," she said, smiling. "Let's get you on board where you can use the rest room." Her nametag said Gwenneth, and the tall beauty had deep green eyes, a sure sign of not being of pure Chinese descent.

"Thank you," Harrison whispered in a little voice. "I didn't want to seem pushy or anything, but, well, you know…"

"My first baby seemed to love kicking my bladder," the woman said in a friendly manner. "I understand. It's okay, come with me, please."

A few of the younger men scowled as the pair moved past the line and onto the plane. But all of the adults merely smiled as they figured out the reasoning behind the courtesy, and remembered similar incidents from their own lives.

A killer a hundred times over, Harrison took hold of the pretty woman's arm and let his hand press against her uniform jacket, savoring the warmth of her full breasts as they walked along the skyway tunnel. Then he felt a flash of real fear at the totally unexpected appearance of a second weapons scanner in the entrance of the waiting 747 jetliner. This wasn't on any of his plans or charts! Relinquishing his hold on the flight attendant, Harrison cradled his fake stomach and pressed on the sides to activate the Chameleon at its lowest setting. The tunnel lights flickered for a brief moment as the field engaged, but then they returned to normal and he passed through the EM scanner without incident.

Inside the plane, he gave a male flight attendant his ticket and shuffled quickly toward the little lavatory. Once inside, Harrison locked the door and reached under his dress to turn on a Humbug. The device silently swept the lavatory for any optical pickups or working microphones. When it checked as clear, he pulled out a Tech-9 machine pistol, worked the bolt to chamber a round for immediate use, then slid it back under his dress into the cushioned sack of supplies hanging from his shoulders. The thing weighed a ton, but there was no other way to accomplish his mission. So what couldn't be changed had to be endured. At least temporarily.

Adjusting the power levels on the Chameleon, he raised the dial from its lowest setting to about halfway, and locked it into position. Soon now, very soon. Using the toilet, Harrison washed his hands and waddled out to his seat, settling down with a contented sigh.

Remembering to read a magazine through his glasses, he waited and watched as the last of the passengers came on board. After the door was latched shut, the pilot made an announcement that the flight was on schedule, and the steward began his mindless song about safety and seat belts, while the female flight attendant checked seat belts and the storage of the carry-on baggage. Gwenneth was working his aisle, and Harrison allowed himself to study her in detail. Slim legs rising to a perfect rear, a narrow waist and large breasts. Midnight-black hair, pouting lips, sparkling green eyes—yeah, maybe he'd keep her alive for a while, before he sent everybody else on this plane straight to hell.

As the pretty flight attendant walked by, Harrison stretched out a fingertip to lightly brush the smooth nylons on her thigh.

Angrily, Gwenneth glanced down to scold the flirt. But when she saw it was the pregnant passenger, she dismissed it as an accident and moved on to help other passengers settle in for the long flight to India.

Yes, do your job, little flower, but nothing can save these fools now. Harrison smirked behind an impassive face. All I need are a few more minutes. Then it will be too late to stop me. And afterward, nobody would ever be able to stop the fall of America.

Stony Man Farm, Virginia

MURMURING SOFTLY, the radio receiver tucked into security chief Buck Greene's ear gave a constant report on the progress of the Black Hawk gunship coming in from the south. The surface-to-air missile bunkers were armed and ready in case it wasn't the Stony Man teams inside coming home. The Farm's mission controller, Barbara Price, had told Chief Greene about the secondary effects of the Chameleon device, so he was taking no chances. If the lights flickered just once, or if there were two Black Hawks instead of one, then he would order the covert fortress to cut loose with everything it had, which was plenty. A mistake could be made, and friends might die. "How could we stop a Chameleon attack?" Greene wondered out loud.

"Yeah, I've been thinking that myself," John "Cowboy" Kissinger stated. "Radar-invisible gunships, armed with invisible missiles—how could we stop those?"

"We couldn't," Greene replied flatly. "That's what worries me. Even our proximity trips wouldn't work."

"Damn."

"That's putting it mildly."

If they were reduced to visually targeting a flying enemy, they'd be slaughtered. Running stiff fingers through his hair, Kissinger scratched his head as he considered possible countermaneuvers, and came up with nothing.

Tall and lanky, Kissinger was the master gunsmith for the covert warriors of Stony Man, his strong and nimble hands constructing nearly all of their speciality weapons. Guns were his thing, and there were damn few better at his job in the entire world. A 10 mm Megastar pistol rode in his shoulder holster this month, the Magnum automatic being personally tested by the gunsmith for possible use by the field operatives. Unless a weapon carried the Cowboy seal of approval, it never made it into the hands of the Stony Man commandos.

"Our heat-seekers are good, but at short range, they'd

never have enough flight time to lock on to the exhaust of an incoming missile or rocket," Kissinger said at last.

"I know," Greene rumbled.

"Just trust to the nets," Kissinger said, glancing at the thick trees surrounding the hidden base, "and keep those land mines armed. Whether it's helicopters, jet packs or pogo sticks, they got to land sometime."

"Amen to that," Greene said, tilting his head to listen to the soft voice coming over the radio. "Heads up, they're here."

Almost immediately they heard the powerful throb of rotor blades approaching from the south. The noise rapidly built in volume until suddenly a sleek Black Hawk came into view over the leafy tops of the trees in the park.

Greene and Kissinger watched the helicopter maneuver into a landing.

As the aircraft landed, the two men caught sight of the grinning pilot through the cockpit windows and relaxed. Chief Greene and Kissinger walked from the building bent over against the turbulence of the spinning blades. Before they got halfway there, the side door of the Black Hawk slid open, exposing Able Team and Phoenix Force. Carrying bulging duffel bags, Carl Lyons, Rosario Blancanales and Hermann Schwarz jumped to the ground, and, bent low, hurried to greet their friends.

Smiling with pleasure, Greene and Kissinger shook hands with the team.

"Glad to see you guys in one piece," Greene shouted. "How did it go?"

"Still in one piece," Lyons quipped.

Kissinger snorted a laugh. "Damn glad to hear it!"

Just then, the men of Phoenix Force exited the aircraft along with their cargo of destruction. The men were still under the blades when the Black Hawk lifted and circled the Farm once, the smiling pilot giving the men on the ground a thumbs-up gesture before leveling out and departing.

"Nice to see you boys again," Kissinger stated as the swirling dust settled. "Barb's waiting in the computer room for a debriefing. Something's going on in Alaska."

"Alaska?" Rafael Encizo asked, shifting the strap of the duffel over his shoulder. "Any trouble with the Chameleon test?"

They already knew? Chief Greene shook his head. "Better ask Barb."

The two teams accepted that and headed for the farmhouse.

Walking onto the porch and up to the front door, McCarter tapped a security code into a keypad and the door clicked open.

The teams headed directly to the basement, taking the stairs rather than the elevator, ceiling-mounted security cameras tracking them along the way. At the landing, Schwarz raised a hand to block a camera, and it gave a nasty warning buzz. Quickly, he took away his hand before the alarms sounded and tear gas began to vent from the ceiling.

"Touchy, isn't it?" Manning said, amused. "Built-in proximity sensor?"

"Yep," Schwarz said with a touch of pride. "The best in existence. I helped design them."

Hawkins frowned. "And if the Chameleon works as promised, they would be about as useful as two paper cups and some waxed string."

Since it was true, nobody bothered to reply to that.

Exiting the stairwell, the two groups continued on to the tunnel that would take them to the Annex, choosing to walk rather than take the tram.

The Computer Room was abuzz with activity, two men typing madly at computer stations, while a red-haired woman wearing a VR helmet and gloves rode the Internet. At the end of the row of consoles, the fourth computer was dark, the chair empty.

"Anything on the railroads or bus lines?" Barbara Price demanded, crossing her arms.

"Nothing so far," Aaron "the Bear" Kurtzman replied, his hands flowing across a keyboard. A former member of the Rand Corporation think tank, Kurtzman was the chief of the electron-riders at the Farm. Although confined to a wheelchair from an attack on the Farm many years earlier, his mind was as sharp as ever. That was, aside from a minor dementia for black coffee strong enough to kill a rhinoceros.

"Ditto with major airlines," Akira Tokaido added, speed-reading a scrolling monitor. "Every plane is on schedule and accounted for." Of Japanese and American descent, the handsome young man was often referred to as a natural-born hacker with "chips in his blood."

"So far," Price said, biting a lip. "Keep a watch on

the private planes. He might try to hijack a Cessna or a helicopter. Are there any crop dusters working in the state?"

"Good idea. I'm on it," Tokaido said, turning on a submonitor while typing with his other hand.

"What are we looking for?" Lyons asked, dropping his duffel to the floor. It landed with a clank that momentarily caught the attention of the hackers.

"Glad you're here," Price stated without preamble.

"Where's Hal?" McCarter asked, glancing around.

"Already back in D.C. talking with the President," Price answered, waving the men toward the coffee station along the wall. "There's plenty of coffee, so help yourself. I expect you're also hungry, so I had the staff fill the fridge with fresh sandwiches. I can brief you as you eat. You go airborne in fifteen minutes."

So fast? Lyons started to ask for an explanation, but said nothing. Price was no fool. If she was sending them into the field this quick, then the shit had already hit the fan.

"Ah, thanks, I think. Did Bear make the coffee?" James asked with a worried look.

Without turning in his wheelchair, Kurtzman laughed. "And you call yourselves soldiers." He brandished a steaming mug. "This'll put some hair on your chest!"

"Or take it off," James quipped.

"Also degreases tractor parts," Schwarz added.

"Heads up!" Carmen Delahunt announced from behind her VR helmet. "I just accessed a NSA WatchDog satellite."

Right on cue, the main wall monitor fluttered with a

wild scroll and settled into a picture of more swirling clouds.

"Damn!" Delahunt cursed. "There's no break in the cloud cover over western Alaska." She sounded as if the inclement weather were a personal affront to her abilities as a hacker.

"Carmen, did you really expect clear sky at this time of year?" Price asked. "That's why the Pentagon set the field test for the Chameleon. No other nation's satellites could watch."

"Advanced technology is so damn primitive," Schwarz said with a flash of a smile.

"Apparently so, this time," Delahunt muttered, going back into the virtual reality of the worldwide Net.

Going to the kitchenette, Price poured herself a fresh cup of coffee, adding a lot of milk and sugar. "Have you all read the report from Hal?"

"In the Black Hawk coming here," Lyons replied. "There wasn't much there."

"Sadly, it's all we have," she said.

"Okay, grab a seat," Price instructed, gesturing at some chairs pushed along the wall. "We're truly operating in the dark on this. We know nothing about how the Chameleon operates, power requirements, distance limitations and so on. Every report and file was destroyed in Alaska. All we can do is make some educated guesses. Everybody connected with the project was at that field test or in the laboratory. The missiles from the USS *Fairfax* killed them all."

"What was the hoped-for size of the unit?" Schwarz asked, leaning forward in his chair.

"About the size of a paperback book," Price replied. "But Hal said that the President believes Professor Johnson was field-testing a shoe box version yesterday."

"The size of a shoe box?" James said, the astonishment plain on his face.

She nodded. "Yes. But once again, it's only a guess."

"Still certainly small enough to be portable," McCarter said, rubbing his chin. "How much did it weigh?"

"We figured it at roughly twenty pounds. But it could be more, a lot more."

"Barbara, was that Professor Torge Emile Johnson by any chance?" Schwarz asked, scrunching his face.

Blinking in surprise, Price turned. "Yes, it was. So you know him?"

"Only by reputation. I've read articles by the man. He was a genius. A real one. Made breakthroughs all the time. *SA* once called him the Thomas Edison of the twenty-first century."

"*SA*?" Manning asked patiently.

"*Scientific American* magazine," James explained.

Manning nodded wisely. "Ah, yes. I have the swimsuit issue at home."

"Oh, shut up," James growled.

"So what is the mission?" Hawkins asked, leaning against the wall. "We're supposed to get it back before anybody get hurts?"

"Over three hundred people are dead already," Price answered sternly. "We want it found, or destroyed."

Going to the fridge, Blancanales opened the door to find it filled with plates of sandwiches, soft drinks and bottles of juice, so he grabbed sandwiches and an orange juice. It was going to be a long day. He could feel it in his bones.

"What about the off-site backup files?" he asked, resting against the counter to unwrap his food and take a healthy bite.

"The what?" McCarter asked, heading for the fridge. There was no Coca-Cola in sight, only some diet Mountain Dew and several bottles of fruity stuff, and the juice.

Blancanales was chewing, so Schwarz answered. "Every project is vulnerable to accidents, or hackers. So all big corporations, and most government projects, have an automatic recording of everything done in the lab located far away from the building. Just in case."

"Smart move," McCarter commented.

"Damn straight it is. The IRS does the same thing, which is why it's pointless to bomb the place."

"The Farm, too?" Hawkins asked.

Turning away from his console Kurtzman said, "No, we're too sensitive. If this place goes, nobody will ever know we even existed."

"The backup files are a good place to start a search, but once again, we don't know where they're located," Price added grimly. "Only the project head and the Pentagon liaison did."

"And they're dead," Encizo stated.

"Exactly."

"So our job is to go through the wreckage and find the location of those backup files," Lyons said, thinking aloud, his eyes half-closed in concentration.

"Yes," Price said. "Able Team goes in as DOD inspectors. Phoenix Force stays in the background to give you three cover in case of trouble."

Lyons frowned. Which translated as, his team got killed, but Phoenix Force found the culprit.

"And then?" Encizo inquired.

"Kill the thief." Price didn't believe in couching terms. If the men could do the job, then she could damn well say the word.

"Any ID on him yet?" Blancanales asked, then added, "Or her?"

"Not a thing," Price replied, placing her mug aside on the counter. "Whoever did this is good. As good as anybody we have."

"Must have been an inside job. Nothing else makes sense," McCarter stated. He took a drink from the bottle, then went on, "So it's a mole."

Lyons shook his head. "Or an ape."

Ape, yes, Price knew the term. Spies stayed out and relayed information for years. Apes hit hard, blew things up and stole things. "Ape" was slang for an AP, which stood for Agent Provocateur. Secret government soldiers.

"So we're facing a James Bond type," Schwarz said without a trace of humor. "Not many of them around these days."

Blancanales lowered his sandwich. "And for just this reason. Everybody is dead, and the prototype is lost."

"Maybe lost," James corrected. "Maybe destroyed in the explosions, or stolen. We don't know shit right about now."

"Could be a solo, or a freelance," Price admitted.

"Somebody not affiliated with any government. Just there to steal the Chameleon and sell it on the open market."

"Or even sell it back to us," Hawkins grumbled. "If it cost us a billion to make, then we'd certainly pay that much to get it back."

"At least."

Rubbing the faint bullet scar on his temple, Encizo sighed. "Hellfire, we really are in the dark on this."

"That's why we have to move fast," Price agreed, "and try to cover every base."

"What was the name of the company doing the research?" Kurtzman asked over a shoulder.

"Quiller Geo-Medical," she said, and then smiled at the surprised expressions. "Yes, it means nothing. But it sounds very scientific, and people seldom ask."

"Or maybe one did," Kurtzman muttered, then wheeled his chair about. "Akira! Check the IRS tax records for a list of employees. Then cross-check that with the state driver's-license files at the Alaska DMV. Carmen, I want you—"

"On it," she interrupted from behind her mask, both hands in their VR gloves caressing the air. "I'll access the video surveillance cameras at the airports and run a facial check as soon as Akira gives me some faces from the driver's licenses."

"He'll be wearing a disguise," Price warned. "And this person is damn good. KGB good. Maybe better."

Delahunt shrugged. "We can adjust for that. It's our ID software that caught that last group of terrorists trying to sneak out of the country."

"Where's Hunt, anyway?" Blancanales asked, glancing at the empty fourth chair at the end of the row of computer stations.

Huntington "Hunt" Wethers had been teaching cybernetics at Berkeley when he was recruited into Stony Man. With wings of gray hair at his temples, and smoking his briarwood pipe, Wethers looked like the stereotypical college professor. Yet he possessed a facility with computers that few other experts had.

"Hunt's on a special assignment with Mack," Price explained after a moment.

That was an unexpected answer. "In the field?"

She shrugged. "Mack asks, and he gets."

Lyons stood. "Good luck to them both," he said with feeling. There had to be a major problem for Striker to request assistance from anybody, and double so for him to ask for a desk jockey like the professor.

"Better save it," Hawkins said, pushing away from the wall. "Because I think we're going to need all of the luck we can get to bust this nut."

"Alert," Delahunt announced calmly. "We have a break in the clouds."

Everybody turned. The main wall monitor filled with a view of western Alaska, then jumped closer in a staggered series of zoom shots until the screen was filled with a real-time view of the destroyed target zone and the smoking ruin of the research lab. The ambulances had come and gone, leaving only chalk outlines everywhere on the ground. Often, there was only the outline of a limb, or a torso, instead of an entire body.

Somebody merely grunted, while another muttered a curse.

"Barbara, tell Jack to get fueled and ready for liftoff," Lyons ordered brusquely. "We'll meet him on the front lawn in ten minutes."

"Cowboy already has your spare equipment ready to go. Along with the proper ID cards, weapons permits, all the usual," she told him.

Both teams headed for the door, and a grim-faced Encizo tapped in the exit code this time.

"We bloody well could be walking into a trap, mate," McCarter commented.

As the armored door started to cycle open, Lyons looked backward at the pictures on the wall monitor, the hundreds of chalk outlines amid the smoking rubble.

"No," he replied in a voice of stone. "They are."

CHAPTER FOUR

Flight 18, above the North Pacific

The recessed ceiling lights in the 747 flickered for a moment.

"Hey," a man said, taking the cell phone away from his ear. "What the hell is going on?"

"What's the matter?" his wife asked, lowering her magazine.

"This damn thing is dead!" he raged, hitting the device.

Gwenneth started forward to talk to the upset passenger, when she noticed that across the plane, a woman was shaking her airphone and also muttering annoyances. Two phones died at the same time? How odd.

"Hu, Yuki," Gwenneth said to the other flight attendants. "Go calm down the passengers. I'll report this to the captain."

Yuki nodded vigorously and started down the aisle, beaming a pleasant smile.

"It's nothing," Hu scoffed, sliding another packaged meal into a microwave to be warmed. "Just a coincidence."

"Maybe," Gwenneth said, biting a lip. "Or maybe it's a freak magnetic storm that'll throw off the navigation and make us hours late. Either way, regulations say that the captain must be informed at once."

Hu shrugged in a noncommittal manner, and Gwenneth pushed past the man to start for the cockpit. Moving through first class, she stopped as the door to the lavatory opened, almost hitting her in the face. It was Mrs. Coleson, the pregnant American woman from coach.

"You really shouldn't be here, dear," Gwenneth started to say, when the woman grabbed her forcibly by the arm and shoved something hard into her stomach.

"I have a weapon," Davis Harrison growled in his real voice. "Stay calm and you may get to live."

Her eyes went wide at the realization that it was a man wearing a disguise. Quickly, Gwenneth started to pull air into her lungs for a full-throated scream, but Harrison rammed the gun into her stomach, almost knocking her out. Gasping for breath, Gwenneth felt her eyes well with tears as she fought to draw in a ragged breath.

"Oh, dear," Harrison said, sounding like a woman again. "You've go the flu, too, eh? Here, let me help you sit down."

Gwenneth tried to fight free from the other person, but his grip was like iron, and every move only earned her another jab in the belly. Her vision was starting to go red from the lack of air, and a wave of weakness swept over her. This had to be a hijacking…terrorists! But how to warn…

Something slammed into her face, and Gwenneth

had a brief flash of the steel-plated door to the cockpit before the universe turned black and she tumbled into a warm darkness.

"Yes?" a voice said from the other side.

Dropping the unconscious woman to the deck, Harrison pushed the door open, its electronic lock disabled from the humming Chameleon strapped to his belly. Stepping inside, he swung the deadly Tech-9 about, marking his targets. The crew was three, pilot, copilot and navigator, exactly as there should be. No surprises here. Excellent.

"Hey, that door was locked!" the navigator cried out in confusion, spinning from his console. Then he raised an eyebrow at the pregnant woman holding an automatic weapon of some kind. Shit! A hijacking!

"Nobody move," Harrison ordered.

The copilot fumbled under his seat, while the navigator snatched a small black box from the wall and lunged forward to thrust the Talon stun gun at the intruder, the silvery prongs crackling with electricity. The Chinese man got only halfway before Harrison fired from the hip.

Hardly any flame or smoke erupted from the muzzle, and only a subdued click was heard, as if the weapon had misfired. But the navigator dropped the Talon as he was slammed backward against his console, blood spurting from his throat.

Harrison fired twice more, only clicks sounding. The navigator writhed under the sledgehammer blows, his chest seeming to explode and a radar screen behind the man noisily cracked as a slug drilled through. Exhaling life itself, the shuddering man fell to the cold deck, blood pouring from the gaping holes in his body.

"Alert, Anchorage!" the pilot said quickly into her throat mike. "Code four, repeat, we have a code four in progress!"

But there was no reply from the airport; not even the soft crackle of static came over her earphones. The radio was completely dead.

That was when she noticed that most of the control board was dead, many of the instruments giving wildly impossible readings. Shit and fire, her ship was in some sort of a jamming field! There was no other possible explanation.

Reaching under the chair, she thumbed a hidden button. Then something hit her shoe, and the pilot glanced down to see a misshapen lead slug on the deck. From the pistol? But there had been no noise. What was going on here?

"That emergency signal will never be heard." Harrison chuckled, enjoying their confusion. On impulse, he reached up and pulled off his annoying wig.

The pilot scowled at the sight of the hijacker's bald head, the skin stubbled with hair. Not bald, shaved, details she would need to remember to help convict him in court before the Red Army firing squad blew off his face.

"Don't hurt anybody else," the copilot said in Chinese, raising both hands. "We will obey. What do you want?"

The hijacker frowned at the copilot, and the pilot realized he didn't speak Chinese. That could be useful in the future.

"This is foolish," the pilot began in English. "Once we move off course—"

"Shut up! Do you need the copilot to fly this plane?"

Not really, no, she admitted to herself. Then the end result of such honesty became horrifying obvious.

"Yes!" she lied, darting a glance at her friend. "Of course. This aircraft is huge!"

Harrison smiled. "You lie," he whispered, and the strange gun clicked twice more. The copilot jerked backward against the hull, then slumped over in his chair, supported only by the safety harness around his chest. Blood began to dribble from his slack mouth, and a second Talon fell to the deck with a clatter.

"Toy, stupid, useless toy," Harrison growled in annoyance.

Then the Tech-9 swung to point at the captain. To her, the muzzle seemed larger than the Beijing Tunnel, and she felt the world shrink to a view of its black interior. A drop of sweat suddenly trickled down her face, and a thousand images and feelings flashed through her mind in a single heartbeat: childhood, family, friends, becoming captain.

"Obey me, or die," Harrison said from somewhere in the distance.

Her attention split in two, the yoke of the jumbo jetliner felt hot in her grip, the elaborate control board only inches away. If it was only her life, she would crash the plane rather than submit. But she was responsible for all the other souls in the aircraft. Honor wouldn't allow her to abandon them. For the moment, there seemed to be no other choice. Yes, she would obey, and hopefully live, and do her best to keep the passengers alive no matter what.

Then a muscular hand gripped the pilot's shoulder and squeezed hard, the sharp painted nails digging painfully into her flesh.

"Well?" Harrison demanded, pressing the gun barrel to her right eye.

As if her head weighed a thousand tons, the pilot slowly nodded.

"Very good." He chuckled and slid his hand down the silken material of her white blouse to cup a soft breast and squeeze with brutal force.

She started to cry out from the pain, then bit back the sound and concentrated on flying the plane as the man lewdly fondled her body. Born and raised a Communist, the pilot didn't believe in any gods, but she still sent a silent prayer into the universe begging for deliverance from the coming hell.

CHAPTER FIVE

Nome, Alaska

The summer wind was warm, gently rustling the bluebell flowers that grew wild in the fields outside the airport.

The unmarked C-130 Hercules transport was parked all by itself on a secluded landing field as far away from the main terminal as possible. All across the Nome International Airport, the staff, crew and TSA guards were staying far away from the military transport. They had been told when it would arrive, and nothing more. But nobody thought twice about the incident. Alaska was so close to Russia, only fifteen miles at the closest point, that the local population was used to covert military landings, odd troops movements and such ever since the cold war. America and Russia were friendly these days, but the military still kept a close watch on its old foe. Just in case.

With a strong whine of hydraulics, the rear of the C-130 Hercules transport disengaged, and cycled down to the ground to form a ramp. Deep inside the mammoth plane, headlights flashed on, and soon a civilian SUV rolled into view and bumped down the ramp to reach the tarmac.

Driving a few yards away from the aircraft, Carl "Ironman" Lyons parked the SUV and waited for the rest of the team to drive out. The vehicle was a dark green in color, so dark it appeared to be black. The windows were tinted, and the license plates carried government numbers.

What couldn't be seen was the composite armor lining the SUV, and its hidden arsenal of weaponry in the ceiling, walls and seats.

Suddenly the massive engines of the Hercules coughed into life, the four great propellers rotating in spurts and then accelerating into a steady blur. Then the rear hatch began to cycle upward as the airplane prepared for takeoff.

Setting the parking brake, Lyons scowled. What the hell was going on now?

The side door near the tail swung open and a pair of duffel bags was tossed onto the tarmac, closely followed by Blancanales and Schwarz. Even as the two men grabbed their bags, the C-130 released its brakes and started to taxi forward, heading for an empty runway. The two men walked toward the SUV, and by the time they arrived, the Hercules was airborne and disappearing into the clouds.

"Trouble?" Lyons asked from behind the wheel.

Blancanales opened the rear hatch and tossed in his bag. "Yes and no," he replied. "We caught the squawk from the Farm that a China Air 747 has crashed in the Koryak Mountains of Russia only an hour ago."

"Sorry to hear it," Lyons said with a grunt. "What has that got to do with us?"

"Its destination was New Delhi," Schwarz said, adding his duffel to the pile of equipment and packs in the rear of the SUV. "And it left Ted Stevens Airport in Anchorage two hours after the attack on Quiller Labs, about six hours ago."

As the men climbed into the vehicle, Lyons did some fast mental math. "So it's hundreds of miles off course. And how did it penetrate that deep into Russian airspace without being challenged or shot down?"

"Only one way that Barb can guess," Blancanales said, snapping on his seat belt.

"The Chameleon," Lyons growled. "Our ape must have hijacked the plane, then killed the crew, jumped out and let it crash to hide that he was ever there."

"Or it could be a diversion," Schwarz offered, pulling the 9 mm Beretta from his shoulder holster and dropping the clip to check the load before reinserting the clip. "But I don't read our ape that way."

Adjusting his DOD identification badge on his suit jacket, Blancanales nodded. "Agree. Our boy is fast and furious. Not really into fancy tricks. He's more the lead-pipe type."

"Anything from the pilot, or civilian cell phones?" Lyons asked, starting the engine again. The big V8 purred into life, and he slipped the shift to start driving for an access road.

"Not a peep," Schwarz replied. "And the emergency beacon didn't activate until the plane was already tumbling out of the sky."

"You mean once it was out of range of the jamming field of the Chameleon," Lyons said grimly.

"That's the idea, yes."

"Gadgets, could the ape have used the Chameleon to mask itself and smuggle it on board past airport security?" Blancanales asked frowning.

"He could have smuggled an Abrams tank past security with that thing," he answered. "But it would have to be operating at very low power. Full force it would interfere with the operation of the controls regulating the jet engines, and the plane would—"

"Crash," Blancanales interrupted. "Goddamn it, maybe the passengers rushed the bastard and that's exactly what happened!"

Pennsylvania all over again. Conversation stopped as only a few hundred yards away, a 707 roared into the sky. Even as it ascended, a small two-seater Cessna daintily arrived to touch the ground on another landing strip. In spite of the fact that it was so close to the Arctic Circle, the Nome airport was always busy with the combined civilian and military traffic, but its safety record was equaled by few other airports.

"So unless we can find the backup files here, this is going to be a race between McCarter and the Russian air rescue service," Lyons stated as the SUV bumped over a small crack in the road. There had been an earthquake in November 2002 that rocked all of Alaska, and the damage was still being repaired on a priority basis.

"Which is why they took off with us still on the field," Blancanales agreed.

"Jack isn't going to try to fly Phoenix Force there, is

he?" Lyons demanded. "He'd never get past the Russian radar."

"Damn right he couldn't. Their EM umbrella is tight," Schwarz stated with conviction. "Without the Chameleon, there's no way to fly into Russian national airspace without getting a SAM up your ass. Maybe two.

"Unless you do it at a height of six inches," he added.

Slowing down at a locked gate, Lyons waited for the armed TSA guards to leave the kiosk. He showed the woman his ID. She gave no reaction, but spoke into her radio, and then waved them past.

Taking a turn onto an access road, Lyons raised an eyebrow at that. "They're going to try a deadman's run?"

"Only way to get there fast enough," Blancanales said, pulling an M-16/M-203 combo from his duffel. "Our ape might not have jumped, and the damaged Chameleon could still be on the plane. They have to get there first, at any cost."

Damn. Then Grimaldi would be taking McCarter to Ketchikan Island. The Coast Guard should have what the team needed. If not…

"Check your equipment," Lyons directed. "We'll be going to the testing area first. That's the last place where anybody would hide their backup files."

"Then why are we going?" Blancanales asked, puzzled, slapping in a clip. Then his face brightened. "Because it's the best place for them to ambush us."

"This crazy son of a bitch is trying to take the pressure off Phoenix Force," Schwarz snorted, thumbing a fat 40 mm round into the breech of his M-203 grenade launcher. He closed the breech with a solid metallic snap. "Fair enough. Let's rattle the trees, Carl, we got your six."

Merging with the outgoing traffic, Lyons said nothing as he checked the .357 Colt Python under his jacket and sent the SUV heading for the coastal highway outside of Nome.

CHAPTER SIX

International Waters, North Pacific Ocean

The white Coast Guard cutter pitched and tossed in the churning ocean, waves crashing over the bow with drumming force. The evening sky was pitch-black, a cold rain pelting sideways through the fog.

Visibility was near zero. Off in the distance, the powerful beam of a Russian lighthouse was only a ghostly glow, and if there was a warning horn, its plaintive cry was swallowed whole by the near deafening crash of the endless waves.

"This weather couldn't be any better!" David Mc-Carter shouted in frank approval over the wild storm.

"God loves the infantry." Hawkins chuckled as the cutter dropped five feet into a wave trench. "But I think He hates the Navy tonight. Hold on, here comes another big one!"

The men gripped the chain railing tight, bracing for the crash. For a full second the ship was in free fall, then it hit hard, the jolting impact almost tearing their hands away. Riding the recoil of the watery landing, Phoenix Force watched and listened to the rampaging storm, getting a feel for its tempo and rhythm. The unexpected squall was helping to mask the approach of the USCGC *Mellon*. That was the good part.

Unfortunately, the Coast Guard cutter was also falling way behind schedule and the team felt the pressure of the lost time bearing down upon them. The numbers were falling and not in their favor. Too many battles to count had been lost because of arriving late. However, they couldn't afford for this to join those ignoble ranks.

"We're going to have to leave early," McCarter stated, wiping the water from his face with a palm. "Got no choice!"

"In for a penny, in for a pounding, eh, David?" Gary Manning joked, bracing himself as a giant wave swept across the lower deck to crash against the hull just below their boots.

"Pity we had to leave Ketchikan Island before seeing the Panama Guns," Encizo said, casting a glance back toward the coast of North America, only a hundred miles away, but in this storm it might as well have been in other dimension.

"Not much left of those cannons anyway," James replied loudly, squinting into the maelstrom. "Hey, I think the squall is easing some!"

"Good!" Hawkins yelled. "Still, they would have been nice to see! The Panamas were designed to stop the Russian navy from taking Alaska. Sort of the American version of the Guns of Navarone!"

"How big were they again?" Encizo asked, swaying to the pitch of the rolling deck.

"A whopping 155 mm!" Then he added with a grin, "Just about the size of decent T-bone steak in Texas!"

"You mean a deep-dish pizza in Chicago!" James shot back.

Whipped by the wind and sea, Phoenix Force shared a brief laugh as the men battled the squall and continued their vigil. Time was short, but professional soldiers knew how to wait until just the right moment, and then explode into action. It was all timing.

Inside the wheelhouse of the USCGC *Mellon*, a young helmsman turned from the joystick-style yoke and gave a scowl at the strangers below on the forward deck. Alaska had been clear sailing, but only fifty miles off the coast they hit this squall. Now cold rain was coming down in sheets, and the triple-blade window wipers fought to keep the bulletproof glass clear. But the raging sea and rain were mightier than the technology of man, and the wipers gave only brief slices of visibility, strobing glimpses of the churning sea and the rocky shore they were heading toward at full speed.

"Look at them out there," the helmsman muttered in disapproval, involuntarily flinching as a wave slammed against the starboard windows. "Standing on the open deck! Crazy bastards."

"Peterson, why are you talking to yourself?" Captain Tyson asked, hands clasped behind his back. In spite of the inclement weather, the officer was neatly dressed in a crisp uniform, his shoes shiny with polish and his hair freshly cut.

On the wall behind the officer was a line of yellow rain slicks, Veri pistol flare guns, fire extinguishers, a medical kit and a dozen lifejackets.

"What was that, Skipper?" the helmsman asked, checking the course and heading on the dashboard instruments.

"You know the standing orders," Tyson stated. "There is nobody on the deck, not a soul in sight but you and me." The captain paused. "And you sure as hell didn't just call your CO crazy, now, did you?"

The helmsman swallowed hard and turned his face to the rampaging storm again. "Sir, no, sir!" he chanted, tightening both hands on the joystick.

"Didn't think so," Tyson muttered, moving to the motion of his cutter. Sonar showed the sea below was clear of Russian submarines, but the radar screen was filled with the storm, the computer unable to recognize a few small dots moving in from the west. They could just be St. Elmo's fire; there was a lot of that out here. Or it could be MiG fighters moving just above the storm on a recon run.

"Maintain course and speed," Captain Tyson said, looking out the windows at the squall.

"Aye, sir." Concentrating on his job, the helmsman switched hands on the joystick to wipe the first one dry on a pant leg. Equipped with autofeedback, the computerized yoke wasn't loose under his grip, but pushed back at him this way and another as the currents slapped the rudder about. It was exactly like holding a wheel and steering a windjammer. In spite of the mechanical interfacing, the joystick gave a man the feel of the water, and that was sometimes even more important than maps and sonar readings. Sailing was a science, but one that was ruled by art. The poetry of the wind was more than a clever saying; it was a way of life burned into the bones of every sailor.

Especially on this combination rescue vessel and warship. The USCGC *Mellon* was the pride of the Coast Guard. A Hamilton-class cutter, the craft was 378 feet long, with a crew of eighteen officers and 143 sailors. She boasted both gasoline and diesel engines, along with a flat bottom for faster speeds and the ability to go into amazingly shallow water without damage. The hull was composite armor over an aluminum frame, making the *Mellon* strong but lightweight. The windows were shatterproof glass, every door a watertight hatchway, and each deck was railed for safety in even the roughest storms. The *Mellon* could sail through a hurricane and come out fighting back, its crew and passengers alive and safe.

As was standard in the Coast Guard, the cutter came with a 76 mm cannon in a small pillbox at the bow, designed to put a whistling warning shot across the deck of other vessels to make them come about for inspection. However, if the warning failed, the *Mellon* also boasted two 25 mm Bofors Autocannons, four .50-caliber machine guns and side-launching Mk49 torpedoes.

OUTSIDE AT THE RAILING, McCarter noted the addition of Harpoon missiles to the cutter's impressive arsenal. Back in 1992 the torpedoes and the missiles had been removed because of budget cuts. After 9/11, the Coast Guard got a massive boost in spending and quickly re-installed the heavy weapon systems. Basically, it was a pocket battleship. More accurately, the cutter was a PT boat for the twenty-first century.

"David, how many of these does the Coast Guard have?" Manning asked, his face into the wind, hair slicked back from the wash so that he resembled a tango instructor or Mafia capo.

"Twelve!" McCarter shouted in reply. "But they should have a bloody hundred!"

"Preaching to the choir, friend!"

"Rocks!" Encizo shouted, pointing at black shapes looming in the storm. Jagged peaks of stone, the broken cliffs stood defiant in the crashing waves, the pinnacles rising higher than the radio antenna of the listing *Mellon*.

McCarter grunted, "About damn time."

"HALF SPEED!" Captain Tyson barked. "Hard to port, two degrees!"

"Aye, sir!"

Shapes rose from the squall, black and imposing.

"Quarter speed! Hard to starboard!" Damnation, the rocks were everywhere! He glanced at the instruments, but they were useless. Too much conflicting data from the storm, rocks and muddy surf.

"Half speed! Hard to port!" More rocks appeared from the rain. "Quarter speed!" A wave crashed across the bow of the turning cutter, and there appeared a wall of black rock straight ahead of them.

"Full speed ahead!" Captain Tyson commanded, his hands clenched white behind his back, but his expression was cool and calm.

"Aye, sir!" the helmsman cried, fighting the joystick. A wave slammed them on the port side, then there came a metallic shriek as something under the water scraped along their hull. The mountain of stone seemed to expand before the cutter as the ship fought the waves. A crash seemed imminent, and then the *Mellon* entered a calm in the storm, the sections of tumbled-down cliffs forming the imposing breakers soon in their wake.

On this side of the barrier, the force of the storm was noticeably less and visibility was greatly increased. The shoreline of mother Russia was barely visible about four miles ahead. No lights showed along the shore, or in the wooded hills beyond. But that was why this section of the coast had been chosen. Near total isolation. Not even smugglers used the deserted cover because of the deadly breakers and underwater boulders that could rip open the keel of a ship like a soda can being crushed in your fist. And if not for his special passengers, Captain Tyson would never have come to this special little slice of Russian hell.

Breathing a sigh of relief, the captain checked the GPS and the navigational chart, and then the compass just to make sure. Okay, the *Mellon* was now in the national waters of Russia and most certainly on their radar screens. The storm should kill visual, but at the first sign of anything suspicious, the Russian navy would hit the Coast Guard cutter with infrared, UV and anything else the local boys had. And if those were indeed MiG fighters in the sky...

"Okay, son, full stop. We now have engine trouble," the captain announced, checking his wristwatch. "Shut her down, and drop the main anchor."

"Aye, aye, sir," the helmsman acknowledged crisply, and worked the controls on the joystick, slowing the huge craft with surprising ease until it was relatively still in the choppy North Pacific waters. Overriding the automatics, he gunned the gasoline engines a few times, making them turn over but refuse to catch.

"Keep doing that until further notice," Captain Tyson said, turning to leave. "But keep the diesels hot in case we have to leave in a hurry."

"Sir?" the helmsman asked hesitantly. "Do you think that this might be a good time to run a gun drill with the crew?"

The captain nodded at that in appreciation. He liked sailors who thought fast. Smugglers were tough and clever, and only touch and clever CGs could do the job of guarding the shores of America.

"This close to the Bear," Tyson said, meaning Russia, "that is generally a good idea, but not tonight. We have engine trouble, the crew will all be down in the hold banging on hatchways and pipes with hammers to make as much noise as possible. So that for the Russian sonar can hear us doing, ahem, repairs."

"Understood, Skipper," the helmsman said, setting his shoulders as he gunned the flooded engines again. "We're dead in the water, but in spite of the storm, we don't need any assistance yet."

"That's what the radio operator will be reporting to Ketchikan base right at this moment," Tyson said, pulling out a cell phone and tapping in a memorized number. "Carry on."

"Aye, aye, skipper!"

THE PAGER in McCarter's breast pocket vibrated, and he hit the pager to turn it off. That was the signal. If they were in the vicinity, the Russians would be monitoring the military channels for transmission, and not be paying much attention to the civilian bands. Unless there was a lot of traffic. So all messages were being sent over pagers and cell phones, and consisted of a yes or no.

"Let's move," McCarter said, starting along the railing toward the stern of the huge cutter.

The deck was wet, but the rubberized covering made their footing secure, and Phoenix Force easily reached the aft helipad.

Two crafts were there, lashed down tight under sheets of canvas by a web of ropes. Pulling knives, the men slashed the ropes free and hauled off the canvas to reveal two rather lumpy-looking rubber dinghies. Each was equipped with a set of tandem motors and filled with bags of supplies.

Going to the first craft, McCarter, Encizo and Hawkins climbed inside and started the engines. They came to life with a muted purr. Manning and James took the other, as the crew of the cutter appeared to pile in additional watertight bags, along with an assortment of flotation boxes—waterproof, cushioned containers designed for hauling delicate electronic equipment through the worst of storms.

"Wait for it," McCarter said, adjusting the radio transponder around his neck, tucking the receiver into an ear.

A hatch opened on the tower, and the captain walked

into view on the aft gun deck, flanked by a pair of Remington .50-caliber machine guns, still strapped down against the squall. Dressed in a bright yellow slicker, Captain Tyson stood with his hands folded behind his back, the very ideal of a Coast Guard officer.

Taking a seat between the two tandem engines, David McCarter gave the man a salute. Nodding for a moment, the captain returned the gesture and then spoke into a radio mike hanging over his left shoulder.

Listening to a response over his earphone, the captain raised a splayed hand and folded one finger down. Then another, a third, a fourth...

Right on cue, the engines of both of the strange rubber crafts roared into full power exactly as the huge rumbling diesel power plants of the massive Hamilton-class cutter started working.

As the rubber skirting of the crafts billowed outward, the vessels rose about a foot off the wet helipad. Moving effortlessly, the hovercrafts sailed off the end of the cutter and skimmed onto the choppy waves of the cove. Bouncing a few times, they settled down into a smooth run and rapidly built speed until the men and machines both vanished.

"Helmsman, our engine trouble is fixed now," the captain said into the radio handset at his shoulder. "Take us back to Alaska."

"Aye, aye, sir!" came the response in his earphone.

Just then, something rumbled in the sky overhead, a different noise than anything previously made by the squall. Looking up quickly, the captain caught a brief glimpse of three MiG fighters streaking through the clouds, and then they were gone.

"Timing," Tyson said softly, grinning to himself, "is everything."

CHAPTER SEVEN

Kobuk Valley, Alaska

The drive from Nome to the Kobuk River had been accomplished with a minimum of fuss. The state took great pride in maintaining its roadways, and what damage the November quake had done was mostly minor this far north of the epicenter.

On the way, Schwarz and Kurtzman had coordinated an effort to sweep the most likely spots in the state for a hidden government computer dump, starting with every existing off-site backup computer. As expected, nothing was found that gave the slightest indication of where the Chameleon files were located, even the locked and encoded files.

Stopping at the side of a deserted road, Lyons and Blancanales stood guard while Schwarz opened the multiple locked doors of what appeared to be an electrical substation. Inside the brick-and-concrete bunker, Schwarz pressed his hand to a palm plate set into the wall and nervously waited while the machine checked his fingerprints against his fake file in the DOD system. Ceiling-mounted Auto-Sentry machine guns kept their deadly barrels aimed at him in a cross-fire pattern that could literally cut him in two at the first sign of suspicious behavior. An expert in electronics, Schwarz disliked being at the mercy of a machine, knowing how easy it was for even the best computer in the world to make a mistake. No matter how much knowledge they contained, it was still impossible to give them even an ounce of human common sense.

With a dull beep the wall plate glowed green, the Auto-Sentries disengaged and the Able Team commando quickly checked over the info dump for any sign of hacking, physical invasion, bugs or any other kind of illicit monitoring. But the site was clean.

Evening had fallen by the time Able Team reached the target range in the Kobuk Valley. As their SUV swung around a huge outcropping, Lyons eased to a gentle halt. The side road they wanted was closed off with orange barrels full of sand, a construction crew working on the berm while a portable concrete mixer chattered alongside. A lone foreman was checking items off a clipboard and talking to somebody on a radio headset, the silvery mike jutting stiffly near his mouth.

"They're Feds," Blancanales said in disapproval. "There's no cars. A work crew drives to the construction site, so there should be cars here. These folks were dropped off in a batch."

"Pretty advanced com link for some gravel jockeys," Schwarz said, checking the EM scanner in his palm. "Okay, it's bullshit. They're using a military frequency."

"Ankles and hips," Lyons grunted, nodding at the assortment of hidden guns carried by the state work crew. "I'd say Military intelligence, or maybe Homeland."

"Up here?"

"Alaska, Texas, Florida, those are the main entry points for illegals into America."

"Wonder if they made us yet?" Schwarz asked.

"Let's find out." Lyons tapped the horn twice.

A nearby workman glance up from raking loose gravel and spoke briefly into his cuff. Instantly, the foreman turned and walked their way wearing a tired expression.

"Hi, folks," he said, as if doing this a hundred times a day. "Sorry, but the road's closed. Some secondary damage from the quake." He pointed to the east. "You'll have to take the main highway just a few miles to get around."

"Get out of my way, cop," Lyons said. "I work for Quiller Geo-Medical."

"What did you say, cousin?" the foreman asked, tilting his head and smiling.

Able Team noticed that at those words, everyone stopped working and started adjusting their clothing or scratching, getting a hand closer to their weapons.

"Or rather, I used to," Lyons continued. "Until everybody went home with the flu."

Lowering his clipboard, the foreman stepped closer, "Yeah, there's a lot of that going around," he said slowly, "ever since the big snow last year."

"Hell, boy, it was a blizzard."

"Acknowledged. ID, please," the foreman said, holding out a hand. Now that the passwords had been exchanged his demeanor was completely different, and several of the workers unzipped their grimy worksuits to place a hand inside.

The team passed over their Department of Defense identification booklets. The foreman checked their photos, then waved the booklets over his clipboard. It beeped as it scanned the bar codes, and then beeped again.

There was no chance of them being detected as fake, because they weren't. The identification booklets were part of the support supplied to Stony Man by the White House, and were as real as any issued to a special investigation agent of Military intelligence.

"Pass," the foreman said, giving the booklets back. "Give 'em a door, people."

Four of the workers placed their shovels aside and rolled the heavy orange barrels out of the way to make a path for the SUV.

Lyons drove through slowly, the tires crunching on the loose gravel scattered over the road to give the illusion of work being done.

Once past the construction, Lyons started to accelerate, and by the time the SUV had reached the top of hill, the orange barrels were back in place, the road closed again.

Following a curve in the road, the Able Team leader turned off the paved road and started down a gravel track toward the target zone. The forest grew to the edge of the road, and the branches closed off at the sky at several spots, the dappled light of the setting sun giving the landscape a ghostly feeling.

Then Lyons took a curve and braked fast at the sight of black Hummers blocking the road. U.S. Army soldiers swung big M-60 machine guns about on the vertical mounts and worked the arming bolts as a dozen more troopers in camouflage fatigues stepped out of the woods on both sides, the men armed with M-16/M-203 combo assault rifles.

"They're ready to repel an invasion," Schwarz muttered, keeping his hands in plain sight.

"Can you blame them?" Blancanales replied softly, doing the same.

"Password!" a colonel barked, resting a hand on the holstered Desert Eagle pistol slung low on his hip. The checkered grip was exactly where his fingers would reach with his arms hanging natural and easy at his side.

Lyons grunted at that. It was a fast-draw holster. This was Military intelligence, not regular Army.

"Call your watch commander," Lyons stated. "The password is Trinity."

"That's a goddamn lie," the colonel snarled, drawing the massive weapon.

"Then shoot me twice," the Able Team leader said calmly, hands on the steering wheel.

Now the shoulders of the colonel relaxed slightly and he holstered the Desert Eagle. "Password confirmed," he said with a nod. "You can pass."

As Lyons shifted back into gear and drove the SUV past the soldiers, the men kept their weapons pointed at the civilian vehicle as if just waiting for any excuse to cut loose.

"They know something is up," Blancanales muttered.

"Be fools not to," Lyons agreed grimly, turning on the halogen headlights.

The bright lights flooded the woods ahead of the

SUV to nearly daylight level. The gravel road curved into tattered trees, the bark missing from one side, and many of the branches missing leaves. With a clatter, the heavy SUV rolled onto a wooden bridge spanning a rocky stream, the roadway made of railroad ties bolted together. The beams should have been strong enough to support an armored personnel carrier, but the wood was badly cracked in spots, and there was the familiar acne-effect of shrapnel along the surface. It looked like an aerial explosion from the pattern.

Past the splintery ruins of what might have been a guard kiosk, Lyons drove the SUV down a sloped embankment, the ground uneven and full of potholes. A vast field spread before the team, and only their maps showed it as a parking lot for the target range.

The area was a disaster, wrecks scattered about as if hit by a wing of bombers. Soon, Lyons had to stop the SUV as driving was becoming impossible through a maze of debris on the ground: smashed windshields, burned shoes, charred lumber, a woman's purse, broken bricks, a single tooth. The sad remains of life, reduced to the effluvia of death.

Braking the SUV in a clear patch of cracked asphalt, Able Team got out and studied the tattered landscape in the beams of the headlights. They were trying to get the feel for the battle zone. Minutes passed in hard silence, with the only noise coming from the ticking engine. Thankfully, the bodies were long gone, taken away in ambulance airships to the nearest military hospital under full security. Only the chalk outlines remained. Hundreds of them. Not one complete, only bits and pieces of the corpses were shown.

"Any sign of a dump?" Lyons asked, frowning. Something was hinky here. The former street cop could feel it in his bones. As if they were under observation.

"Nothing yet," Schwarz said, operating the EM scanner once more. "But all of this metal is making things…"

A shot rang out, and something ricocheted off a half-melted engine block.

Diving for cover, the team hit the ground with weapons drawn. Their senses heightened by adrenaline, the men listened for any movements, but the field of destruction seemed clear.

Sliding on a pair of Starlite goggles from his pocket, Blancanales scanned the surrounding hillside, boosting the magnification to maximum.

"Looks clean," he said reluctantly. "If there's a sniper, he's very well hidden."

Another shot was heard, but this time Lyons caught a brief motion out of the corner of his eye.

"Goddamn, it's the ammunition in the belts of the dead guards," he said angrily. "The rounds near the fire are cooking off from the heat."

"Great," Blancanales muttered, using a thumb to ease down the hammer on his .380 Colt pistol. "Let's finish our EM swept and get the hell out of here."

"I'm with you, Pol," Schwarz agreed, slowly rising to his feet. Checking the scanner, he boosted the range to maximum and started meandering through the rubbish and wreckage, swinging the device back and forth as if probing the ground for mines.

"No underground cables so far," he announced, leading the way through the darkness. Their shadows extended before them, the deeper pools of night only dimly illuminated by the dying fires. Busted masonry and torn pieces of clothing were everywhere. A broken M-16 lay in the dirt, black ants covering a brownish stain on the stock. The men said nothing at the sight, concentrating on the mission. Death was part of the job. Soldier or cop, you learned how to handle it, or got into another line of work.

"Any idea on the number of vehicles?" Lyons asked, walking around a crumpled sedan lying on its side. The tires were gone, burned off the rims, the doors smashed inward, and the interior upholstery was slashed in a thousand places, the stuffing well out like pus from a wound.

"According to Aaron, forty-five," Blancanales said, sweeping the destruction with his goggles. "So that gives us a minimum death toll."

"Most of these were limousines," Lyons corrected, brushing a hand over his short blond hair. "And nobody drives in one alone. So I'd place the minimum at 250, a maximum of, say, six hundred."

"Okay, heads up. The primary detonations were there," Schwarz said, pointing at another location. "And over there. But there were a lot of secondaries in the parking lot."

"Gas tanks in the cars?" Lyons asked.

After a moment, Schwarz shook his head. "More likely fragmentation bombs hidden in the trunks of a few cars that sent out dozens of bomblets that then detonated."

Carefully, Blancanales sniffed the air. "No smell of willy peter. Could have been thermite, or napalm."

"How hard would those be to obtain?" Lyons asked, dodging slightly as another round cooked off in the distance.

"We've been using them for forty years, England, China, heck Australia has its own version. They're expensive, and you have to know what you doing or else you only get a big-ass flash and not a damn thing is damaged."

"But do it right and whole towns could disappear off the map." Lyons said grimly. "And this is what they used merely to cover their tracks?"

"Whatever they used, I'm convinced now that it was for the Chameleon," Blancanales said, walking among the smashed cars, a tattered scrap of Navy uniform fluttering from a jagged piece of twisted metal. "It took a lot of effort to achieve this. Sure as hell wasn't done to get revenge on some congressman or senator."

While Schwarz continued his EM scan, Lyons surveyed the smoldering ruins of the grandstand. Okay, he was forced to agree with his teammate. If this had been a personal grudge against somebody, a simple car bomb would have done the job. In spite of what the Secret Service said, it was relatively easy to kill a man if you didn't mind dying with him. This level of destruction was done to cover the theft.

The somber atmosphere of the site was disturbed by a buzz from Lyons's jacket pocket. Switching his gun to his other hand, he pulled out his cell phone and flipped the lid.

"Able," he said.

"Cain," replied the voice of Barbara Price. "Good news. Aaron found gold. Professor Torge Johnson was spotted driving his car through a red light an hour after the explosions in Fairbanks."

"But MI identified the professor from his dental records and a finger found at the bunker," Lyons said, then added, "So we have a duplicate."

"Agreed. Unless the professor was kidnapped in front of a hundred VIPs."

"Highly unlikely."

"Agreed."

"A duplicate of a dead man, a stolen prototype, goddamn it, I remember something about a similar incident in France a few years ago," Lyons growled. "A politician was killed in an explosion, but his duplicate showed up minutes later at a national depository and emptied his personal safe-deposit box. God alone knows what state secrets were in there."

"Anybody claim the job?" Price asked.

"No."

"I'll find the incident and have Aaron and Carmen compare the records of everybody killed in the French explosion to the dead in this one. Somebody is going to match somehow, and that could be our man."

"Or woman," he said.

"Yeah, I already considered that. The professor was slim, and had a bushy beard. An easy man to imitate." Price sighed. "Too bad Hunt isn't here. He knows the French government systems inside and out."

"Help design them?" Lyons asked.

"No, but a student of his did."

"And Hunt taught the kid everything he knows?"

"She knows," Price corrected with a chuckle. "We almost recruited her, then Carmen came our way."

Lyons whistled. "That good, eh?"

"Very few better."

Somewhere in the woods, an owl began to hoot, then abruptly stopped as another round of ammunition ignited from the asphalt fires.

"Sorry, I missed that," Lyons spoke into the cell phone.

"I said, how is the search going?" Price asked.

"Zero so far. I'll call back when we find something."

"Confirmed," Price said, and the line went dead.

The Able Team leader closed the lid on the cell phone and slipped it away. "Okay, let's go see the target range," he ordered, heading briskly into the darkness. The sooner his team was out of here, the better. He simply couldn't shake the feeling of being watched.

Firebase One

THE MISSILES WERE ready to fly.

Gigantic, gleaming columns of metal, the four North Korean monsters stood in a neat line, each supported by an individual gantry. Brick fire pits yawned open beneath each titan to contain the fire blast of a launch. Power cables hung in clusters, while fat fuel lines kept the tanks of liquid hydrogen and liquid oxygen constantly filled to the absolute maximum level. Wisps of cold fog drifted around the exhaust vents of the colossal ICBMs, and a thin layer of ice covered the housings where the huge fuel tanks were located.

The sum total of the organization's resources had been used to make these four missiles. There would be no more. But they would suffice. The design of the missiles was unique: a mixture of American electronics,

Chinese alloys and Russian engines. They were marvels of technology, fully capable of traveling halfway around the world to deliver a payload of staggering destructive power. Not nukes. Those had proved impossible to obtain. But something almost as deadly, supplied by their comrades from Vietnam.

Standing behind a thick Plexiglas window, a slim Oriental man looked upon the towering missiles with near fatherly pride. He was dressed in a well-cut suit from the finest tailor in London, and a tiny red flower was in his buttonhole. A gold Rolex watch shone on his left wrist, and a cryptic tattoo adorned the back of his right hand—three interlocking circles.

"Are the coordinates programmed in for the new targets?" Major Yangida Fukoka asked in flawless English.

It was odd. The technical staff was from several nations, and at first, communication had been a problem. Then he discovered that many of them were amateur pilots, which easily settled the matter. English was the chosen international language of airport flight controllers. Every pilot in the world knew a little English. Brothers bound together by their knowledge of the hated enemy's tongue. The irony was almost poetic.

Crouched over a console of instruments, an elderly man turned and smiled. "Yes, sir," Dr. Owatari Tetsuo replied, pulling a pack of cigarettes from the pocket of his lab coat. "We can launch at your command."

Major Fukoka merely grunted, trying to ignore his own reflection in the Plexiglas. His face was horribly pockmarked with acne scarring, a combination of starvation and filthy living conditions as a child. Only his eyes were beautiful, shining with intelligence, although without the warmth of humor or compassion. Women of many races were drawn to his wondrous eyes, until they discovered the mind behind them, and by then it was too late. The major's tastes in bed ran to the extreme, and few of his partners ever saw the light of day again.

Lighting a cigarette, the scientist drew in a deep lungful of smoke, letting it trickle slowly out of his nose. "My technicians are ready to copy the device as soon as it arrives. Maybe a day, perhaps only an hour. Depending on the design and complexity of its circuits."

"Good," Fukoka said, glancing at his watch. "Now it is simply a matter of waiting for the arrival of Chameleon."

"And Davis Harrison."

"Yes, him too," the major said with a cold smile.

CHAPTER EIGHT

Kolyma Hills, Eastern Russia

Watching the glowing green radar screen, David Mc-Carter stayed alert for boulders in the nameless river. The pelting rain of the squall was far behind them now, the ocean mist replaced by a thick fog moving along the calm surface of the country river. Briefly, McCarter had a flashback to London at midnight. But this was not the time, nor the place. The former SAS officer cleared his head of such pleasant memories and concentrated on the work at hand. But it was difficult to forget. This was his fifth mission in a row without a break. McCarter knew he was starting to get edgy, his infamous short temper becoming dangerously tetchy. He needed some R&R. Hell, his whole team needed some rest and relaxation soon, or else their next mission would be their bloody last one!

The radar flashed a mute green light.

"All stop," McCarter subvocalized into his throat mike.

At the rear of the hovercraft, Encizo was operating

the engines, and he carefully began to slow the vehicle. Wearing night-vision goggles, Hawkins stood guard at the port side with an assault rifle draped over a shoulder and a silenced tranquilizer gun held loose in his gloved fist. This was civilian territory, and even if the U.S. and Russia were at war, the Stony Man commando would refrain from killing innocent civilians at all costs. The narcotic dart of the gun would put a person to sleep for hours, and by then Phoenix Force would be long gone. As always, the danger was encountering a child. The darts carried an adult dose to put a man down fast. The same amount could cause heart failure in a small child, but there was no second gun. If the team was spotted by a kid, they would have to run for it and take their chances against the entire Russian army.

Manning and James, in the second hovercraft, pulled alongside the first and as the engines went silent, the vessels lowered into the sluggish river. The fog carried a faint aroma of wood smoke, but there was no sign of a flickering campfire in the billowing mist covering the two shorelines.

Rising and falling with the gentle currents, the hovercraft headed downstream toward the ocean. The waves slapped against the moss-covered boulders rising from the river like baby mountains. Manning jerked about his assault rifle as a fish broke the surface, jumping after an insect. He relaxed with a sheepish grin, then went stiff as a soft buzz came the sky. The big Canadian whistled softly in warning, but the others had already caught the sound. A single-engine plane, or a small one-man helicopter. With the masking effect of the fog it was hard to tell, and McCarter didn't dare use the radar again. If that was a military aircraft, the pilot would spot the signal instantly and backtrack it directly to the hovercraft. That would blow the entire mission.

"T.J., toss it," McCarter said gruffly, keeping a steady hand on the small control board for the craft.

Sliding the tranquilizer gun into a holster, Hawkins pulled the pin on a fat tube that resembled a pipe bomb. Whirling it above his head at the end of a short rope, he built momentum and then let it go. The bomb flew into the fog and disappeared. If it hit water, the sound was lost in the noise of the waves on the rocks.

At first nothing seemed to happen, then the sound of the plane began to drift away in the direction of the pipe until it could no longer be heard. Lifting a pair of infrared goggles to his face, McCarter scanned the sky and found nothing. Switching to UV, he still saw nothing. Feeling the pressure of time, he decided to risk the radar and the screen came up clean. The plane was gone.

"Engines," he whispered into the mike, and the motors were cut back in immediately. "We used this long enough. Head north by northwest, half speed."

Rising off the river, the hovercraft moved forward once more and soon made up the lost distance. Skimming across the rocks and water, they floated over a submerged log and up onto a pebble shore. Continuing onward, the hovercraft moved up the slope and onto bare soil, then smooth grassland. Now their speed noticeably increased, and the team felt as if they were flying across the dark Russian countryside. After a hundred yards the sounds of the river were left behind, and there was only the low moan of the wind and the steady purr of the hovercraft engines.

"Looks like the plane bought the singer," James said, one hand tight on the joystick of the little craft.

The singer was a decoy that generated the radar ghost of a flock of birds. A sensor set for aerial pursuit would switch off the ghost as soon as the plane got close. The team also carried one set for a school of whales if they had been in danger of becoming exposed at sea. That one would sink while making the sounds of a dying whale, then turn itself off as it touched the seabed. The singer was designed by some unsung genius in the Pentagon as cover for Navy SEAL incursions and emergency evacuations. This was the first time Phoenix Force had used one, and so far it was receiving high marks.

Floating along the ground at fifty miles per hour, the men stayed alert for obstructions coming out of the thick fog. Now and then a tree zoomed out of the mist and they had to separate fast to go around. But mostly the terrain appeared to be farmland, the soil churned by tillers for the spring planting. Once a giant shape appeared on the horizon, and the team swung their weapons around. But it proved only to be a combine tractor sitting idle until the next day of work. Minutes passed in hushed quiet, only the purr of the engines and the rush of the ground-effect that keep them airborne disturbing the night. The craft dipped as they took a ravine filled with reeking garbage and stagnant water. But they rose again on the other side, sailing past some loose bricks scattered on the ground.

A soft glow became noticeable in the rushing fog, and McCarter checked a map on his PalmPilot. Ah, just a local village. This part of the Kolyma Mountain Range was mostly deserted, aside from a few farms and a couple of mining towns. The CIA believed it was also the training ground for a Russian terrorist organization, but that was unconfirmed.

Chancing the radar once more, McCarter slowed the hovercraft until it stood still, drifting slightly in the wind of its own creation. James did the same with the second. Some loose gravel on the ground kicked out from the spinning turbines, creating a small dust cloud. The men backed away until it stopped.

Just then, rapidly building in volume, a great shape came rushing out of the fog with blazing lights, and then it was gone.

"Clear," McCarter announced, nudging the joystick forward.

Moving on, the two craft flowed effortlessly over a low rock wall and across a smooth concrete highway. The two American craft paused above the grassy strip, separating the opposite lanes until another truck went by. Then they proceeded once more, down a gravel hill and out across a rough terrain of broken shale and small ponds.

As they crested the top of a low hill, the mountains were now in sight, impossibly tall peaks surrounded by a dense forest. If they stayed on the roads, the team might be seen. But if they stayed in the woods, soon the trees would be so close that the men would be forced to abandon the hovercraft and proceed on foot. But the forest gave them vital cover, so they'd keep flying until the very last moment.

"Any sign of the crashed plane yet?" McCarter asked.

"No response from the ILM system or the black box,"

James replied over the earphone. "But the GPS says we're smack on track."

"Stay alert," McCarter said, squinting into the foggy night. "Watch for wreckage on the ground, or broken treetops."

"Roger that."

In the second hovercraft, Manning and James shared a thermos of coffee and zipped up their suits a little tighter. Cold. The Russian night was surprisingly cold.

Trees rose in the darkness, and the proximity sensor gave warning in time for the hovercraft to be turned in time to avoid a collision. Minutes later, their forward speed was cut by half as the two craft wove through the dense greenery, the trees dangerous close to one another. The branches formed a canopy overhead, and the sky was gone. Dead leaves swirled in the wake of their turbofans, and birds screamed in terror at the mechanical invasion, but there was no help for that. Time was of the essence.

The team knew that, while America and Russia were on genial terms these days, political friends became economic enemies at the drop of a stock market, and there was still a strong anti-American feeling in many of the former Soviet Union soldiers. The Chameleon would give the Russians a killing advantage in stealth technology—invisible spy planes and unstoppable missiles. Even incursions like this by Phoenix Force would be next to impossible to control if the hovercraft were masked by the blanketing field of the Chameleon. Recover or destroy. The words rang in their minds. It was seldom they received such a command.

The craft slowed at a rushing river, the mist fading

away and a cold, clear moonlight bathing the primordial woods. Encizo did a scan with the infrared and found nothing. The same for James and the tracking beacons. This was starting to worry McCarter. A crashed commercial jetliner was one of the easiest things in the world to find. Aside from the great fan of wreckage in its wake, the jet planes carried numerous devices for rescuers to find the passengers. There were backup systems on the backup systems. So unless Flight 18 had slammed into the side of a mountain and been blown to smithereens, there should be a beacon beeping for help. But the airwaves were clear.

"I don't like this," Hawkins commented, sliding an AK-105 off his shoulder and working the bolt.

The deadly assault rifle had a 40 mm grenade launcher attached under its barrel. Normally, the covert team carried a favorite weapon for close-order combat, the incredibly reliable 9 mm Heckler & Koch MP-5 submachine gun. But this was politically dangerous territory, and so the AK-105 had been chosen as the support piece for the mission. Any shells found would be traced back to the Russian army, not American soldiers. As backup weapons, the second hovercraft also had the team's MP-5 subguns, but those were for emergency use only.

Holding the sleek, tubular weapon, with a pair of UV goggles on his face, McCarter felt like a starship trooper in some sci-fi flick. But the characters in those movies only had robots and alien monsters to battle. His team was facing the most dangerous opponent known: other men, highly trained, heavily armed and on familiar ground.

A sudden flurry of motion from the trees made the

team swing their weapons in that direction. But they withheld firing at the sight of a flock of bats, the creatures squeaking and flapping through the night.

"Must be near the mountains," Manning said, resting the barrel of the AK-105 on a shoulder.

"Most species of bats live in trees, not caves," James corrected. His breath fogged at every word, but the cold didn't really bother the tall former Navy SEAL. Born and raised in Chicago, anything sort of standing naked at the North Pole was merely chilly.

Taking another drink from the thermos, Manning glanced about. "Trees we already got," he muttered, screwing the cap back on.

Checking the fuel gauge, McCarter saw the hovercraft were nearly at the halfway point. Soon they would have to stop or risk going on foot to the pickup point. A fishing trawler was waiting at a coastal village to the north to take the team, and any survivors, hide them and the passengers in its hold and sail them straight through the underwater sonar buoys of the Russian navy and into international waters where they could rendezvous with U.S. Navy ships. The plan was good, but as an old campaigner, David McCarter knew that virtually no battle plan ever survived first contact with the enemy. Some young wag in MI-5 had once said that a battle plan was merely a list of things that wouldn't happen in combat.

"I have a reading," Encizo said, checking the scanner in his gloved hand.

"The beacon?" McCarter demanded, checking his own.

"No, a fire. But it's in a triangle pattern. Just due north of us, 210 yards."

Could be the crash site. His hopes for some survivors rose at the news. A triangular pattern would mean a sideways approach. A deadly vertical impact would read as a circle.

"Let's go," McCarter commanded, working the bolt on his AK-105 assault rifle. "Full speed!"

Kobuk Valley, Alaska

THE FLIES WERE THICK near the ruins of the grandstand, and flocked to the flashlights carried by Able Team.

But Lyons and his teammates were prepared and sprayed themselves with insect repellant before working their way through the splintered timbers. Only vestiges of flagstones in the ground told them where the grandstand had originally stood. A single Delta Four didn't leave much behind, and a salvo even less.

Half-melted poles bent low to the ground, the only reminder of the safety nets erected to prevent clumps of soil from hitting the spectators when the missiles hit the distant hillside. Beyond what might have once been a railing was a flat field with a large charred hole in the center. Thumbing his flashlight to a tight beam, Lyons played it about, but not even scattered debris remained to mark the exact location of the annihilated bunker.

"Nothing we can salvage from that," Schwarz muttered unhappily, tucking away the scanner.

"That looks like a direct hit," Blancanales said slowly, rubbing his jaw. "Without a gunner washing it with a laser light, there must have been a homing unit in the blockhouse to make sure it was struck dead center. Deltas are good, but not that good."

"I'm betting on a homer," Lyons stated, resting a shoe on a chunk of concrete as he fanned more of the field. The breeze from the nearby inlet carried a faint smell of saltwater, the clean air helped reduce the charnel-house reek of the killzone. "Our guy likes to plant hidden bombs. Bombers are very monogamous. They find one type of explosive and stick with it."

"You don't," Blancanales said to Schwarz.

His teammate shrugged. "I'm a professional."

"Maybe our ape is, too," Lyons growled, returning the flashlight to its usual setting. Then he stood. "Okay, we've seen ground zero. Let's go check the lab."

The men were quiet on the ride out of the parking lot, each deep in thought about the attack. The homing beacons would have needed to be placed by hand, while the missile tests were going on in all likelihood. That took a particularly cool operative.

As the SUV jounced onto the gravel road, Schwarz cast a look backward.

"I'm willing to bet that if there were any intact bodies," he muttered, "that we'd find several of the Marine Corps guards dead."

"Bombers aren't usually face-to-face killers," Blancanales reminded him. "But yeah, I'll buy that. Whoever this guy is, I'm surprised we haven't encountered him before. Nobody this good just falls out of the sky."

"Maybe we have," Lyons said grimly, shifting gears as he started up the rough incline. "But this is the first time we know about it."

The two soldiers frowned at the grim notion, but said nothing.

After driving to Quiller Geo-Medical Laboratories, Able Team went through another search pattern, with equally poor results. The destruction was on a staggering level. There were no signs of additional bombs being planted in the complex, but they wouldn't have been necessary. A pair of Delta Four missiles hitting a fully stocked chemical laboratory would reduce the building to a memory.

Running an EM scan of the tattered lawn far outside the blast crater, Schwarz boosted his equipment to the maximum while Lyons and Blancanales swept the grass with their flashlights. The off-site backup file would be carefully hidden. Most likely the feeder cables snaked, or twined, with the local power company.

Twining was something the federal government had been doing for decades. When a technical installation was being built near a civilian area, when the telephone company crew arrived to lay the cables, there would be a switch done by NSA agents, and the original cables replaced with an NSA special. The new cable would look exactly like a standard heavy-duty phone line, and would responded properly to the civilian instruments. But afterward the NSA would return to splice additional lines to the hidden wires inside the main cable, and run them to the listening post, off-site dump or whatever they wished. The utility did all of the hard digging, but the cable was under NSA control, and best of all, there were absolutely no records of the installation.

"Anything?" Lyons asked, walking alongside his friend.

"Not yet." Schwarz pulled out his personal computer to check a map of what the area had formerly looked like. Changing direction, he moved out of the headlight beams of the SUV and headed for a broken clump of trees, then abruptly stopped.

"Wait a second," he said quietly, adjusting the scanner.

Scuffing his shoes along the ground, Schwarz found something large and metallic. Kneeling, he pushed away the loose soil to expose a manhole cover.

"Bingo." He grinned in triumph. "Give me a hand, will you?"

The three men wrestled the heavy cast-iron plate out of its rimmed recess and uncovered a dark hole. Lyons played his flashlight around inside and found a ladder welded to the side of the steel pipe, but the bottom was out of range of the beam.

"Want some company?" Blancanales asked, using a strip of Velcro to attach his flashlight to the barrel of a .380 Colt pistol.

Loosening his tie, Schwarz started down into the pipe. "No need. This should only take a few seconds." Then he paused to wriggle his shoulder through the tight fit. The opening of the access pipe was an oval now instead of being circular from the crushing shock wave of the missile hits.

Standing guard on top, Lyons and Blancanales watched their friend descend until he was gone from sight.

"If this is a bust, we check the apartments of the staff next," Lyons stated, switching his attention to the surrounding forest and the distant hillside. The military cordon thrown around the valley should have been enough to keep out any civilian witnesses, but he still had the odd feeling of being observed.

"And after that?" Blancanales asked, brushing away some gnats.

"We start from the beginning to see what we missed," the big man stated. "And we keep going it until Barb tells us to stop, or we find the files."

"Or the thief. You know, I've had fun before, and this ain't it."

Lyons cracked a rare smile. "I hear ya."

Dark clouds blocked the stars overhead, and flying insects gathered around the bright halogen beams of the idling SUV across the lawn. Faint taps sounded as the bugs hit the glass and bounced off again and again.

Clicking off their flashlights to save power, the men waited until their eyes adjusted to the darkness. A cool breeze rustled what leaves remained on the battered trees, but aside from that the silence was oppressive. No birds, no crickets, no night creatures. Just silence.

Time passed slowly in the Alaskan field. They were starting to get concerned when a bobbing light appeared at the bottom of the pipe, then they heard Schwarz muttering curses as he climbed back up the ladder.

Switching their lights back on to help him see, the men waited until their teammate reached the ground and wiggled free, ripping his jacket on the recessed rim.

"Damn it, that was new," Schwarz cursed, getting to his feet.

"Screw that. Did you find anything?" Blancanales demanded anxiously.

"Yes and no." Schwarz sighed. "I found the dump computer, but it was wiped clean. Our ape had been here long before the missiles arrived."

"How can you tell?" Lyons scowled.

Reaching into a pocket, Schwarz pulled out a small lump of C-4 plastique. "He left this behind to blow the site. See here?" He touched a small silvery disk dangling from a broken wire. "That's a pressure switch. This charge was supposed to blow the dump site when the concussion wave from the missiles arrived."

"So this was done first."

"Yes."

"Damn!"

"You were expecting something like that," Blancanales stated. "That's why you wanted to go down alone."

"No, I just work better by myself," he lied to his teammate with a toothy grin, tucking away the C-4.

Pulling out a cell phone, Lyons started tapping numbers. "I'll tell Barbara," he said, then frowned as the device changed functions. Then did it again, and again. What the hell?

With sudden understanding, the Able Team leader went cold. Son of a bitch. The cell phone was being hit by an infrared beam of some kind that was randomly activating its programs. It wasn't an attempt to hack the phone; an infrared beam couldn't do that. No, this was a concentrated beam and the only thing he could possibly think of was the tracer of a sniper rifle sweeping the team to zero in for a kill. Adrenaline flooded his body.

They had flushed out a source of information. Now all his team had to do was stay alive to question him. Time to move!

"Incoming!" Lyons yelled, and sprinted for the SUV.

Blancanales and Schwarz responded instantly and spread out in different directions to not offer a single target. Almost immediately a hard metallic belch sounded from the trees on the hillside, closely followed by muffled thump as a canister hit the grass alongside the open pipe in the ground. It burst apart and began spewing out volumes of gray smoke.

Catching a glimpse, Lyons doubled his speed for the car. That was sleep gas! Somebody had to have been following the team from the distant hilltop, waiting for them to find something and now was coming to collect the team alive for questioning. He wanted them alive just as much as Able Team did him. Not the thief, then. So who was he?

The answer to that question was duck soup, Lyons thought as he pounded across the open ground. Step one—capture a duck. There were heavy weapons hidden in the ceiling panels of the SUV that would tip the balance in their favor. If he could just get hold of an M-203, or another grenade launcher...

The Stony Man commando was only ten yards from the SUV when the hillside belched again and something crashed through the windshield of the vehicle, filling the interior with greenish smoke.

Vomit gas! Okay, change in tactics. Shifting direction, Lyons raced across the open ground and dived headlong into the ragged bushes. The belch of a grenade launcher sounded again as the Able Team leader fought his way free and jumped off the top of the embankment. He landed with a splash into the trickling creek at the bottom and sprinted into the blackness of the storm drain set under the road. A figure rose before him, and Lyons almost fired from the hip when the shape gave a two-tone whistle. He responded and stepped closer to Blancanales and Schwarz.

"Well, we found the end of the rope," Blancanales said, checking his .380 Colt pistol. The weapon was woefully underpowered for a duel with a sniper, but everything else they had was in the SUV. "Anybody catch his direction?"

"Toward that big peak to the west," Lyons said. "That's the direction my cell phone was facing when it triggered from the tracer beam."

"Good thing he's using infrared. If it was UV, we'd be facedown in the dirt," Schwarz commented. "And a pro would have known better than to point IR at civilian equipment."

"So this isn't our ape, then? Damn! Then again, he might know who our guy is."

"We take this asshole alive," Lyons stated.

Just then, something splashed into the stream outside the storm drain and green smoke rose from the bubbling water.

"More vomit gas," Schwarz said, covering his mouth with a pocket handkerchief.

Kneeling, Lyons dipped his handkerchief into a puddle before covering his mouth and drawing in a deep breath.

"That wasn't a mortar round," he stated, tying the

cloth behind his head. "It sounds too weak. Maybe a Russian RPG or a 40 mm American M-79." If he caught some of the smoke, the wet cloth would help, but not for long, and not against tear gas.

Or VX nerve gas, Lyons observed. How long would the sniper try to take them alive before he changed to more lethal tactics?

"He's firing too fast for those. I'd bet it's an MM-1," Schwarz replied. "That holds eighteen rounds, and he's only sent five our way so far."

There came another crash of glass, and the hissing from above became noticeably louder.

"Make that six," he amended.

Blancanales frowned. Twelve more rounds before reloading. And the shells for an MM-1 came in a wide variety. The person on the hill could start lobbing anything at them, from aerial flares to light up the night, to antipersonnel shotgun rounds that could cut an oak tree in two.

"Anybody else have a grenade?" Lyons demanded, pulling the explosive charge from his pocket. The colored stripes marked it as a stun grenade. It was perfect for this sort of work. Unfortunately, it had a very limited range, while that weapon on the hill could easily sweep the whole valley.

"Just the C-4," Schwarz said, patting a lumpy pocket. "Why, got a plan?"

"Yeah, we make a run for the SUV and get more weapons," Lyons said, pulling out the keys. He pressed the fob and there was an answering horn honk from the vehicle as the engine turned off.

"Okay, in about thirty seconds the headlights will automatically cycle off, and with this cloud cover we'll be almost invisible," Lyons stated quickly.

Blancanales took some mud from the floor of the drain and smeared it on his cheeks in lieu of combat cosmetics.

Smart man. Lyons copied the trick. "We hit the car from both sides and get the Sabers from the trunk. The ceiling panels take too long to open for the other weapons. After that we can—"

He was interrupted by a loud explosion from above, followed by a soft explosion and a crackling noise.

"That sounded like the SUV got hit with an explosive round," Blancanales said, furrowing his brow. "So much for the Saber assault guns in the trunk."

"Damn things are too heavy anyway," Schwarz muttered, blinking hard against the stinging gas. The wind was blowing through the tunnel from the western ocean. If the sniper figured that out and hit them with gas on both sides, they would be forced into the open. Easy pickings.

"I don't think our boy wants us alive anymore," Lyons said, liberally adding more mud to his white shirt. The rest of the suit was nicely dark, but the clean white shirt would only be a beacon asking to be shot in a night attack.

"That second blast was the gas tank. I recognized the sound," Schwarz said, shifting his stance in the muddy water. "The ammo will start cooking off soon, and when that goes, it'll set off the C-4 satchel charge hidden under the seats."

"We can use the explosion as a diversion," Lyons

said. "We'll break for the trees and go after the bastard when the C-4 charges blow."

"How long?" Blancanales asked, looking at Schwarz, who shrugged.

"Any time now."

With those words, the entire world seemed to shake, and a harsh red light banished the night, the concrete tunnel cracking slightly overhead and sprinkling fine dust. Without pause, Able Team dashed out of the storm drain and into the night.

Scrambling up the steep slope of the culvert, the three men barely reached the top when a canister dropped into the space behind them. Spreading out fast, each man was going in a different direction across the grass when the charge loudly detonated. A vertical wall of flame rose upward, channeled by the embankment, the hellish light brightly illuminating the night for a terrible few seconds. And then it was gone.

Waiting for shrapnel to hit him in the back, Lyons tensed his muscles, but kept going headlong into the bushes. Immediately, he ducked behind a tree for safety, then charged off at an angle to make it impossible for the gunner above to track his movements. Sure enough, a few moments later, an explosion shook the tree, followed by the rustling rain of leaves and debris falling back to earth.

Okay, the gloves were off now, and the gunner knew that he had trouble coming. That had been willy peter, white phosphorous, used in the drain and HE on the tree. He was going for a kill now. But what the gunner didn't know was that Able Team wanted him alive much more than he needed them dead.

Finding a break in the canopy, Lyons fired twice in the wrong direction, trying to make the gunner think his position was still unknown. More gunfire sounded as his teammates did the same thing. Good men. Lyons charged into the bushes again, trying to disturb the foliage as little as possible and betray his own approach.

The gunner wouldn't be at the very crest of the hill. The moonlight coming from behind would silhouette the man and make him a perfect target. Okay, but not too low, either, or else he wouldn't have been able to see the target range as well as the ruined lab. Lyons paused at the sight of a creek flowing down the hillside. He studied it for a heartbeat and then moved onward. The creek was a natural and fast route to the top of the hill. So if that wasn't mined, then the gunner was a complete fool.

A metallic belch sounded once more, louder than before, and without warning a bright light filled the sky. Lyons froze as a Starshell slowly parachuted toward the ground, the terrain and valley brightly illuminated by the sizzling magnesium flare.

The moment it died away and darkness returned, Blancanales and Schwarz both fired their weapons, but Lyons didn't. This high up the hill, the gunner might be able to track the sound and start lobbing in more phosphorous grenades. Stay low, go fast—that was the rule this night. Then came the unexpected chatter of an Uzi machine pistol. The burst went on and on, then abruptly stopped, and the 30 mm weapon belched again, followed by two loud explosions.

He's shooting blind, trying to force us into cover,

Lyons thought with a grimace. So, either the gunner was an amateur, or else he thought they were. Which made no sense. The ape was highly trained, so why would he team up with a fool? Something very odd was going on here, and Lyons was starting to smell a rat.

Zigzaging up the steep grade, he caught a movement in the bushes and spun with his blaster at the ready. But at the last moment, the Stony Man commando held fire and allowed himself a small smile. It was only a red ribbon tied to a bush. Excellent. That was an old hunter's trick to mark the area for other hunters that this was a good area filled with game. It also meant there would be a hunter's platform hidden in a tall tree somewhere close. The ideal spot for a sniper.

The Uzi spoke again for a full clip and then the 30 mm, but with a pause between the two. That meant there was only the one gunner, with no backup, or else the weapons would overlap. More bad news. Anybody they found had to be taken alive. There could be no blind firing on their part.

Taking a position behind a wide tree, Lyons pulled out his cell phone and plugged in an earphone, then hit a programmed number. There was a buzz, followed by a soft click.

"Ethel?" Schwarz asked.

"No, this is Lucy, Fred," Lyons whispered back. "What's your twenty?"

"We're ghosting the creek. Found a couple of trip wires. Our boy was expecting trouble."

An explosion shook the night.

"He's dug in tight," Lyons said, ducking his head as more dirt and leaves fell from the sky. "However, I think I know where Ricky is located."

"So do I. He's in a hunter's platform."

"Found a ribbon, eh? Me, too."

"Lazy bastard."

"Confirm." There came a violent explosion and a fireball rose from the trees, sending broken branches outward in an umbrella of destruction.

"Heard that? I'm ten yards northwest," Lyons stated, knowing that Schwarz would translate that into twenty yards southeast. There was no scramble function on civilian cell phones, so the team would only use coded phrases.

"Got a plan?"

"See the big rock ledge to the east? Concentrate your guns there. I'll flush him out."

The Uzi split the night once more. But the big-bore MM-1 grenade launcher didn't cut loose. Unless Lyons lost count, the gunner still had two more rounds to go. So he was either holding them in reserve, or was reloading. Both of which were bad news.

"Our boy is getting smart," Schwarz warned.

"Roger on that."

In rapid succession, the MM-1 fired six times and several trees in the sloping forest violently disintegrated under the assault of the antipersonnel rounds. Slowly bending over, a massive oak dipped lower and lower until its branches snapped off as the trunk hit the ground with a strident crash. Twice more the gunner fired into the forest, leaving patches of destruction.

"Son of a bitch reloaded," Blancanales remarked calmly.

"Think our pals from down the road might come to investigate?" Schwarz growled.

Lyons cast a glance in the direction of the military cordon. "The cops would want to, yes. But the troops know better. We're on our own," he stated with conviction. Then he added, "But just in case, stay alert for friendlies. We move in six."

"Roger that."

"Ten-four, Lucy."

Lyons removed the earplug and tucked away the device. Okay, he had three minutes to get closer before they cut loose.

Going down a hill a little ways, Lyons found a thick clump of blackberry bushes. He knew from past experience that animals often left tunnels through dense bushes, paths actually, as they tried to reach the juicy berries in the middle of the bushes. He didn't know how high up the hill it might go, but the tunnel would offer excellent coverage. That was, as long as he didn't meet a bear coming down the hill. But the gunfire should have frightened away any wildlife.

Going on hands and knees, the Stony Man commando crawled through the thorny darkness as fast as he could, staying alert as the sound of the grenade launcher and then the Uzi got steadily louder.

Slowly kneeling, he waited for an explosion before spreading some of the prickly bush for a better view. The thick cloud cover kept out most of the moonlight, but Lyons could vaguely make out a dim figure standing in a crouch. The gunner or a cop come to help, he couldn't tell. Then the Uzi chattered once more, and in the strobing light of the muzzle-flash, the Able Team leader could see it was their quarry.

Dressed in dark clothing and hiking boots, the man was sweeping the hillside with the Uzi. An MM-1 hung at his side from a canvas strap, and a pistol rested at his hip in an oddly shaped holster. A dirt bike leaned against the rock face of a small cliff behind the man, the outcropping neatly blocking off any chance of sneaking up behind him. A stone-filled gully cut sideways across the hill in front of him, and beyond that was a sharply angled open field. Certain death for anybody trying a frontal assault. That was what he had been trying to force Able Team into. The position was good, but like all amateurs, the gunner hadn't properly checked his flanks and had missed the bear tunnel.

Moving slowly to avoid making any noise, Lyons tucked the Colt Python into a forking branch of the bush and retrieved the grenade out of his pocket. Pulling the pin, he released the arming handle and placed the bomb on the ground, ignoring the thorns cutting into his skin. Any moment now...

Gunfire exploded from the other side of the hill, and as the gunner pivoted toward the noise, Lyons rolled the grenade through the small opening in the bushes. It moved along the ground heading for the gunner as he discharged round after round into the night. Then Lyons bit back a curse as it started to angle away, following the natural incline of the ground. It rolled into the gully before igniting.

With a strident roar, the stun grenade cut loose, the light flash washing across the open field. But the cant of the gully shielded the gunner from the effect, and he stayed masked in relative darkness.

"Jesus Christ!" he screamed, blindly firing the MM-1 in every direction.

A clump of bushes near Lyons was completely blown away by a barrage of the steel buckshot from the 30 mm round, and he involuntarily grunted as some thorns raked his face. The gunner's eyes went wide at that, and as he swung the wide maw of the deadly weapon toward Lyons, the Stony Man commando stood amid the prickly thorns and fired. The roar of the .357 Magnum Colt Python was matched by the scream of the gunner as his right elbow exploded with blood and he dropped the launcher. Clutching the hideous wound, he staggered backward against the low cliff.

Fighting his way through the bushes, Lyons placed his next two shots with extreme care, going for the flesh of the thigh where there were no major arteries. They needed this man alive!

With blood pumping from his wounds, the gunner fell to the ground.

"Freeze or die!" Lyons growled, his finger tight on the trigger of the Colt Python.

Snarling something in a foreign language, the gunner brought up the Uzi that lay beneath him. Lyons had only the briefest glimpse of the barrel of the dropped weapon blocked with mud before the breech of the weapon exploded. The chest of the gunner erupted into a ghastly spray of bones, blood and organs. Flopping sideways, the man sprawled on the ground, his exposed back offering a clear view to the crimson-soaked soil beneath him.

A few moments later, Blancanales and Schwarz exited the bushes on top of the cliff.

"What happened?" Blancanales demanded, looking down upon the scene.

"He refused to surrender," Lyons said, turning over the warm corpse. The man's face was contorted in a grisly rictus of pain and shock. "Come on down and help me go through his pockets."

"Better hurry," Schwarz warned, craning his neck.

Down in the valley below, lights were bobbing along the sides of the access road leading to the ruins of Quiller Geo-Medical.

"It looks like the military finally decided to come investigate anyway," Blancanales observed curtly. "We have five minutes, maybe less."

Turning out the wet and bloody pockets of the dead man, Lyons found only breath mints, spare ammunition clips for the handgun and some loose change.

He frowned at that. The guy carried loose change into battle? This was a real amateur, but also a fanatic who refused to surrender. That was a bad combination.

Blancanales and Schwarz remained on watch from the top of the cliff as Lyons checked the ground for anything that might have been dropped. He was about to give up when something metallic crunched under his shoe. Shielding the beam of his flashlight with a cupped hand, he carefully looked under his foot just in case it was another booby trap like the ones set along the creek.

Gold and silver winked back at him, and Lyons smiled as he pulled out a set of keys. The plastic fob carried the logo of a car-rental company, and as he pressed it, there was an answering bleep and headlight flash from the top of the hill.

Instantly, the lights in the valley below stopped, and started coming straight up the side of the hill.

"Let's move," Lyons commanded, blending into the darkness.

CHAPTER NINE

Orkormev Plain, Eastern Russia

Broken treetops marked the initial descent of the plane, then broken limbs, followed by smashed tree trunks mixed with pieces of wreckage. Manning and James held back as reserves as McCarter and the others went straight in with weapons at the ready.

The crash site spread out for yards, wheels and debris scattered in every direction. Small brushfires burned out of control, but there was no general blast nimbus indication of burned aviation fuel. Following the natural rise and fall of the land, the team suddenly came upon the downed plane. The wings were crumpled, the fuselage bent at impossible angles, but the plane was mostly intact, some of the windows still intact.

"One hell of a pilot," Hawkins said in admiration as the hovercraft swung around the plane on a fast recon. Bodies lay on the ground, mostly men, and one rested against the cracked hull, a line of bloody holes across his chest.

"Land," McCarter ordered. "Unit Two continue the sweep, watch for enemy troops. A passenger has been shot."

"Shot? That's a confirm. Roger, Unit One."

A woman's scream came from the darkness, followed by a pistol shot.

Revving the hovercraft to full speed, James swooped around the tail section of the aircraft, working the joystick even as he pulled a weapon. Bodies were scattered across the ground, oil lanterns adding a yellow tint to the orange light of burning debris. A suitcase was open on the ground, filled with wallets and jewelry, another with cell phones and in-flight liquor bottles.

Two women were tied spread-eagle on the bare ground, ropes lashed around their wrists and ankles tied to wooden stakes jutting from the hard dirt. One was a young woman, no more than a teenager, the other a mature woman in her fifties or so. Both were naked, their clothing ripped away, the remains shoved out of the way onto their bound arms and legs. The older woman faced the sky with her head thrown back, her throat slashed open and blood pooled around her shoulders. The teenager's head was flopped sideways, a gaping red hole in the middle of her forehead. Blood was smeared on their thighs and breasts.

Manning worked the bolt of his AK-105 assault rifle and concentrated on the group of bearded men standing near the corpses. A bald man in heavy clothing was zipping up his pants, as another pumped a second round into the dead teenager. Standing nearby, several other men in civilian clothing were laughing among themselves, one of them displaying a pair of lacy panties.

Working the joystick of the hovercraft, a cursing James slowed the craft as Manning cut loose with the Kalashnikov. The time for stealth was over.

The first burst went wild from the moving hovercraft, and the men looked into the darkness beyond their lanterns with shock, and then anger as they drew an assortment of weapons from their clothing. As the craft landed firmly, Manning and James both cut loose with their AK-105 assault rifles, sweeping through the murderous group. Three of the men threw their arms to the sky as the hardball ammo punched straight through their chests, blowing red life out the front of their flannel shirts. The big man with the Tokarev pistol got off two shots, one of the bullets humming past James. In reply, the Phoenix Force commando stitched the killer from groin to face, the heavy-duty combat rounds almost cutting him in two.

As the body fell, a fifth man stepped around the tail section of the plane firing an AK-74. The weapon jammed, and the gunner screamed vulgarities as he savagely worked the bolt to clear the ejector port. Centering his weapon, Manning put a burst into his adversary's chest and the man went flying backward, his repaired weapon discharging into the uncaring sky. He landed on some wreckage, a sliver of metal piercing his throat completely, the needle-sharp end glistening with fresh blood. His fingers twitching, the killer dropped his weapon and went still, his own blood dripping down upon his lifeless face.

"Stony Two to Big Dog, we have scavengers," Manning said, dropping a spent magazine and slapping in a fresh one.

"Roger, Two," McCarter said crisply. "We heard. On the way."

Suddenly, two more men appeared at the gaping rift in the fuselage, firing Kalashnikov assault rifles, the fiery muzzle-blasts lighting up the night. Ducking behind the rubber gunwale of the hovercraft, James loosed a burst their way. The Russian lead ricocheted off the exposed struts of the body of the plane, and one man crumpled into a ball, his arms wrapping around the bleeding ruin of his stomach. His comrade ducked inside, then a gun barrel poked through a rift in the hull and started firing blindly.

Leaping out of the hovercraft, Manning zigzagged across the debris-covered ground as James gave cover fire in short bursts from his assault rifle. There was a 40 mm round in the grenade launcher attached under the main barrel, but that was loaded with a Starshell. The aerial flare was useless for this fight, since there was more than enough light coming from all of the small fires.

Passing the suitcase full of wallets and purses, Manning involuntarily flinched as a horrible smell hit him like a punch in the face, and he tried not to gag. It was vaguely like burned pork, but he knew better. A cold fury flooded the big Canadian. Roasting human flesh reeked like nothing else in the world, and once you smelled it, the odor was branded into your brain. He could only pray the passengers were already dead when the fires overtook them.

There was a motion near a rent in the side of the

crashed plane, and Manning fired. There was a flutter of clothing, but no cry of pain. Damn, it had to have missed flesh by less than an inch.

"Shoot no more! I have a hostage!" a man inside shouted in heavily accented Russian. "Come closer, and I kill her!"

The accent sounded Georgian, and it took Manning a moment to decipher the words. German and Japanese were his specialties, but every member of Stony Man knew a little Russian from their long battles with the KGB and Moscow Mafia.

Moving low and fast, McCarter and the rest of Phoenix Force appeared from the night, their hands full of destruction. Silently, James relayed them instructions with a few curt gestures, and the others moved into position.

"Do not hurt my wife!" Manning cried out, pulling out a pistol with his left hand. "Here! I surrender!" Tossing the AK-105 into the twisted hatchway of the craft, Manning dropped flat and aimed his Tokarev pistol as the rest of the team assumed a firing stance behind the hovercraft.

"Army fool!" The man chortled, stepping into view with the Kalashnikov level at his hip. "Time to die!"

The entire team cut loose in an orchestrated barrage, the incoming hail of lead driving the killer backward until his riddled body crashed through the door to the lavatory. As he slid to the floor, his twitching hands released the assault rifle and it hit the ground, banging off a single round. Rushing forward, Manning grabbed his rifle and slammed his body against the bent fuselage of the jumbo jet alongside the hatchway. Keeping the pistol in his left hand, Manning listened hard for any motion inside the plane. He heard nothing, but the smell of death of was strong, almost overpowering. The coppery tang of spilled blood mixed with the reek of emptied bowels. Death in any fashion was always ugly.

Darting along the ground, McCarter came closer, using the pieces of wreckage as cover. Going to a window, he pulled out a small plastic mirror from a pocket on the thigh of his fatigues and looked about inside. Turning to the others, he raised an empty hand to show it was clear, then slashed it sideways as the go code.

With a stubby AK-105 in one hand and a long AK-74 in the other, Hawkins hit the opposite side of the hatchway, and Manning swung in with both of his weapons sweeping for targets. James and Encizo took sniper positions near empty windows, their faces masked with IR night goggles. Then McCarter slammed the butt of his AK-105 onto the cracked glass of the window. As it shattered, Hawkins slipped inside the hatch as backup for Manning.

Sliding down his own night goggles, McCarter started for the hatchway when there came a brief burst of machine-gun fire. The Briton froze at the sound. With both sides using the same weapons, he couldn't tell if that had been from one of his people or from the raiders looting the plane!

"Give me a sit-rep, Stony Two," McCarter subvocalized into his throat mike. "Are you green?"

"Confirm, David," Manning said over the earphone. "Green and clear. We found somebody trying to hide among the dead passengers. I fired a burst as a diversion so T.J. could go for a capture, but the stupid bastard pulled a knife."

"Is he alive?"

"Me, yes, him, no," Hawkins stated matter-of-factly.

"Damn it, we could have used a prisoner to question," McCarter said, walking into the plane. There was rubbish and blood everywhere, yet the aircraft was in amazingly good shape. Most of the destruction seemed to have occurred after the crash.

"Must have been an amazing pilot at the controls," Encizo observed, walking in with James. "Especially considering the rugged terrain."

"Trees and planes are natural enemies," Manning muttered gruffly. "But, yes, these people landed alive."

"Then the raiders came." James scowled. "I wonder if that was part of the plan for our thief, or just bad luck?"

Tiny sparkling squares of broken green glass from the safety windows were scattered across the slightly tilting deck. Mixed among them was shiny gold, spent shells casings from the automatic weapons. Hawkins knelt to pick one up, then picked up a warm shell on the floor. The cold shell was longer, 7.62 mm, rather than 5.45 mm.

"This is from a brand-new AK-104," he said, frowning. "These clowns were carrying AK-74s." He raised the two brass shells. "Somebody else was here."

Kneeling carefully to avoid a dried pool of blood, McCarter touched a few of the shells on the floor until finding a cold one. He sniffed inside the brass carefully.

"This is more than two hours old," he finally said. "Three at the most."

"Handload?" Encizo asked, furrowing his brow.

McCarter shook his head. "Factory fill. Military grade." He tossed over the brass.

Encizo made the catch and checked the stamp on the bottom. Standard Russian army ordnance. "Why the hell would the army not take all of the surviving passengers with them?" he demanded, his breath fogging into cold air.

"Maybe it wasn't the Russian army, just their guns," Hawkins said, closing the eyes of a dead woman still strapped into her seat.

McCarter frowned deeply. Yeah, that was his call on the slaughter, too. The Russian army had a civilian review board to answer to these days, just like the American and British armed forces. The old blood and thunder time of the Red Army running amuck was long gone, with nobody happier about the change than most of the Russian army. Most, but not all.

"T.J., go back to the hovercraft and watch the radar for incoming. Cal, cover the door. Gary, check for survivors pretending to be dead. Encizo, hit the cargo hold," McCarter ordered, heading straight for the cockpit.

As he expected, everybody there was dead, the copilot and navigator still at their posts. However, the pilot chair was empty. A jacket was draped over the near of the chair, the nametag indecipherable Chinese. A long hair on the collar was jet-black. So the flight had a female pilot. Yeah, made sense—China had a lot of those. Women had naturally faster reflexes than men, and could take more G forces. Most of the top fighter pilots in the Israeli air force were women, and there had never been any complaints about their work.

Glancing out the cracked port-side window, McCarter frowned. Neither of the two women assaulted outside by the raiders could be the pilot; one was far too young, and the other much too large. Both were blondes.

"Check over the crew," McCarter said, touching his throat mike. "We're looking for the pilot, female, black hair, most likely Chinese."

"On it," Manning replied.

"Keep me posted," McCarter growled. Going under the control console, he looked for the black box and discovered it was gone, and the emergency radio beacon had been deliberately smashed. Nobody involved had wanted this plane found but the crew and passengers.

As he started to leave, McCarter stopped as something on the floor caught his attention. It was just another brass shell case, similar to the hundreds of others on the dirty decking, but something about it had triggered his attention.

Picking up the shell, his face got hard as he realized it was too big for any Kalashnikov rifle. The damn thing was a 9 mm cartridge, but trimmed down to a 7 mm, and the opening was blocked solid with a smooth piece of steel. Steel inside a brass cartridge. Their thief had been here!

"Look at this," McCarter said, walking back into the main section.

Accepting the cartridge, Manning scowled. "This is a silent round," he said in surprise. "That's KGB weapon technology. These aren't available on the weapons market. Nobody can make these but Russian and American Special Forces."

The shell was an invention of the Soviet special forces. The standard-issue cartridge detonated a half-powder charge that shoved forward a tiny piston blocking the narrowed-down mouth airtight, but the impact shoved forward a smaller-caliber bullet. With the propellant gas completely trapped inside the cartridge, there was no bang, or muzzle-flash. The shells only made a soft click of the piston ramming forward that sounded remarkably similar to a misfire. Yet the tiny piston hit hard enough to throw a bullet forward at subsonic speed. The silent rounds had terrible range and even worse penetrating power. But for a spy it was the ultimate covert weapon, and could be used in any pistol of the correct caliber.

Even reduced to 7 mm, there was still sufficient firepower to blow open the cockpit door and kill the crew. But checking, McCarter found it was undamaged. Which meant the hijacker tricked his way inside, maybe with a hostage, or else he used the Chameleon to neutralize the magnetic locks.

"Yeah, he was here," McCarter said.

Manning nodded. "Looks like, David."

"Everybody accounted for?"

Something in one of the small fires popped, and both men swung about with their weapons at the ready, then relaxed.

"Not quite," Manning said with a scowl. "The manifest says 118 passengers and crew, and there are 115 bodies."

"Including the two outside?"

Manning cast a sideways glance out a busted window. Hawkins had already cut the dead women free from their ropes and covered them with blankets. It wasn't much, but all they could do at the moment.

"Yes, counting them, too," Manning said softly.

"So we have three missing people."

"One of them is the pilot, one is our thief and somebody else. A hostage, maybe."

"Unfortunately, we don't even know if our thief is a man or a woman."

"Could be a team, and they took the pilot."

"Maybe so," McCarter conceded.

"Head's up," Encizo said, and threw some clothing on the floor. "I found this in the cargo hold."

It was a woman's dress and handbag, with a wig and glasses stuffed inside. But the dress was out of shape, lopsided and distended in the middle.

"Pregnant," Manning said in sudden realization. "The bastard was disguised as a pregnant woman!"

"Any pregnant women among the dead?" McCarter asked.

"No, thank God," Manning stated.

"It's not a woman," Encizo said, turning the wig over for the others to see. There was double-side tape lining the inside.

Both McCarter and Manning frowned at that. Not bobby pins or clips. Tape. That meant a bald head.

"A man," McCarter stated, his breath fogging slightly. "Our thief is a man, disguised as a pregnant woman."

"Probably had the Chameleon strapped around his belly with some padding," Manning agreed, resting the stock of his AK-105 on a hip. "Along with that KGB silent gun. And probably a lot more."

"Well, he wasn't carrying a parachute," Encizo stated. "Not if the Chameleon was as big as we were told."

"Any missing?"

"I already checked. There are slots for ten emergency parachutes, and two are missing," Encizo said, "and the seal covering the belly hatch is ripped to pieces."

Two parachutes gone, but three people were missing. The only scenario that made any sense was the thief hijacked the plane, and jumped with the pilot as a hostage. With the rest of the cockpit crew dead, he could leave the plane on autopilot, and it would eventually crash far away from where he left.

"Only somebody broke in and landed the damn thing," Manning said, obviously following the same train of thought. "Crew maybe, or a passenger with flight experience."

"Then the raiders arrived," Encizo started, then frowned. "No, we killed all of them. Somebody else was here first and the raiders came later."

"Or their boss took somebody for questioning, and left the rest for his men," Manning said, standing straight. "If that's right, they might know when our thief jumped."

"Alert. Company coming," James said over the earphones. "One large plane, two helicopters."

"Military gunships?" McCarter demanded, striding from the wreckage.

"I'd say no. But the Russians still use a lot of stuff that we'd consider obsolete, so who knows?"

Fair enough. After the fall of communism, the country was still reeling financially, and the lower military services often had to use equipment left over from World War II. On the other hand, most of it still worked. Say what you wanted about their politics, but the Russkies built machines that lasted.

"ETA?"

"Twenty minutes."

"More than enough," McCarter said, heading through the debris and corpses for the hovercraft. "Okay, mates. I want a recon sweep of the area right now. Somebody took a prisoner and we need them back. These assholes got here from somewhere else, and I want to follow their tracks home. We have nineteen and counting. So, move!"

Snapping on flashlights, Hawkins and Encizo took off at a trot in opposite directions around the huge craft, their beams playing along the ground looking for tracks. Near the tree line, James stayed in the hovercraft, watching the blips moving on the glowing screen.

"David?" Manning said, his face cast in shadows from a kerosene lantern on the ground.

McCarter turned. "Yeah?"

"It just occurred to me that our thief might have simply shoved the pilot out of the plane when he jumped using a chute," Manning suggested.

"Yeah, I thought of that, too."

"If he did, we're dead in the water."

"True," McCarter said, lighting a Player's cigarette and drawing the smoke in deep. "But the only way to be sure is to find the leader of these bastards and see for ourselves."

CHAPTER TEN

Ungalik City

"This'll do," Lyons said, pulling the stolen Jimmy to the side of the highway.

With the tires crunching on the loose gravel, he set the vehicle behind a large boulder where it couldn't be easily seen, set the brakes and turned off the engine. Able Team got out of the vehicle.

Rolling up the sleeves of his shirt, Blancanales knelt along a tire pretending to work on the lug nuts in case somebody drove by.

Meanwhile, the others walked to the edge of the cliff and scanned the horizon. Even though the men of Able Team were all world travelers, they had to admit that the view from the simple Alaskan hilltop was extraordinary. In front of them was a rocky shoreline, the blue-gray waves of the Northern Sound crashing white onto the rusted steel-and-concrete shipping piers of Ungalik City. Lazy smoke rose from a hundred chimneys in the sleepy town to join the slate-colored clouds blanketing the sky, mystically connecting Earth and Heaven into a single, homogenous whole.

Behind the men were nameless rolling hills stretching past the raging Yukon River and onward to the imposing, distant, snowcapped Kaiyuh Mountains.

Standing on the gravel berm, Lyons and Schwarz could feel the wild power of Nature filling the air like the aftereffects of a lightning strike. Man wasn't the dominant force in Alaska. Nature ruled here, untamed and defiant. This was raw land, still bleeding from the fresh scars of live glaciers and constant earthquakes.

"Got any change?" Lyons asked, rubbing at the numerous thorn scratches on the back of his hand. Nearby was a bulky telescope set on an iron stand for tourists to use. The machine was low powered, but their binoculars had been destroyed in the SUV. Unfortunately, the machine was coin operated, and better armored than an ATM, probably more against the inclement weather than vandals. But the end result was the same. There was no way for them to break open the coin box without using explosives.

"Nope," Schwarz replied, reaching inside his torn jacket. "But I have something that we can use."

Lyons raised an eyebrow. "Not one of those telescope pens?"

"Better." Schwarz grinned, and, resting a shoe on the line of small boulders that served as a safety rail, he pulled out a small set of survivalist glasses. They were about the size of a cassette tape and weighed virtually nothing. With one hand, he pressed the release on the side, and the flat box sprang open into a triangle formation with exposed plastic lenses.

"What kind of magnification does that have?" Lyons asked, trying to keep the amusement from his voice.

"Thirty power," Schwarz replied, looking over the city below.

"Not bad," Lyons grudgingly admitted, then jerked a thumb. "Better than that coin-operated thing."

"Of course," Schwarz replied, trying to keep the amusement out of his voice. He didn't carry this stuff around because he was a tech buff. Well, okay, he was. But all of it was useful, in one way or another.

In the city below, people wearing sweaters and jeans were walking about in the chaos of ordinary life. A drunk waving a bottle seemed to be singing to a tree, and a huge caribou was strolling across a parking lot, pausing now and then to nibble on the vinyl rooftops of cars.

Wood and fieldstones were the main components of the homes, with only the government buildings made of red brick. There were no sidewalks, as with most towns near the Arctic Circle, and few buildings above five stories. Schwarz could identify the hospital by the heliport on the flat roof. Ungalik was a typical Alaskan town, the streets wide, the main artery six lanes across, and every building was spaced far from its neighbor, making the whole place seem oddly deserted. But that was necessary for snow control when the brief days of summer were past and the North seized the world once more in its white fist of indomitable snow.

"Anything happening?" Lyons asked, squinting at the sky. The cell phone weighed heavily in his pocket, but he didn't want to make a coded report to Price at the Farm yet until they had completed the job at hand.

"Looks clear," Schwarz said, putting the compact binoculars away again. "No sign of any activity at the police station."

"Good," he muttered, rubbing his hands together for warmth. "Let's finish the search."

Returning to the Jimmy, Lyons replaced Blancanales at pretending to work on the wheel, and the other two men began a more detailed search of the Jimmy 4WD, now examining the places that they couldn't when it was in motion.

After locating the dead gunner's rental car hidden behind some bushes, Able Team had quickly checked for traps. There was a tear gas cartridge rigged behind the passenger-side visor, obviously for getting rid of unwelcome guests, but aside from that the vehicle was clean. Clearly, the gunner hadn't been expecting serious trouble.

With the bobbing flashlights of the military coming up the hill, the Stony Man commandos climbed inside and drove off into the night without using headlights until they went around a curve. Then Lyons flipped on the beams and hit the gas.

Trying to put as much distance between them and the Kobuk Valley, the Able Team commander raced along the interstate road without stopping, cutting through the Waring Mountain pass and crossing Hog River. The deep gorge was still choked with pieces of floating winter ice in spite of the seasonal warmth.

While Lyons drove, the others tore the vehicle apart, searching for anything useful about the identity of the assailant or possibly whom he worked for. But there wasn't so much as a used gum wrapper on the floor mats. No spare ammo, no maps, not even a thermos of coffee for the cold nights.

Opening the rear area, Schwarz lifted up the carpet to discover there was no spare tire or jack. Those had been removed to make space for spare ammunition, a medical kit, handcuffs, leg irons, a ball gag, blindfolds and a case of torture instruments.

"He badly wanted something our thief had," Schwarz said grimly. "And wasn't squeamish on how he got it."

"Has to be the Chameleon," Lyons muttered. "Or who he was planning on selling it to."

When he was a cop in Los Angeles, Carl Lyons had done business with several bounty hunters who used items similar to the leg irons. This wasn't new equipment, and had been well used. Could their gunner have been a collector for a turkey doctor? It was a chilling thought. Turkey doctors were brutal torturers for organized crime: the Mafia, the Jewish mob, the Russian Mafia, the Colombian drug lords, the Rastafarians, Yakuza, everybody used them. Maybe this whole thing was a play of some crime family to steal the Chameleon, and not a covert mission by a foreign government. That would expand the scope of their search for the device a hundredfold. Shit!

Standing, Lyons wiped his hands clean on a pocket handkerchief, pulled out his cell phone and tapped in a memorized number.

"Hello, Stone House," he said. "There may be new guests at the party."

As Lyons made a brief report to Barbara Price in Virginia, Blancanales crawled out from below the steering wheel, where he had been checking under the carpeting below the floor mats. Another zero. That left only one more spot. During the two-hour trip to Ungalik, the only spot that hadn't been fully inspected was the driver's seat. Now Blancanales expertly ran his fingertips over the leather and twilled cloth and stopped as he encountered a poorly glued seam near the back, where the driver wouldn't be putting any pressure. Holding his breath, he pulled out a knife and carefully split open the material. Loose pieces of foam padding puffed out of the opening. Gently teasing them aside, Blancanales allowed himself a brief smile as he unearthed a clear plastic bag containing a wallet, a ring of keys and an airline ticket folder.

"Eureka." He exhaled, placing the bag on the front passenger seat.

Avoiding the pressure seal, he sliced open the side of the clear plastic and extracted each of the items, checking for more traps before placing them aside.

"The name was James Dunbar," Blancanales said, flipping open the wallet. "Which was most likely as false as the names that we're traveling under."

Schwarz looked down at his nametag of Shawn Lane. "Why?" he asked. "Don't I look Irish?"

"What else is in there?" Lyons asked, joining the others.

Pushing the seat back to gain more room, the men gathered around the items and examined them. There were no markings on any of the keys, not even a manufacturer stamp, which meant they were illegal copies. Which was interesting, but not useful. The wallet was full of cash, nonsequential, large bills, well used, with a crisp hundred tucked behind the driver's license clearly intended to be used as a bribe to a traffic cop. Lyons scowled darkly at the implication, but said nothing.

However, aside from the money and license, the wallet contained nothing else. No credit cards, video store card, ATM card, family photos, dry-cleaning receipts, nothing.

"That would set off alarms in any cop that sees it," Schwarz said, scowling at the empty leather. Their own wallets contained an entire false history, including movie stub tickets. Details made lies believable, not a lack of them.

"This guy was an amateur," he continued. "Ruthless, and well financed. An MM-1 isn't a Saturday night special. But he really didn't know what he was doing."

"Here's the license," Blancanales said, rifling through the wallet. "Sure looks like the real thing."

Accepting the card, Lyons barely gave it a glance. "No, this is a fake," he declared. "Top-notch quality, but a fake. It's too thick and the picture is too clear. This is better than the DMV of a state would issue to the governor."

"Carl, I can hear it in your voice," Blancanales replied slowly. "We have gotten hold of the end of a rope."

"Maybe," Lyons muttered, turning the license over and over in his hands. His ice-blue eyes glinted hard as any glacier. "Just maybe."

"Well, the airline ticket is real," Schwarz said, holding up the paper to the dome light to check the watermarks. "Same name as on the driver's license, James Dunbar, first class, open ended, good on any flight, final destination is Memphis."

"Any stops along the way?" Blancanales asked, chewing a lip.

"Let me check." He flipped the booklet open and thumbed through the flimsy vegetable-paper copies. China Air didn't exactly use SOTA printers. "Yeah, there is a twelve-hour layover, O'Hare at Chicago."

"So that was his real destination," Lyons said, tucking the license into his shirt pocket.

"Yeah, makes sense," Blancanales agreed. "He burns the extra fare to hide his hometown. Smart move."

"Must have been done for him, then," Schwarz stated. "We've already figured out Dunbar was no rocket scientist."

"That's the truth," Blancanales snorted.

Lyons started around the Jimmy. "Okay, with all of our equipment gone, we need to buy a high-density scanner to send a jpeg of this card to Bear to run for analysis." He slid behind the steering wheel and started the engine. "Ungalik is too small for high-end computer equipment. They'll have office scanners and such, but nothing like the quality we need."

"Fairbanks will have what we need," Schwarz said, closing the door and buckling his seat belt. "They have a large enough tourist industry to carry what we need."

"Good." Lyons slipped the vehicle into gear and drove off the berm. Reaching the highway again, he hit the gas and started building speed. The hunt was on at last, and he could feel the electric tension building.

"Then we can charter a helicopter to Anchorage, meet with Grimaldi and fly to the Windy City."

"And start burning the rope," Blancanales stated grimly.

Feeding the Jimmy more gas, Lyons nodded. "With hellfire, my friend," he stated, "and then some."

CHAPTER ELEVEN

Russia

Footprints in the soft ground, scuffed leaves and a cigarette butt gave Phoenix Force a clear trail into the forest. Using the hovercraft, the men circled the crash site once to scramble the trail and prevent anybody from air rescue coming after them. They needed to find the perps first for several reasons, not the least of which was getting the missing crew member back alive.

Hopping out of the hovercraft, Encizo and Hawkins hit the ground and started into the woods, probing the ground with their pocket flashlights. The rest of the team stayed far behind them to prevent the wash from the belly fans of the hovercraft from destroying the faint trail.

Killing their lights, McCarter and James kept the rumbling machines at their lowest setting, knowing that the noise of the rescue helicopters would mask the sound of their engines until they landed. Hopefully by then, they would be far enough away to not be heard. It was a gamble, but they really didn't have a choice in the matter.

Away from the fires and lanterns of the crash site, the stygian night ruled the land, the occasional breaks in the heavy cloud cover showing a moonless sky. Progress was slow, and McCarter said nothing as he watched the fuel gauge steadily descend. Unfortunately, the quiet hovercraft engines used aviation fuel, not gasoline. So unless they found an airport in the middle of nowhere, his team would be on foot a hundred miles away from the pickup point. Not good. There was probably some spare fuel cans on the rescue helicopters, but not enough to make a difference.

"We lost a few packs in the storm," McCarter said into his throat mike. "Any chance we still have those bags of civilian clothing?"

"Negative," James replied, his words marred by a soft crackle of static. "They went over the side."

"Damn. Any Russian money?"

"That was with the clothing, David."

"Maybe the perps can loan us a couple of bucks," Hawkins growled over the radio from the darkness. "I'm sure we can make a trade of some kind."

"Lead for green?"

"That was the idea."

"Heads up," Encizo whispered. "There's a break in the trees ahead."

Easing down on the power, McCarter and James hung back as Manning jumped over the side to join the others in probing ahead. Floating above the ground, the two men felt oddly detached from the world. With the leaves rustling all around them from the wind of the hovercraft, it was impossible to hear anything nearby. The low hills and trees blocked any sight of lights from the crash site, and the radar screen showed only empty sky above. It was as if they were all alone on an undiscovered continent.

Reaching the edge of a small clearing, Hawkins and Encizo paused to allow Manning to join them. Silence filled the Russian forest, and not even the muffled engines of the Navy hovercraft could be heard above the softly moaning wind in the treetops. Then the big Canadian appeared from the shadows carrying a Barrett Light Fifty rifle. The cap was on the telescopic sight, and the barrel was wrapped in camouflage-colored cloth to prevent any unwanted reflections.

Giving the others a nod, they started forward in a search pattern while Manning stayed near a tree to give protective cover fire for the other two if it was needed. Pulling out the 9 mm Tokarev with his left hand, Manning thumbed back the hammer. His preferred weapon was the Barrett, a sniper rifle that fired .50-caliber cartridges about the size of a cigar. The weapon had a maximum range of two miles, punched through most armored personnel carriers as if they were made of balsa wood and at close quarters would literally blow the arms and legs off a man when the monstrous 750-grain slug hit. The Barrett was also louder than doomsday and would be kept out of any battle until absolutely necessary.

With their AK-105 assault rifles at the ready, Hawkins and Encizo moved like smoke across the uneven ground of the clearing. Every sense was keyed to a combat pitch, but the area proved to be clear. Most the soil was gnarled with roots, or lumpy with rocks, but off to the side were a few muddy patches. Perfectly impressed into the material they found some tire tracks. Lifting up their night-vision goggles, the Stony Man commandos followed the tracks until finding an area near some bushes with oil stains on the rocks, a crushed cigarette butt and a woman's black leather shoe lying on its side.

"No heels," Encizo commented, picking it up. "Exactly the same as the dead flight attendants wore on the China Air flight."

Kneeling on the ground, Hawkins ran his fingertips along the flat rocks. There were muddy tire tracks here, and another oil stain. "Two vehicles," he said. "A truck of some kind and a small jeep. Damn me if it doesn't look American."

"It is. World War II surplus," Encizo added. "I'm surprised one of those is still running."

"Won't be for long," Hawkins added with a hard expression, studying the clearing. "They came from that direction," he said, indicating the south, "but they went due west."

"Let's go," the little Cuban said, then stopped. There were footprints on top of the tire tracks. A bare foot and a shoe, then just bare feet. Looking off to the side, he saw the shoe under a bush.

"They walked the prisoner behind," he announced into the throat mike. "So unless they want her dead, their base is close by."

"Roger that," McCarter replied crisply. "You're on point. Let's move."

Flipping down their night goggles, Hawkins and Encizo took off at a jog as Manning slid out of the bushes, his massive rifle held in both hands. A few seconds later, the two hovercraft were floating around a copse of trees. Instantly, their wash flooded the clearing, obliterating any trace of the tracks.

Privately, David McCarter was unhappy about the close proximity of the raider's base. There was no way this was a coincidence. The hijacker wanted the plane to crash in this vicinity so that the raiders would loot it and help destroy any evidence that might lead back to him. The man was good.

The clearing turned into grassland, thick with bushes and cut by countless rain gullies and small streams. Wary of traps, the teams proceeded as fast as they could over the rough terrain, the hovercraft staying far away to not disturb any tracks. After a mile or so, a gentle dip in the ground turned into a small valley that rose to a ridge thickly crested with pine trees. A dried stream made a natural road leading to the top, and the men found traces of tire tracks, and traces of blood. And a single brass cartridge.

"Not enough blood showing if they shot her," Encizo stated, fighting a rush of anger. "The ground must be cutting her bare feet, is all. That's just stupid. Leaves a hell of a trail to follow."

"They must have fired a round to keep her going," Hawkins agreed. "We're either going to find their base soon, or her dead in the bushes."

"Double time," McCarter order brusquely. "We need that woman alive!"

The men took off at a full sprint, eating the distance to the top of the crest. More forest filled the landscape, with black mountains rising high on the horizon. The team stayed on the dried stream, knowing their boots would make less noise on the hard-packed earth. They were also fully exposed, but the lack of bushes to push through let them move faster. The stream was a trade-off. Speed for cover.

"Radar check," McCarter asked brusquely.

"Screen is clear," James replied. "But the radio is crackling with traffic. Air rescue back there is calling for everybody but the Bolshoi Ballet."

"How long till daylight?" Manning asked, squinting at the cloudy heavens.

"Four hours."

"Good."

Suddenly, Hawkins raised a clenched fist and everybody froze. "Hold it," he whispered. "We have a sentry, two o'clock, twenty yards."

"I see him," Encizo said, pulling out a tranquilizer gun. Thumbing off the safety, he paused, aimed and fired once. The weapon only made a tiny spitting noise, but they heard a little gasp of pain from the darkness ahead of them. Then a body flopped over sideways out of a bush and rolled into the stream, landing face upward.

With their weapons at the ready, Phoenix Force waited for any reaction to the hit, and when nothing happened, they moved in quickly. The man was dressed in rough clothing and used boots, but wore a Rolex watch. A Kenwood portable radio lay near the unconscious man, its power light off, probably to save the batteries until they were needed.

"Bad move," Encizo whispered, going through the man's pockets, which yielded only cigarettes, chewing gum and a few speedloaders.

Kneeling, Hawkins merely grunted in agreement as he removed an arsenal of weapons. There was a Red Army REX .357 Magnum revolver riding in a stained-leather shoulder holster outside the sentry's heavy jacket. Emptying the weapon, Hawkins tossed the shells into the bushes and then returned the revolver to the shoulder holster. Just a little insurance in case of trouble later.

The guard also had a rifle bayonet sheathed on his left side, and an old Soviet army flare gun at his right hip, with fat flares tucked into hand-sewn loops on the gun belt. On the ground was an RPK-74, the 40 mm grenade launcher and assault rifle both splashed with different color paint in a crude job of camouflaging.

Inside the bush was a camouflage-colored tent, with a pair of binoculars hanging from the front post. A wooden chair was situated at the entrance, with a black-and-red-checkered thermos nearby, the cap balanced on top. Inside the tent was an antique cherry-wood dining table that was badly scarred, its top covered with American MRE packs, tin cans, a box of cigars, piles of sex magazines, boxes of ammo, a crate of grenades and a small cardboard container with a roll of toilet tissue.

Closing the flaps, Encizo and Hawkins shared a brief smile. This was no temporary site, but a permanent sentry post.

"I'll take the bottom," Hawkins said, grabbing the guard by the boots.

Encizo took the shoulders, and they carried him inside the tent, draping the unconscious man over the table in what they hoped was a natural position. Now he merely appeared to be asleep on duty if anybody found him.

Returning to the creek, the team spread out to do a fast recon until finding a wall of thorny bushes that cut off the mouth of a small ravine with steep hills on either side. Good enough.

Retreating into the forest, McCarter and James moved the hovercraft out of the way, and then spent a few minutes cutting branches to hide the craft. Helping with the task, Hawkins noticed the fuel level, but made no comment. First things first. Get the woman. Then they could talk about escape.

When they were satisfied that the hovercraft couldn't be found by a casual search, Phoenix Force circled around the hills and crawled on their bellies over the top until they could see down into the ravine. It was filled with men and machinery.

The ravine was more like a river backwash, almost circular in shape, and a double layer of camouflage netting was stretched across the top, the anchor cables set into thick tree trunks. Perfect cover against aerial recon. Dim lights on poles were set in steel bowls to shine downward and not reveal the base. Unfortunately, most of them were turned off. Taking cover in the shrubbery, the Stony Man commandos switched to the UV setting on their goggles, and the mountain base instantly became clearly illuminated, although an eerie black and white. Three Quonset huts spread out like a duck foot at the end. A barricade of logs and cinder blocks blocked off the only entrance. The steel-plated gate was padlocked shut and braced with a thick wooden beam.

Thorny bushes were visible on the other side, effectively hiding the gate, and beyond was the dried riverbed.

"Good layout," McCarter said into his throat mike. "If we hadn't already known it was here, it would have been a bitch to find this place."

"Nobody ever said the Russians were stupid," James said, adjusting the focus on his goggles. Ah, better.

The still of the night was broken as they heard the soft chatter of a motor from one of the Quonset huts. Electrical wires spread outward from its roof to the rest of the enclosure, clearly marking it as the power house. Set between it and the next hut was a sandbag nest armed with a belt-fed Finnish 20 mm antitank gun mounted on a swivel so that it could sweep the sky or the hills alongside the camp. An old but formidable piece of weaponry. More sandbags formed an open garage where a truck and two battered jeeps were parked, and, set off by itself, a third sandbag redoubt was piled high around a large tank clearly marked as the water supply.

"That's their fuel dump," Hawkins stated. "That old water gag only works against green troops. Keeps them from hitting that first and setting the place ablaze."

"That wouldn't work here," Manning stated. "The dump is too far away from the huts. Blowing that would only block the entrance."

"Yes," McCarter said slowly, almost smiling. "Yes, it would."

Laughter sounded from somewhere, followed by a woman's scream.

"David, someone's being raped," Encizo growled, his hands tightening on the AK-105.

McCarter nodded, his sharp eyes sweeping the camp. "Yeah, but where?" he asked. "We go in blind, and they'll be picking their teeth with our bones. And then go right back to finish with the woman."

"Must be one of the huts," James said, controlling his breathing. "The electrical generator, the barracks or the storage."

"Barracks makes the most sense," Manning suggested.

Easing the safety off the military crossbow, McCarter scowled. "Yeah? And are you willing to bet the farm on that?"

"Sure am," James said, working the bolt on his AK-105. The Starshell round had been replaced with an HE charge, and he knew exactly where it was going.

Another scream sounded from below, the cry changing into a wail of pain.

"I agree," McCarter commanded, cocking his Barnett military crossbow. "Okay, Gary plays God. Cal opens the door. T.J. blows smoke. Move!"

Slipping into the bushes, McCarter, Encizo, Hawkins and James spread out and moved toward their targets while Manning stayed on the side of the hill. Scuttling into a bush, the big Canadian laid the Tokarev pistol on a nearby rock as backup, and slid the long barrel out of the greenery, snapping off a twig that was in the way. The Barrett had a range of almost two miles under ideal conditions, and the base was no more than three hundred yards away. But heavy foliage could turn a bullet as easy as a sheet of glass, so he needed a clear line of fire to the base.

Watching the smoke drifting from the exhaust stack on top of the barracks hut, Manning checked the wind drift and adjusted the scope two clicks. Carefully sweeping the camp with the telescopic sights, he couldn't see the rest of Phoenix Force moving through the underbrush, but he did spot the enemy.

"Payback's a bitch, boys," Manning whispered, working the bolt on the massive rifle and marking his first target.

CHAPTER TWELVE

Merlyk Ravine, Russia

Smoking Turkish cigarettes, the two guards were loung-ing near the gate of the base talking about the Chinese woman prisoner, and passing around a bottle of airline Scotch whiskey. Both were named Ivan and they were always assigned to work together as a sort of crude joke; aside from the mutual name, they really had noth-ing in common.

"When it's my turn she'll be begging for more," the elder Ivan said, winking.

"More like begging for death," the younger Russian said, sighing, then taking a swig from the bottle. "Here, fill your mouth with this and shut up."

"Certainly, my comrade general." Ivan grinned, ac-cepting the Scotch with a mock salute.

The other man snorted. "If we were in the army, we would both have been shot long ago."

"And that is another good reason to drink the fine Scotch!" Ivan chortled.

Raising the bottle high, the man started to chug the whiskey when he violently jerked backward against the wall. Dropping his AK-74 and the bottle, he clawed at his throat and started making gurgling noises.

"Idiot! It might have broken," the second guard scolded, retrieving the bottle.

Wiping the neck clean, the younger Russian took a moment to finally realize that his friend wasn't putting on an act. Then he stared in shock at the bloody quarrel sticking through his friend's neck, pinning him to the log wall.

"Mother of God," he whispered, and threw the bottle aside to grab a whistle hanging around his neck. But before he could place it in his mouth, there was a blur of motion, and something white-hot exploded in his belly. Pain! Doubling over to clutch the quarrel jutting from his shirt, the guard tumbled sideways, his hand spasming on the grip of the AK-74. The assault rifle chattered a burst into the night, chewing apart the corpse of his partner nailed to the wall.

Almost instantly, the door to the middle Quonset hut slammed open and a large man holding a 40 mm grenade launcher stepped into view.

"What is happening?" he demanded loudly, squinting into the darkness. Wearing only boots and pants, his bare chest was covered with a network of scars from a hundred fights. Snapping open the breech, he thumbed in a fat brass shell and looked over the base.

"Guards! Report!" he bellowed, then flew backward into the hut with a spray of blood. A split second later, the thunderous discharge of the mighty Barrett .50 rolled over the camp, shaking the windows.

"Invaders!" a man shouted inside the sandbag nest. Slapping on a helmet, he worked the heavy arming bolt of the Finnish antitank gun and swiveled it about to started randomly firing at the hillside. The tracer rounds stitched across the air to punch through the camouflage netting and hit the trees in fiery detonations. The stark coloration of the shells proclaimed them white phosphorous rounds.

The Barrett spoke again and a sandbag on the nest exploded, throwing loose dirt everywhere. Cursing wildly, the gunner grabbed his face and tried to clear his eyes. Then an AK-105 chattered in the darkness, and he fell over minus a throat.

Shouting men were running everywhere in the small base by now, and suddenly the pole lights slammed on to full brightness.

Unexpectedly, a canvas pack flew out of the bushes to hit the ground near the fuel dump. The U.S. Army satchel charge was still moving when the C-4 blocks cut loose and a strident blast ripped apart the gasoline tank, sending out a fiery spray that engulfed the vehicles in the garage and covered the front gate, making escape for anybody impossible. Charging out of the third hut came a group of men fully dressed and well armed.

"Hell's demons, we've been cut off!" a short man wearing an eye patch shouted. "Section two, go hard! Delta five, hike! Cover the points and squeeze!"

From the hillside, Manning cursed at the bad luck to encounter somebody who knew better than to shout uncoded instructions in the heat of battle. That wouldn't work with regular troops because it was too difficult to keep track of who knew what code phrase for retreat, or open fire. But in Special Forces teams it was the only way. This guy had to go away and fast.

Turning aside, the short man heard something hum by and then a rolling boom echoed from the eastern hills.

"Sniper!" he shouted, pointing. "All guns fire!"

Aiming his own RPK-74, the gang leader braced himself and pumped a 40 mm shell from the attached launcher toward the densest group of shrubbery on the hill. If there was a hidden gunner, that would be the location. A full heartbeat later an explosion formed a fireball into the trees, throwing out a corona of branches and leaves.

"You got him, sir!" a man cried, brandishing his AK-74 and shaking the weapon.

"Shut up, fool. I see no body parts," the leader said, adjusting his eye patch. He flinched as a secondary explosion came from the burning vehicles in the garage. "Have Ivan and Ivan get the smoke generator working! We need cover!"

"They're both dead, sir!"

"Then you do it, but move!"

As the hardmen scattered across the base, the door to the power shack was slammed open and a big man wearing NATO-style commando garb knelt in the doorway to fire an AK-105 into the camp. Three of the hardmen were cut apart before the rest dived for cover.

As smoke from the fire blew across the camp, the leader charged for the sandbag nest and frantically scrambled inside. Swinging the 20 mm gun around, he started to aim for the stranger when a lance of flame stretched across the camp and slammed into the Finnish weapon with a doomsday clap.

Inside the Quonset hut, McCarter ducked out of the way as tattered sandbags and body parts went flying. He dropped the nearly spent clip and slapped in a replacement just as the linked belts of 20 mm rounds started detonating in their ammo boxes like firecrackers. A hellish umbrella of shells streaked away in every direction, slamming into the ground, the gate and the huts, filling the camp with explosions and ricochets. One man started to shriek as his left arm was removed at the shoulder and tried to staunch the flow with a bare hand. Stepping out of the bushes, Hawkins aimed his AK-105 at the man, then started to turn away, paused and pivoted to put a burst into his chest. The screaming stopped instantly.

The deadly sound of AK-74 assault rifles on full-auto filled the night, and a spray of bullets impacted on the sandbag walls with meaty thumps, sounding horribly similar to lead hitting flesh. The AK-105 rifles answered with deadly force.

Wasting no more time, McCarter turned away from the door and went back into the hut. The air reeked of exhaust fumes, and the wooden floor was dotted with barrels of diesel fuel. At the back was the humming generator, and to the side were several freezers, thick gloves stuffed inside the door handle. A work bench was filled with tools, wiring and a black-and-white television showing one of the *Die Hard* movies with Russian subtitles.

Turning off the television, McCarter moved to a Russian lying on the floor with a quarrel through his neck. The razor-sharp tip was still dripping blood. Taking the AK-74 assault rifle from the hand of the dead man, McCarter shot the master control panel to pieces. A spray of sparks erupted from the panel, the ceiling lights winked out and the humming generator quickly died away until it was still.

"Rabble, this is Rouser," McCarter said into his throat mike, tossing away the empty weapon. "It's midnight at the oasis. Time to rock and roll."

Now the rest of the Stony Man commandos came out of hiding, their shadowy figures distorted by their night-vision goggles. Avoiding the reddish light of the dying fires, the team swept through the encampment ruthlessly cutting down the enemy on sight. Most of the Russians fought back, diving for cover and tossing grenades. But a few threw down their guns and begged for mercy. However, each and every member of Phoenix Force still had the fresh memory of the dead and raped passengers from the crashed airliner fresh in their minds. Any desire to offer clemency was negated by recollection of the dead women tied spread-eagle on the filthy ground.

The Barrett boomed once more and a man trying to operate a flamethrower was engulfed in a fiery blast. A human torch, he dropped to his knees waving both arms as he howled in anguish. The Barrett sang its song once more, and the burning man went silent.

Taking advantage of the distraction, the men of Phoenix Force called in their status to their team leader, and it was soon obvious that the enemy had been neutralized. That left only the two remaining Quonset huts.

Converging on the middle hut, Encizo chewed off the hinges with a long burst from his Kalashnikov. Hawkins kicked it open and charged inside as his teammate reloaded, and followed close behind. A few seconds later, the men appeared at the tattered doorway and ran a thumb across their throats showing the building was empty.

Suddenly, the door to the barracks was thrown open and a half-naked Chinese woman came into view, her flight uniform hanging off in strips. Her bruised skin appeared golden in the reflected firelight, and her slim wrists were bound with black tape to her throat, her ankles lashed with rope. The combination effectively hobbled any effort to run. Tears were streaming down her cheeks, but her head was held high, and defiance showed in her eyes.

"Leave now, or we kill the hostage!" a man shouted, only the barrel of his Kalashnikov showing past the doorjamb.

As if in response, the Barrett fired. The incoming round punched a hole through the roof of the hut and knocked over some of the sand bags from the front wall. The echo was still in the air when the Barrett fired again, and another hole appeared in the prefabricated metal structure.

"Stop firing or the girl dies!" the gruff voice ordered.

"Surrender the woman or you die!" McCarter answered in halting Russian. Then he worked the bolt on his AK-105 as loudly as possible, ejecting a live round. The rest of his team did the same several times, making them sound like a small army.

"Do not shoot!" the man yelled, prodding the shivering woman with his rifle. "Perhaps we can make a deal!"

A pistol shot rang out inside the hut, and the woman moved back as a big man with a beard stumbled into view. McCarter and the rest of Phoenix Force pointed their weapons at the man, but with the prisoner directly behind him they couldn't shoot from this angle without endangering her life.

Then the mysterious pistol fired again, and the Russian collapsed out the doorway and onto the ground. Now the team cut loose, the converging fusillade of rounds tearing him apart, the body twitching madly from the hammering blows.

As the gunfire stopped, James appeared on the roof holding a 9 mm Beretta pistol.

"Thanks for the gun holes," the former Navy SEAL said into his throat mike, holstering the piece.

"No problem," Manning answered from the unseen hillside.

With smoke blowing across the camp, McCarter and Hawkins entered the hut and checked for any other survivors while Encizo cut the Chinese woman free. James stayed on the roof as lookout.

"Do you speak English?" the little Cuban asked, rubbing her ankles to help restore circulation.

She flinched at the contact at first, then seemed to understand its purpose and relaxed slightly.

"Yes, I speak English," she replied haltingly. "All pilots know little."

"It's clear," McCarter announced, touching his throat. "Cal, keep an eye out for air rescue coming this way."

Then he gave the shivering woman a heavy coat. Gratefully, she pulled it on, covering herself. Then Hawkins handed her the .357 Magnum REX revolver he had taken off one of the Russians. Her eyes went wide at the action, then she sadly smiled and gave it back.

"I understand you not hurt me," she said. "No need gun."

"Keep it," Hawkins said. "I'll rustle up some clean pants and boots, too."

The pilot blinked at the unknown word, but nodded again in acceptance. However, she cracked the cylinder of the weapon to make sure it was loaded before tucking the massive revolver into a pocket of the coat.

Yanking open several lockers, Hawkins found some suitable garments and gave them to her. Then the soldiers turned their backs to give the pilot a moment of privacy as she got dressed. There was almost nothing to hide as the men had already seen her nearly naked. Helplessly bound like an animal. So the gesture was more than mere courtesy; it was done as a psychological return to civilization. It would help her know that the ordeal was over, even though she would carry the mental scars for the rest of her life.

"Thank you, gentlemen," she said, her voice breaking into a sob. "You can turn now, please." As they did, the woman started to cry, then stopped and stood up straight.

"You're a hell of a lady," Encizo said, passing over a sealed bottle of vodka. There had been several liquor bottles from the airline in the collection, but he was sure those would only have upset the woman greatly.

And they desperately needed her lucid. Every minute put them farther behind the escaping Chameleon.

She gratefully accepted the vodka, unscrewed the cap and took a long draft that even impressed Hawkins. Damn, she could drink like a Texan!

"Thanking you. I am Captain Lee Twan Su, pilot for China Air," she said, wiping her mouth on a sleeve. "You are not air rescue." Su didn't phrase it as a question.

"No, ma'am, we aren't," McCarter said, replacing his British accent with an American Midwestern twang. "But they're near. But time is important. We need to know exactly when and where the hijacker left your plane."

"In here, Russia. Ten kilometers before crash," Captain Su answered drawing the heavy coat tighter about herself. Then she frowned. "That would be eight American miles."

McCarter politely waved that aside. "Was anybody with him?"

"A stewardess, yes. Gwenneth." The Irish name was garbled slightly by the pilot. "They use parachute."

"Chinese?" McCarter asked pointedly.

Su shook her head.

No, he hadn't thought so. An Oriental companion in Russia would make the thief rather noticeable.

"Gwenneth, Hong Kong," Su said. "Look American, but Chinese. You understand?"

As a loyal British officer, nobody knew better than David McCarter. The island was owned by mainland China these days, along with its hodgepodge of international citizens.

"Can you describe him?"

"Bald, but blond below," Su said, gesturing below her belt. That rape had been canceled by rough weather caused by an unseasonable squall over the Pacific. However, the other attacks...

She violently shook the memory from her mind and stepped outside. The pilot was startled by the extent of the destruction done to the base in such a short period of time. The battle had only seemed to last for a few minutes! Spinning about, she stared at her rescuers. Who were these men? Soldiers, obviously, but from where?

"His appearance, ma'am," McCarter insisted. "Please. Time isn't in our favor."

Ah! So they weren't there to rescue her, but to capture the hijacker. All was made clear now.

"Slim, many scar," Su continued stoically. "Tattoo arm, blue eye, but contact lens make black."

"He had a tattoo?" Encizo said, frowning.

"Yes, I saw it while he changed into the clothing of Lieutenant Ma Joong, my dead copilot."

"Can you describe it?" McCarter asked. "Was it an anchor, or a line of numbers, a bird?"

"It was knife, with wings."

A dark frown creased his face, and McCarter removed some equipment and began to open his fatigues. Su thrust a hand into the pocket of her coat containing the gun, until McCarter lowered the sleeve off his shoulder and turned toward the nervous woman.

"Like this?" he demanded.

"Yes," Su cried. "Exactly like that!"

Hawkins whistled. "Holy shit, he's SAS?"

"That's not possible," McCarter growled, getting dressed. "Must be somebody who got thrown out, or a recruit that never made it all the way through training. Or just a wanna-be with the tat."

Resting his rifle on a shoulder, Hawkins grunted. "Or a rogue SAS operative gone freelance merc. No wonder the guy was so good. SAS. He might even be ex-intelligence. Sweet Jesus!"

"Pierre," McCarter said, pointing at Encizo, "radio our friends about this."

The Cuban nodded and stepped outside for privacy.

"Now you know about him," Su asked softly, "what happens me?"

"Texas to Canada," Hawkins said, touching his throat mike.

"Canada here, Texas," Manning replied.

"Time to call for the cavalry."

"Way ahead of you, Texas. Now that the fight is over, I've already done the sentry. Just say when."

"Now would be good," Hawkins said.

Looking to the east, a streak of light shot up into the sky and blossomed into a blazing nimbus of light. Slowly, the flare began to drift back down to the earth when another streaked into heavens, followed by another and another.

"Okay, Captain Su, Russian air rescue will be here in five minutes," McCarter stated. "But we have to go right now. Will you be okay?"

"I can survive," Su muttered, casting a glance at the men sprawled lifeless on the ground. "I tell that special army unit kill these men, but chase more of them…"

She made a vague gesture with her hand and paused, waiting.

"West," McCarter said, grinning in spite of himself. "Due west."

Respectfully, Su gave a slight bow. "West. Of course. That is what tell."

With unspoken sentiment, McCarter placed a gloved hand on the woman's shoulder and gave a gentle squeeze. She raised her chin defiantly.

"Death to our enemies," she said proudly in Chinese.

McCarter didn't know what she had said, but could make an educated guess from her expression and tone.

"Long life to our friends," he replied in English, "and Godspeed."

Standing guard in the doorway of the hut, Su watched as the masked soldiers moved silently across the ground to vanish into the trees. Sitting on the front step, she tried to make herself comfortable in spite of her many aches and pains. But less than a minute later, a bright light rose above the hills in the east and she could heard the muffled thumps of helicopter blades.

At the sight, her long denied tears finally came, and she released all of the pent-up emotions into hysterical sobbing. Su lost track of time, and the next thing she knew doctors and nurses were all around her, asking questions in Russian and halting Chinese. Su shook her head at the people as if too weary to speak but let herself be placed on a gurney and carried into the medical helicopter.

As it lifted into the sky, Su felt as if the pain in her heart became too heavy to be airborne and slipped through her body to fall upon the base below. She sighed in relief at the sensation, feeling clean and alive once more. At last, it was over. She was safe, and the ordeal was finished. But somehow the battered woman had a feeling that for the soldiers who had rescued her from the jaws of death, this long night was only beginning. A devout Communist, she couldn't pray for them, but Su asked the universe to help guide their way.

CHAPTER THIRTEEN

Stony Man Farm, Virginia

"Okay, we have an ID," Akira Tokaido said, pulling out his earbuds.

Pausing in typing on his computer keyboard, Aaron Kurtzman swung around in his wheelchair. "You know who the thief is?" he demanded. "Did that French thing Politician suggest work?"

"Well, not quite," Tokaido admitted. "But from the digital pictures of that license sent in by Able Team, I know how to find him."

Kurtzman made a gesture. "Start talking."

The young man tapped a few keys on his console, and a submonitor at Kurtzman's station came to life with a picture of the driver's license. "Just as Carl reported," Tokaido said. "It's too good. In fact, it's top notch. Some of the best work I've ever seen."

"CIA good?"

"Better," he stated firmly.

"Svenson in Oslo is the best at forgery of fake identification," Carmen Delahunt said, masked by her VR helmet. "But he is way out of the price range of some amateur gunner. Only governments and major corporations can afford him."

"Tucholka is just as talented," Kurtzman muttered, thinking aloud. "But Uncle Richard retired a few years ago."

"Where did he go, South America or Australia?"

Kurtzman had to chuckle at that. Poor Australia had more retired spies and forgers than they would ever want to know about. Twenty years ago Brazil had been the place to go, but after the creation of the brutal secret police called the S2, another location had quickly needed to be found, and Australia won. Or lost—it all depended on how you looked at the situation.

"Actually, no," Kurtzman said, scratching the back of his neck. "He went back home to Michigan. Detroit, I believe."

Starting to slide a CD into the slot on his player, Tokaido looked up sharply at that statement. "And Able Team is on the way to Chicago following the trail of their attacker."

"They're both major cities in the Midwest," Kurtzman admitted slowly. "But, yeah, that's one hell of a coincidence."

"I'll hack the FBI files and find out where Tucholka is," Delahunt said, her hands already caressing the air to open programs and activate macros files. The submonitors flanking her main computer screen began scrolling lines of code and government ciphers.

"Akira, you go after Tucholka," Kurtzman ordered. "I'll continue working on the French angle."

"The Justice Department and the CIA both still like to use Tucholka occasionally, so we really can't put much pressure on him," the young man reminded.

"Screw the CIA," Kurtzman barked angrily. "Get Tucholka!"

"How?"

"Hack his bank records, take all of his money and then make a deal. His illegal life's savings for the name and description of one customer."

"Our mole." Putting in his earbuds, Tokaido turned the music up all the way. "Now you're talking," he said, and started typing on the keyboard with both hands.

Pushing away from his workstation, Kurtzman wheeled about in a circle and started for the coffee-maker to make a fresh pot of coffee.

"Alert," Delahunt said out of the blue. "Able Team has just landed at O'Hare Airport."

Kurtzman stopped in the middle of the floor "What?" he bellowed. "Impossible! They're an hour ahead of schedule!"

"Jack picked up a tailwind over North Dakota," Delahunt replied, like the blind oracle of Delphi. "Hey, these things happen."

The big man growled a curse and rolled back to his workstation. "Did we get the codes yet from the White House?" he demanded, slamming into the edge of the station. The arms of his wheelchair slid underneath, stopping the chair at exactly the correct distance, and his hands went straight for the keyboard.

"Hal sent them a few minutes ago," Tokaido answered, closing programs and opening new ones at lightning speed. "We'll be good to go in just a couple of minutes."

"Not fast enough! Their plane is taxiing to the main terminal right now," Delahunt warned. "Move it or lose it, my friend!"

"Damn it, I'm being challenged by the NSA and Homeland Security!" Tokaido raged. "I can't handle both!"

"No problem. I'll block them, and you hit that power grid!" Kurtzman commanded, his computer dissolving through screen after screen of government security logos.

"I'm slaving my console to yours…now!" Tokaido announced.

Their controls fused into a single unit, the two men electronically charged into the fray, accessing, deleting, denying and overriding at breakneck speed.

Casually walking into the room, Barbara Price started to speak, then caught the tension in the air. She bit her tongue. Any distraction now would only slow the cybernetic experts.

Aside from the belief that O'Hare was the real destination of the assailant in the Alaska hills, Able Team had nothing else to go on. So with some help from Kurtzman and his team, the Stony Man commandos were going to try to shake the bushes, hopefully making the enemy reveal itself. It was a long shot to say the least, but she just had to trust to their skills, and hope this wild gamble paid off.

O'Hare International Airport, Chicago

WEARING CIVILIAN CLOTHES, Able Team strolled through the security checkpoint of O'Hare without any trouble.

Even Schwarz had removed all of his trick pens to facilitate an easy entrance.

A milling throng of people moved through the busy concourse, their hushed voices combining into an indecipherable roar. Crying and laughing, a huge crowd of anxious people stood behind the new Plexiglas dividers, waving goodbye to people heading for the weapons scanners, and waving in greeting to the folks coming off a flight.

Flight arrivals and departures were announced over a PA system of surprisingly superior quality, and the air smelled faintly of flowers and hot pretzels from a vendor by the escalator going to another level. In the crowd, a limo driver raised a placard with a corporate logo, and a small girl lifted a handpainted piece of cardboard with just the word Mom on it. A young couple was passionately kissing goodbye, or maybe it was hello, but since they didn't stop it was impossible to tell. A baby cried shrilly someplace far away, and a man in an expensive suit was chomping an unlit cigar and glancing hatefully at a prominent No Smoking sign.

As Able Team rode the slow conveyor belt past the weapons scanner for boarding passengers, a couple of the new armed TSA guards gave them a hard glance, as if sensing that these three weren't typical holiday or business travelers. But as the men moved by, the TSA guards turned their attention back to the people and luggage trying to get on board the waiting commercial jetliners.

"Remember when you could walk onto the tarmac and simply board a plane as if it were a cab?" Schwarz asked with a sigh as he loosened the collar of his red flannel shirt. Hiking boots and faded denims completed the ensemble, the empty knife sheath at his hip the finishing touch of believability.

"You're showing your age," Blancanales said. "That was long ago, and far away." He was dressed like an off-duty banker in a three-piece silk suit with a gold watch chain across the front. His Italian shoes gleamed with polish.

"Yeah, guess so. But life goes on, eh?"

"Always has, brother, always will."

"Come on, Bear, we're almost at the crowd," Lyons whispered, shifting the duffel bag draped over a shoulder. "Now would be a good time."

The former L.A. cop was in California casual: white deck shoes and matching pants with a Hawaiian shirt covered with multicolored orchids. The shirt alone should have set off the fire alarm, but it was a Christmas gift from his son, Tommy, and Carl wore it whenever possible.

"He won't fail us, Carl," Schwarz said, then stopped as the ceiling lights flickered across the airport.

At the ticket counters, the computer monitors scrolled madly, and the arrival-departure boards went wild, displaying only gibberish for a few moments. Then everything went back to normal.

"Son of a bitch!" somebody gasped among the confused murmurs of the crowd. "He's here!"

Even as they separated, the members of Able Team spun about to lock their attention on that one man. Pushing his way through the frightened people was a big man, his shirt bulging with muscle. His black hair was buzzed in a military crew cut, and there was a rolled-up copy of *Soldier Of Fortune* magazine held in his left fist.

Backing away from the incoming passengers on the conveyor belt, the large man stuffed the magazine into a hip pocket and turned to leave quickly for the nearest exit.

Bingo. Lyons had hoped there would be somebody waiting to meet Dunbar when he returned to Chicago from his mission, to either debrief the man, or pay him off with a bullet in the back of the skull. Having Bear access the Chicago city power grid and flicker the lights in O'Hare as if the Chameleon had been activated had seemed the obvious ploy to use to make the associates of Dunbar think that he had failed and the intended victim was now coming after them. Standing guard in an airport was a shit job for a trusted but low-echelon personnel. With any luck, the man was now calling his boss to relay the bad news, and Bear was already scanning the cell phone traffic for any outgoing calls. The trap had worked, and the noose was tightening.

Surreptitiously following their prey, Able Team converged in the parking garage, just as a black sedan raced away.

"There goes our pigeon," Lyons said, pulling out a cell phone.

"Did you get the plate?" Blancanales asked, craning his neck.

Schwarz nodded and rattled off the letters and numbers. "It was an Illinois plate, but that doesn't mean a thing unless this guy is an idiot."

"He was reading *Soldier of Fortune* magazine."

"True enough. Okay, he's an idiot."

"Or a rank beginner," he amended. "Which makes him doubly dangerous, because we can't predict what he'll do."

"Hello, Birdman," Lyons said quickly. "The quail has left the nest."

"Dark sedan, driving like hell? Yeah, I see him," Jack Grimaldi replied over the steady whomp of helicopter blades in the background. "I've already rented a chopper and will discreetly keep track from above while you boys get some transportation."

"Don't lose him," Lyons warned, watching the weaving car disappear into traffic.

"Not likely." Jack laughed. "Let me know when you're mobile."

Closing the phone, Lyons slipped it into a pocket as the team went back in the airport and headed for a rental agency.

"I called ahead, so there should be a Cadillac waiting for us under the name Jason DeMille," Blancanales said.

"Good." Hardware was the next priority. There was no way to smuggle their weapons through airport security; the TSA was new but good at its job. However, Grimaldi should have their stuff with him. All they had to do was rendezvous with his helicopter somewhere and they would be back in business.

Just then, Schwarz was buzzed and he pulled out a cell phone. He listened for a moment, then grunted and tucked it away again.

"That was Bear." Schwarz stopped for a moment as a group of laughing people walked by them, then he continued. "Our boy just made a frantic call to a local number."

"Anybody we know?" Blancanales muttered, tilting his head.

"No. But the property is owned by Peter Woods."

"The leader of Cascade?" Lyons asked, a frown creasing his face.

Stuffing his hands in his pockets, Schwarz exhaled slowly. "The one and only."

"Well, shit. That certainly explains the *Soldier of Fortune* magazine."

Lyons agreed. Even as a street cop in Los Angeles he had heard of Cascade, a group of fanatics who called themselves neopatriots and encouraged acts of terrorism by foreign nations in the insane belief that constant warfare made America strong. They had a slogan about being Forged In Fire And Quenched In Blood, or some nonsense like that. The possibilities of what Cascade could do with the Chameleon were endless. And all them would involve thousands of dead civilians. Maybe millions.

"Better hope it's a fast Cadillac," Lyons said out of the corner of his mouth as they approached the rental counter.

MILLIONAIRES WERE the royalty of America. In Los Angeles the top lived in Beverly Hills, in New York they preferred the Upper East Side, but in Chicago all of the rich and powerful lived in the Miracle Mile.

Situated along Lake Shore Drive, row after row of luxury apartment buildings faced Lake Michigan. Museums and theaters were sprinkled about their bases like offerings to nobility, a sprawling marina edged the clean, sandy shore, the pristine slips filled with gigantic yachts and sleek powerboats. The toys of the ultrarich. Every building had its own security force, and was topped with a helipad for busy executives too harried to bother with the touch of the ground among the mere mortals. Some of the apartment buildings were old and stately, with astronomical rents. Others were brand-new and trendy, utilizing all of the cutting-edge technologies, with even higher rents. Situated among the towers of power was the crown jewel known throughout the nation as the New Yorker.

The New Yorker was a brand-new style of the oldest form of human habitat, the communal lodge. Forty stories tall, the building was a miniature city set within the city of Chicago. Designed so that the tenants never had to leave the building, the rents were staggering, and the waiting list to get in was as long as the lineage on many of the superrich drooling to gain access to the ultimate downtown living experience.

The basement was an armored fortress to store the cars of the tenants, the first floor a liveried military camp that all nonresident visitors had to pass to gain entrance, even city inspectors and police. There was a kindergarten and elementary school on the fifth floor, high school on the sixth, movie theater and shopping mall on ten, grocery store on fifteen, a wooden park on twenty-five, an indoor saltwater pool on thirty, a brothel on thirty-five and a double helipad on the roof.

A city within a city—no, the New Yorker was more like a small nation with its own aristocracy. Its undisputed king, the only tenant who owned a whomping thirty percent of the building, was the retired billionaire, Peter Adams Woods.

Sprawling on a chaise longue, Woods was on the thirtieth floor soaking up some sun streaming through the bulletproof glass windows and listening to gentle sounds of the artificial surf casting gentle waves upon the pristine white sand beach. Dressed only in silk trunks, Woods was clearly a large man, heavily muscled and deeply tanned, with the build of a professional weight-lifter. His face was clean shaven and handsome, but without warmth or humor, like the chiseled features of a marble statue. Expert plastic surgery had removed the scars of his youthful endeavors to reach this social pinnacle, but no amount of washing could clean the blood off his hands. Nobody wanted to do business with Peter Woods unless it was absolutely necessary, the same as nobody wanted to go swimming in the ocean with a shark in the water. And the results were often similar; the shark got fatter and the swimmer simply disappeared.

Forming a circle about Woods were seven other men, also dressed in swimwear in case their boss went into the water. But these grim professionals also wore loose Hawaiian shirts, and when they moved right it was possible to view the butts of the massive handguns riding in shoulder holsters underneath the colorful attire. These men moved with the grace of panthers, betraying their skills in the martial arts. Several of them had discolored patches of skin on their arms where military tattoos had been expensively removed with lasers, and plain black gym bags lay on the sand nearby, the tops partially unzipped to almost expose the wealth of weapons packed inside for quick access.

These were the Magnificent Seven, as they had been humorlessly dubbed by the terrified staff of the New Yorker, the private bodyguards of Peter Woods who traveled with him everywhere, even the bedroom. Many a young socialite, seeking to improve her standing in the register, had been startled to learn that going to bed with Peter Woods meant having sex before a live audience. And if the girl complained too much, Woods would toss her to his men, like giving table scraps to hunting dogs. Afterward, the weeping girl would never speak of the matter to anybody, and soon another pretty fool would offer herself to the beast of the New Yorker, positive that she would be the one to land the most eligible bachelor in town.

At the moment, two topless women, one in a red bikini bottom, and the other in a black thong, were massaging Woods's legs with scented coconut oil. Both of the woman tinkled musically as they moved, the blonde from the silver bells dangling from her nipple ring, the redhead with the same from her elaborate earrings. They thought it was merely a fetish of the billionaire, but in truth, Woods merely wanted to keep track of them in the dark. Twice assassins had come disguised as whores to service his Herculean sexual appetite. One was buried in the concrete foundation of the New Yorker itself; the other had been strangled by Woods inside his limousine while on the way to meet the mayor at the Firemen's Annual Ball. He stuffed her lifeless body out the window while crossing a bridge, and arrived with a smile on his cold face. The ball was long remembered as the nicest Peter Woods had ever been in public. The billionaire thug loved to kill.

"Shoulders," Woods said, turning his face to make sure his tan stayed even. "And put some muscle into it."

"Yes, Mr. Woods," the blonde said, and they both began fingering the knotted muscles in his upper torso. Jingling, the redhead made sure that her full breasts brushed against the man's arm on a regular basis. He grunted at the contact and reached out to slide a hand up the inner thigh of the blonde.

The woman gasped as he roughly kneaded her flesh, but managed to change it into a laugh.

"Now, don't be fresh, Mr. Woods," she chided in a friendly manner, tears in her eyes.

"Shut up, and take 'em off," he ordered, rolling onto his back. Then he looked at the redhead. "You, too," he snapped impatiently.

Forcing smiles onto their faces, the women stripped and started to climb on top of the man when a cultured voice called his name.

Pushing them rudely off, Woods sat upright to see a waiter for the indoor beach hurrying across the artificial grass near the bar, holding a silver tray covered with a white linen napkin.

As the servant stepped onto the white sand, two members of the seven blocked the way and quickly checked the man thoroughly, before parting and allowing him by.

Kneeling near the billionaire, the waiter removed the white cloth to reveal a cell phone lying on the silver tray.

"Excuse me, Mr. Woods," he whispered urgently. "Sorry to disturb you, sir. There is an urgent call from your mother."

Already reaching for the phone, Woods paused to frown. "Give me that again," he growled. "Who called?"

"Your mother, sir," the waiter gushed, feeling a drop of nervous sweat trickle down his spine. "Naturally, I would never disturb a guest in the no-call zone, but you specifically asked me to do so if your mother ever called."

Inhaling slowly, Woods narrowed his eyes to stare at the waiter. "Yes, of course, thank you," he said, then glanced over a shoulder. "That will be all today, ladies. See you tomorrow."

The naked women nodded assent and gathered their clothing to pad across the sand toward the elevator banks. Woods watched their hips swinging to the motion of their young bodies for a moment, then clicked on the phone.

"Woods here," he snapped into the phone. "Is this a secure line?"

"Damn straight it is, Chief," the familiar voice of Tommy Mannix replied. "And the shit has hit the fan."

The man's real name was Tomasinoro Marnix, but on the street that had quickly become Tommy Mannix. Tommy the Hammer. Unlike Woods, Mannix didn't try to hide his true nature and relished the fact that people were uneasy to even speak his name out loud in the town he controlled. Mannix had money; Woods kept him well supplied. But as the commander of Cascade, his authority came from the end of the sledgehammer he liked to use on his enemies, not a ballpoint pen and checkbook.

"Trouble with Cascade?" Woods demanded, reaching for a remote control. He thumbed a switch and the windows polarized over until they were darkly tinted. Twilight at noon.

"Yes and no," Mannix replied. "Apparently Jimmy failed to do the job in Alaska."

Woods snorted in reply. "Big deal. So Jimmy the Dumbass Dunbar had failed. Well, it had been a long shot at best. No real loss."

"The hell there ain't, Chief. Davis has come to Chi."

"What?" Woods roared, standing. "Are you sure?"

"Better believe it. When his plane landed, everything electrical in O'Hare went haywire for a few minutes. Must have been when he was going through security."

Sneaking weapons through was what he meant. "So the limey bastard is here," Woods stated, clenching a fist.

"And now after us," Mannix stated. "Who knows what that idiot Dunbar might have told under torture?"

"How did you find out? Who was at O'Hare when Davis arrived, Harry or Ivan?"

"Charlie."

Charles Raugh, a good man. "At least he knows how to keep his yap shut," Woods muttered angrily.

"Damn straight he does. Charlie scooted the moment the lights flickered. He's racing up 94 right now headed away from us and into Wisconsin. Just in case he's being followed."

That was SOP for any unexpected event. You never ran to base. The Feds obeyed the law, but they weren't stupid. Rubbing a hand across his face, Wood inhaled deeply, then let it out slowly as a smile.

"I have a better idea," he said with a chuckle. "Have Charlie turn around and let him lead Davis to us. Only we'll be ready to capture him alive. Davis thinks he's coming to burn us down, but all the asshole is doing is delivering the jamming unit to our doorstep."

"Sounds good."

"Meet me at headquarters. Davis was going to e-mail us the schematics for the jamming unit at ten o'clock." He glanced at a clock above the bar. "That's a couple of hours from now. We have until then to get ready before he gets wise."

"No sweat. I'll call in the troops, Chief, and we'll fill this place with guns. The son of a bitch will have a real fight on his hands when he arrives!"

"We want him alive," Woods barked. "Got any stun bags, tranquilizer darts, nets, gas grenades, that sort of shit on hand?"

"Some," Mannix said slowly. "Dunbar took our only MM-1, but I know where to get another."

"Than do it. Is the turkey doc on hand?"

"Sure thing. And he's itching to get to work."

"Good," Woods said, starting across the warm sand for the elevator. "Tell him we'll let him start scratching real soon now."

CHAPTER FOURTEEN

Aboard the White Pearl

Stepping naked out of the steam room, Davis Harrison took a towel from the counter and started to dry himself. His body was smooth and nearly hairless, almost feminine in its contours.

"Sorry to keep you waiting, my dear." He chuckled, vigorously rubbing his head. "But I wanted our first time to be—shall we say?—special."

There was no reply from the next room.

Drying off his legs, Harrison flinched as always as the towel passed over his genitalia. He had been a courier, merely carrying a message to an SAS commando unit in Beijing when he was captured by the infamous Chinese counterintelligence group Red Star. Harrison was beaten, stripped, tortured and finally mutilated and released to be a warning to other British operatives.

Unable to reveal what had been done, he got himself cashiered from the service, and then sold his skills on the world market to anybody with hard cash. Soon, he had enough money, and delicate plastic surgery made him function normally again. But by then he was a wanted criminal on four continents. Unable to risk retirement and chance being found and imprisoned, Harrison found he had no choice but to continue his work. Spy, agent provocateur, smuggler, assassin—they were all the same to him now. Merely jobs to be done without any emotional involvement. That was, unless China was the target, and then he worked with a ferocity that startled even the hardened agents of the Red Star.

Toweling the rest of his body dry, Harrison wrapped the terry cloth low around his waist. But this mission would be his final revenge. China would never recover from the aftereffects of the Chameleon, and at last maybe he could turn the memory of that night of screaming in his head when the Red Star had strapped him into a cane chair and stolen his manhood with a pair of scissors.

Shuddering at the recollection, Harrison bent over clutching his stomach. Fighting the urge to retch, he regained control of his breathing and wiped a sheen of sweat off his face. Payback is coming, you bastards, he snarled at his reflection in the foggy mirror. Oh, God, yes, payback like you could never imagine!

Settling down, Harrison tossed aside the towel and slid on a pair of pants and slippers before going to his open suitcase and choosing a knife from the small assortment hidden inside the lining. Even without the Chameleon, smuggling things into and out of Russia had never really been a problem. Their army was formidable, but their security was a joke.

Parachuting down into cropland, Harrison had dragged the unwilling flight attendant with him to the nearest farmhouse. After killing the family, he bound and gagged the woman into a trunk, tossed it into the family's car and drove away into the night. Although Gwen looked English, she spoke Chinese perfectly. For some reason that offended him deeply, so Harrison decided to keep her as both a hostage in case of pursuit, and for some private retribution later on should the opportunity arise.

At the train station, he stayed with his secret hostage until the diesel locomotive was well under way, and then settled in for a good meal in the dining car. Long gone were the days when Russian food was something to be tolerated, or at worst, simply avoided. Huge corporations were spreading across the wild frontier of Russia, bringing in civilization and modern conveniences as fast as possible. At the end of a gun when necessary, and most of the larger corporations had a sweetheart deal going with the Russian Mob. A little bribery here, a few killings there, and suddenly an entire district now had cable television and washing machines.

Arriving at the Kamchatka Peninsula, he had the trunk delivered from the train to his stateroom on board the *White Pearl,* and stood guard until the boat was well under way before releasing the woman and tying her to a chair. His heart beat faster at the thought that a cane chair would have been better, but he would make do. He always did before.

Then Harrison chuckled at the thought that he was sailing directly toward some of the largest fields of cane in the world. The Kuril Islands.

For over a hundred years, Japan and Russia had been fighting over possession of the mountainous archipelago, a curved line of islands that almost formed a land-bridge connecting the two nations. But after World War II, America gave the archipelago to Russia as a punishment to Japan.

The ninety-three islands ranged from small to colossal, and nearly all of them were deserted. Mostly because of the dozens of live volcanoes in the area, both under the water and amid an impassable mountain range set deep in the lush jungles. The mineral wealth of the islands was sparse, the animals were numerous, but not rare or valuable. The wealth of the Kuril Islands lay in the fact that there were underwater volcanoes. The countless steam vents kept the entire surrounding ocean at a pleasant ambient temperature, and the schools of fish bred all year round. There were no better fishing grounds in the entire world than the hotly disputed Kuril Island chain. Tuna, sharks, crabs, whales, everything seemed to like living there, and the Russian fishing fleets pulled in an endless bounty of food from the warm rumbling waters.

Oddly enough, about a decade ago, the local hatred melted away when a Russian trawler foundered in an unexpected storm and started to sink near the Japanese end of the archipelago. Hundreds of Japanese civilians rushed into the storm to save the Russian fisherman, the bond of sailors overcoming the political machinations of the governments. Now greatly embarrassed, Russia and Japan allowed travel to and from the islands for both sides, and the tourist trade boomed like never before.

Ecologists swarmed out to visit the colonies of sea lions, otters and huge pods of whales. Geologists and volcanologists crawled over every inch of the main volcanoes, even though many of them didn't return from the dangerous climbs up the steep, jagged mountains. And hundreds of the descendants of the original Japanese settlers to the islands returned if only to place flowers on the graves of the ancestors. Finally, a deal was negotiated and one single ship was designated free passage, the *White Pearl*. Formerly a tramp steamer, the *White Pearl* was slowly rebuilt into a luxury liner, with sumptuous state rooms and every conceivable amenity—along with a captain and crew who were fiercely determined that no smuggling would ever take place on board the craft to threaten its fragile neutral status.

Happily, people were people the whole world over. A few bribes and his trunks were delivered unopened. Later, Harrison would kill the purser to cover his tracks. But for the moment, he would let the purser enjoy his newfound wealth, secure in the knowledge that the man planned on turning him in as a smuggler anyway once the *White Pearl* reached Japan. Russia may have stronger prisons, but the Japanese paid larger rewards. Money made the world go around. Money and sex. And revenge.

"Are you ready, my dear?" Harrison called out, testing the edge of the blade on a callused thumb. "Don't worry, you'll soon be with your friends from the plane. Oh, I promise that!" Rocking slightly to the rhythm of the boat, he padded barefoot into the next room humming a tune, but then froze at the sight of the empty chair, its ropes dangling to the floor.

Snarling in rage, he dived for the dresser only to discover his pistol gone. Along with his wallet. Bloody hell!

Grabbing a glass off the dresser, he threw it hard on the floor, where it shattered into a million pieces, the shrapnel shooting under the bed. When there was no cry of pain from underneath, Harrison stepped back into the bathroom and grabbed a spare gun from his suitcase. No KGB special this time, just a standard black matte 9 mm Heckler & Koch with a bulbous sound suppressor.

He pumped two rounds through the closet door, then spun and fired three times into the cabinet under the bathroom counter. But aside from punching splintery holes in the polished wood decor there was no other reaction.

Starting for the door, Harrison paused and returned to the bathroom. It wasn't possible. He knew that. But something in his gut told him different. With a nervous hand, he flipped back the cover on the other side of his suitcase. Harrison sighed in relief at the sight of the two shoe boxes lying side by side.

Chuckling in relief, he nudged the boxes with the sound suppressor of his weapon just to make sure. The lid of the first box came off, exposing a pair of shoes. But when the second lid was knocked aside, Harrison felt his guts turn into water. The box contained only a radio-alarm clock, identical to the one on the table near the bed. But the Chameleon was gone.

Screaming in rage, he yanked a belt of ammunition clips from the lining of the trick suitcase and stormed out of the suite. Gone! It was gone! Six months' undercover work stolen by some Chinese bitch! Betrayed. He had been betrayed by the stinking Chinese again!

"Sir?" a waiter gulped, coming to a ragged halt in the hallway. His hands were filled with a dinner tray covered with a silvery dome from which wisps of steam rose.

Contorting his face in mindless rage, Harrison fired twice, the first bullet slamming aside the dome with a bell-like ring, and the second plowing into the throat of the waiter.

Staggering away, the young Russian dropped the tray and grabbed his ruined neck in both hands, gagging for breath. Viciously, Harrison kicked the teenager aside and started shooting off the locks on the doors in the hallway. The first two rooms were empty, but the third contained a young couple sitting in bathrobes clinking champagne glasses. He shot them both in the head and moved onward.

Suddenly, a woman started screaming in the hallway, and Harrison stepped out to kill a maid holding towels.

"Where are you, bitch!" he screamed at the top of his lungs, prowling along the corridor. "Give it back, or you'll beg for death!"

A door was slammed open by a slim man in boxer shorts who bellowed at Harrison in Russian. Harrison pumped a 9 mm slug into the man's flat belly, and he crumpled to the thick carpet shaking all over, his face a rictus of shock and pain.

Yanking open a supply closet, Harrison found only mops and cleaning supplies. Slamming it shut, he kept walking at a steady pace, trying to regain control of his temper. A dozen people would be telephoning the purser by now, and soon ship security would arrive. He could easily kill them all, but he didn't have enough bullets to terminate everybody on board the *White Pearl*. The passengers could take him down by sheer numbers. He'd be captured again. *Captured. Imprisoned. Helpless as their filthy hands ran over his screaming body...*

Forcing the nightmare visions from his mind, Harrison took a deep breath, and a wave of cool washed over his body. Stay calm, stay low, get the unit, kill the bitch. In that order! Now, move, soldier! Move!

Slipping the hot pistol into his pants, he returned the room of the Russian man and used his knife to slip the lock. Easing inside, he found the man curled in a fetal position on the floor with bloody towels wadded around his stomach, one hand fumbling to reach the telephone on the nightstand.

By now, Harrison could hear people shouting somewhere on the ship, so moving swiftly he got a pillow from the bed and used it to muffle the sound of the silenced pistol as he shot the dying Russian in the heart. The sound of the 9 mm round was reduced to no more than a cough, and death came instantly.

"Consider it payment for the clothing," he whispered, as footsteps went running past the closed door, and people started yelling in the hallway.

Rummaging among the dead man's clothing, Harrison found the clothing was a very good fit, but then the SAS taught its agents fashion and how to gauge sizes for similar situations. Although the scenario played in training had been for German uniforms and Arab business suits. Different countries, different targets.

Neatly dressed, Harrison spotted a pair of glasses on the nightstand and tucked them into a pocket by the earstem so that they hung out of his breast pocket. Reloading the 9 mm HK, he racked the slide and tucked the weapon under his linen jacket. Glancing in a mirror, he avoided his own eyes, then abruptly departed, throwing open the door and coolly stepping outside.

Half-dressed people were flooding into the hallway, shouting in a dozen different languages. The crowd parted for a burly woman carrying a medical bag, but closed in her wake, making passage impossible again. Everybody was trying to get closer to the corpses, which was the opposite of the direction Harrison wanted to go. Slapping a hand over his mouth, he started making gagging sounds. Instantly, people moved away to not be splattered by his vomit, and Harrison staggered into the stairwell at the end of the corridor. Once out of sight, he sprinted up the steps, taking two at a time. Reaching the main deck, he breathed in the clean salt air and planned his next move. A flight attendant would know about undertow from a sinking plane, so she wouldn't be stupid enough to jump into the water. She might have some survival training, but did that mean she knew anything about releasing a lifeboat? Harrison would have to say no, and hold off checking the berths as his last option.

Then he twisted his head about and looked at the bridge rising above the clean white deck of the *White Pearl,* its little radar mast spinning about amid the radio antennae. Then he smiled. No, she wouldn't try to leave. Her training would impel her to seek the captain. Idiot.

Calmly walking along the deck, Harrison reached the main stairs and stopped only long enough to pull the fire alarm. Now with bells clanging across the ship, he walked up the stairs, staying close to the wall and out of the way of the officers rushing out of the bridge to see what was happening on their ship. By the time he reached the observation deck, people started running about in panic on the deck below.

Off to the side was an access door clearly marked No Admittance in Russian, Japanese, English and Chinese. Using his knife to slip the lock, Harrison eased into a short corridor with only two other doors. One was partially ajar, but the other had a grim steward standing guard in front. The big Russian frowned at the sight of the intruder, and he raised a hand to block the way. Harrison pulled the Heckler & Koch and fired a fast three times, the impacts driving the steward backward against the closed door. Spinning, the killer kicked open the other door and killed the helmsman at the wheel. There was a grunt of surprise as an older man wearing a captain's uniform pulled a huge revolver from a holster at his side and thumbed back the hammer.

Ducking low, Harrison shot under the chart table, blowing off the captain's knee. The man yelled in agony and dropped to the deck, losing the pistol. Harrison stroked the trigger, sending a messenger of death directly into a startled eye, and the captain's head rocked as the back of his head exploded into a horrible froth of bones and brains and blood.

Standing slowly, he listened for any reaction to the shooting, but the rest of the crew and passengers seemed to be more concerned with the fake fire and the very real corpses on C deck. Checking the controls, Harrison saw the *White Pearl* was starting to veer off course. He flipped a few switches to set her on autopilot. The warm water currents were strong in the Sea of Okhotsk, but the computer would suffice until somebody came to regain command of the vessel.

Starting to go, he paused to throw a few more switches and set off fire alarms in the engine room, and fuel pump room. That should put fear in the crew, and keep them out of his way until he was done.

Returning to the corridor, he stepped over the dead steward and started to slide his knife into the jam alongside the lock when suddenly the wooden panel of the door burst into small holes and something hummed past his face to smack the far wall.

Throwing himself sideways, he shot a fast four times, blowing off the lock and both hinges. More holes appeared in the door as a weapon fired twice more, and then the door began to topple into the room. A woman's voice cried out in surprise, and Harrison came in fast and low over the door, throwing lead at everything in sight. A small Japanese woman wearing a white doctor's coat tumbled sideways out of a chair, her cell phone flying away. Across the surgery, a table had been flipped on its side and crouched behind was the flight attendant. She aimed the KGB gun and Harrison dived out of the way. He hit the deck rolling and firing, the steel-jacketed rounds smacking into the heavy wooden table with the sound of hammer blows. Gwenneth aimed back, and Harrison threw a chair in the way as protection. Stupid bitch! The blasted weapon could be empty, but there was no way of knowing until a slug hit and blew him to hell. He couldn't take the chance.

Dropping the clip, he reloaded and fanned flame at

the wall behind the woman. The glass front of an emergency case shattered, raining glass down upon her. Crying out in pain, Gwenneth raised an arm to shield her face and he shot her in the elbow. Shrieking in pain, Gwenneth tried desperately to crawl through the glass, cutting her legs badly, all the while wildly pulling the trigger to only subdued clicks.

"One more step and I blow your little box to pieces!" she sputtered, tears of pain in voice.

Laughing softly, Harrison stood and leveled his gun at the cringing woman. "That is only a nine shot," he said, advancing slowly. "And you pulled the trigger a dozen times already. Thanks for letting me know it's empty."

Snarling something in Chinese, Gwenneth threw the empty gun at her tormentor. He didn't move and let it smack into his chest before returning the favor. The Heckler & Koch recoiled slightly as the coughing weapon sent half a clip into her face, blowing her beauty away forever.

Pushing the table aside, Harrison put two more rounds into her chest just to make sure, and then began searching for the unit. Starting in the most obvious place, his impatience steadily grew until he at last found it tucked inside a pillow case on the small bed in the ship's surgery. Forcing the device into a pocket of his jacket, he reloaded once more to make sure he had a full clip, then slipped out of the control area and back into the companionway.

Mingling with the rest of the frightened passengers, Harrison mimicked their expressions and tried to appear equally bewildered and nervous. Personally, though, he was wondering how long it would take for things to settle down and lunch to be served. His evening of torture with Gwenneth had been interrupted by her futile escape, so the least he could do was console himself with a nice dinner.

Upper Kamchatka Peninsula

"ALL STOP," McCarter said into his throat mike.

Surrounded by the whirlwind of their own turbines under the rubber skirt, the two U.S. Navy SEAL hovercraft settled onto the ground and went silent. Directly ahead of them was a set of railroad tracks on an elevated berm of gravel. Off to the side was a small weather-beaten wooden shack to serve as a depot for passengers. Nearby stood a battered old truck that seemed to be held together almost entirely by baling wire and gray duct tape.

Flipping down his night-vision goggles, Hawkins switched to infrared. "Engine and exhaust pipe both read warm," he said, then turned slowly. "Nothing else in the vicinity."

"Perimeter sweep," McCarter ordered, leveling his Barnett crossbow and starting for the shack.

Spreading out, the rest of Phoenix Force covered the area, and then the dilapidated truck, before joining their leader at the shack. It was completely empty, without even a schedule on the splintery wall. There was only a plank resting on some cinder blocks as a bench, and a rusted barrel with holes in its side to serve was a crude firebox to warm the shack in the bitter Russian winter.

"Cold," Encizo said, resting a bare hand on the metal rim. Then he frowned and reached down into the barrel to come up with a crumpled piece of silvery foil.

"Now, I don't read Chinese," he said with a half smile, sniffing the scrap, "but this sure smells like honey-smoked airline peanuts to me."

"Bingo," Manning muttered, hoisting his weapon. "And that's the logo for China Air. We're back in the game."

"Maybe," McCarter growled, flipping down his night-vision goggles and scanning the area first in UV, then infrared.

Following the directions of the Chinese airline captain, the team had easily located the downed parachutes of the thief and his prisoner. Spiraling out from the farm, they found the railroad, but now the big question was, did their quarry grab a ride here, or was this a diversion? That peanut pack was just the sort of subtle clue the ape would leave to fool professional trackers. Or had he had a mistake? Everybody slipped up now and then.

Walking onto the railroad tracks, McCarter looked in both directions. The track stretched into the night and out of sight in both directions.

"Any ideas?" James asked.

"It's a crapshoot," McCarter growled. "There's no way to tell which direction he went."

"Unless this was the rendezvous point," Hawkins added. "And now the Russian Mob or some terrorist group is driving away with the Chameleon in the back seat."

Encizo shook his head. "That doesn't make any sense. Then why didn't they simply meet him at the drop zone?" he said. "Why kill a family to steal their truck? It's much more logical to simply call for a pickup."

"And who says he's being logical?"

"Besides, stealing the Chameleon took months and millions of dollars," McCarter stated forcibly. "This is way out of the league of the Moscow Mafia, or some half-assed Ukrainian terrorists. Even the Hammers of Stalin couldn't finance this big an operation, and they're the local big boys on the block."

"Agreed. My gut feeling is that he is still on the move," James said from the hovercraft. "Our boy is way too smart to jump out this close to his rendezvous point. He's taking the train somewhere, getting lost in the crowd, hiding in plain sight."

"With a woman in tow?" Hawkins scoffed, pulling out a candy bar. "Must be crazy as a shithouse rat if he did." Ripping off the wrapper, the man consumed the bar in a few bites and washed it down with a long draft from his canteen.

"So what's north of us?" Manning asked, looking in that direction.

"Farmland, foothills, mountains, mines and then a million acres of nothing," Encizo answered, then added, "and the old Soviet nuke testing range. Their version of White Sands, New Mexico."

"To the south is more farmland, some major mountains, a few industrial cities and then some fishing villages," James commented, checking a map in the beam of a flashlight. "After that is the Kuril Islands, and Japan."

"Lots of folks in Tokyo would pay big for the Chameleon," Hawkins stated grimly, flipping up his goggles.

"Don't I know it," McCarter said. The Kuril Island archipelago. Nothing much there but sea lions, bamboo, pine trees and volcanoes. But beyond the chain of islands was Japan, and then North Korea. Pyongyang missiles protected by the jamming field could rain death upon cities across the world. The U.S., U.K. and NATO would be forced to strike back, and then China would protect their Communist ally, and...

"Nuclear holocaust," the Stony Man commando muttered, the soft words carried away by a chill night wind. "The end of the world."

Long minutes passed as Phoenix Force stood in the dark alongside the railroad tracks fighting to clear the nightmare images from their minds. The clock was ticking and they needed cool heads to catch the nameless thief.

"Incoming," Encizo said quietly over the radio.

Instantly, the Stony Man team scattered into the darkness. Moments later, headlights appeared in the darkness as a police car rolled into view from behind the dense trees. The wide tires of the heavy vehicle crunched loudly on the loose gravel as it went directly to the abandoned truck. In the wash of the headlights a dome could be seen on the roof of the car, as well as lettering along the sides that clearly marked it as a police vehicle.

The car was parked so that its headlights bathed the truck, the handbrake was set with a loud ratcheting sound and then both of the front doors swung open in unison. Two large men stepped out of the vehicle with big pistols in their hands. The Russian cops stood still for a minute listening to the night, their eyes sweeping the area. One man wore steel-rimmed glasses that sparkled in the darkness with reflected light, while the other sported a trim, square-cut beard like somebody in a painting from the sixteenth century.

Both were wearing dark blue sneakers and light gray sweaters with some sort of an official emblem stitched on the right breast, instead of the left as in America. Leather rigs framed their powerful chests, spare ammunition clips for their guns balancing the shoulder holsters.

"That is the stolen truck," the man with glasses rumbled, his hoarse voice sounding like a broken machine. "I recognize it from the photograph on the kitchen wall of the farmhouse."

The other racked his pistol, chambering a round. "Perhaps you are right and the killer took the southbound train."

"Radio district headquarters," the first policeman said, starting forward. "I believe the madman is heading for the *White Pearl*'s dock. I'll sweep the truck."

"Be wary, my friend. This madman has killed five already," his partner said, reaching for a mike from the dashboard of the running car.

But before he could finish, soft coughs came out of the darkness and both policemen slapped their necks. Staggering, the cops dropped their guns and fell to their knees, then incredibly they each pulled out a small backup revolver. The man with glasses fired blindly into the night, while the other lurched into the car and grabbed the microphone.

"Alert..." he croaked, the radio nowhere near his mouth.

More coughs sounded, and the men recoiled from the impacts of the narcotic darts, their faces going slack from the onslaught of the drugs. Still fighting to try to stand, they finally collapsed sideways onto the ground and went still.

As silent as ghosts, Phoenix Force stepped into the beams of the headlights, the tranquilizer guns still in their hands. McCarter and the others stood guard while James checked the pulse and respiration of the fallen police.

"They're okay," James reported at last. "No sign of overdose or anaphylactic shock. They'll wake up in a couple of hours feeling like boiled crap, but they'll live."

"Are these policemen or dinosaurs?" Manning asked with a grimace, sliding out the compressed-air cartridge from the butt of the pistol and slipping it into a loop on his belt. He extracted a fresh cartridge and inserted it into the pistol, snapping the cover shut with a flourish. "These darts should have stopped them dead in their tracks."

"Pretty tough cops for the sticks," Hawkins drawled, eyeing the snoring men suspiciously.

Flipping down his goggles, Encizo glanced overhead. "Think they're air rescue?"

"Don't care. Just put them in the car," McCarter directed brusquely, "and lose the key."

Holstering their weapons, the team gently conveyed the gargantuan officers to the vehicle. Putting them into comfortable positions, James threw the ignition key away while Manning rolled up the windows and closed the doors.

Hawkins shot the man a silent question.

"They'll sleep longer out of the fresh air," the Canadian explained with a grin.

"Smart," Hawkins grunted, but he suspected a more genial reason.

"T.J., Rafe, watch for any more friendlies coming," McCarter directed, changing the frequency of the powerful uplink radio on his belt.

The men nodded and slipped away.

"Stone House, this is Firebird," McCarter subvocalized into the throat mike. There was only crackling static. "Stone House, this is Firebird, do you read?"

"Roger, Firebird, this is Roosevelt," Kurtzman replied through the hash.

McCarter frowned. Who? Oh yes, the old American president who used a wheelchair. Clever.

"Are you requesting pickup at the rendezvous point?" Kurtzman asked.

"Not quite yet, Roosevelt," McCarter answered gruffly, resting a boot on an iron rail. "We have lost the ape and need some intel on the *White Pearl.*"

There was a crackling pause. "Repeat, please," Kurtzman demanded.

"The *White Pearl,*" McCarter repeated slowly. "If our boy is going for sushi, that would be the way."

"Firebird, this is Opera Star," Delahunt said, cutting into the conversation. "We're way ahead of you, and have been monitoring all major transports in the area for anything unusual. There was a fire and several deaths reported on the *White Pearl* less than an hour ago."

"Has there ever been any similar incident on the

ship before?" he snapped, his stomach tingling with excitement.

"Negative, Firebird," Delahunt said. "A few stolen purses, and several fistfights in the bar, but nothing like this."

"It's our boy!" James said, starting for the hovercraft.

"Sure as bloody hell sounds like him," Hawkins grunted, running alongside the other man. "We got enough fuel to reach the *White Pearl* while it's still at sea?"

"No way," James said with a frown. "We'll have to drop everything we can and transfer all of the fuel into one hovercraft just to reach the end of the peninsula!"

"Stone House, we'll need a long cool drink very soon," McCarter subvocalized as he climbed into a hovercraft. "Can do?"

"Roger, Firebird," Kurtzman replied. "Will send details in thirty, repeat, three zero, minutes."

"Confirm."

"Anything else?"

The sky rumbled just then, and lightning flashed briefly, casting the landscape into stark relief. McCarter scowled. Was that a leftover from the big squall, or some new storm front moving in?

"Yeah," he muttered. "More time, some luck, and bit of fair weather."

"I'll see what we can arrange, Firebird. Stone House, over and out."

CHAPTER FIFTEEN

Chicago

The black sedan moved through the southbound traffic on Interstate 55 as if it owned the world. Other cars got out of the way, or were tailgated to the point of collision. The driver of the sedan was unseen behind the tinted glass, but the other drivers still flashed him the middle finger, along with a chorus of colorful profanity.

Staying a good distance away, the rented Cadillac containing Able Team drove at a steady pace and maintained contact by the use of binoculars.

"The crazy bastard couldn't make himself any more noticeable," Blancanales said, working the bolt of the M-16/M-203 assault rifle combo lying across his lap. "He wants to be followed. This is a trap."

"Good," Lyons said, accelerating slightly.

Busy with his radio, Schwarz said nothing as he adjusted the scrambler to a new code to get in touch with the Farm. This close to two major airports, O'Hare and Midway, the TSA and Homeland Security would be monitoring the airwaves very carefully. One slip on the radio, and Able Team would be surrounded by armed troops with a shoot-first-ask-questions-later attitude. That would mean an end to the mission until Hal Brognola could get the team sprung, and by then the Chameleon would be long gone.

The glistening towers of Chicago were falling behind the rented Cadillac, as Lyons drove steadily along the concrete highway. Traffic was light, mostly taxicabs heading for Midway airport and semitrailers heading for St. Louis and beyond. Plus, one black sedan with tinted windows.

Glancing out the side window, Lyons noted a few jetliners moving across the empty sky. O'Hare and Midway carefully coordinated their arrivals and departures in a complex ballet. Personally, he didn't know how the air-traffic controllers stayed sane doing their impossible job. First as a cop, and now as a covert operative for Stony Man, Carl Lyons had faced death a thousand times in combat, making split-second decisions that risked innocent lives. But he couldn't imagine doing it for eight hours a day, nine to five, five days a week, for years on end.

"And they call me an Ironman," Carl Lyons muttered softly, flipping a salute to the unseen guardians of the skyways.

"Hello, Stone House? This is Trinity," Schwarz said into the compact radio. Trinity was that week's code name for the three-man team. Schwarz started to add something, then frowned and touched the receiver tucked into his ear.

"Say again?" he muttered, arching an eyebrow in surprise. "Well, I'll be… Yes, continue, please."

Hearing a familiar deep throb, Blancanales tucked the

M-16/M-203 out of sight as a sleek police helicopter rose into view from below the elevated highway and swung across to head into the east. Grimaldi had been surprised, then suspicious, when the car that raced out of O'Hare had suddenly done a U-turn on Route 94 and started heading south. Kurtzman had registered that the cell phone call made from O'Hare had been to an abandoned automobile-manufacturing plant in the heart of Gary, owned by a company that was owned by Peter Woods.

Now the reasonable thing for the observer at the airport to do would have been to inform his boss and then to drive away from Gary to confuse anybody trying to tail him. But by the time Able Team had gotten their rented car and headed onto the highway, Grimaldi reported that the black sedan was heading toward Gary. It didn't take a great leap of logic to figure out that Peter Woods had ordered an ambush for anybody following the car.

Able Team and Grimaldi had briefly discussed the matter, and arranged for a fast rendezvous with Grimaldi at a deserted weigh station to acquire weapons and supplies. Afterward, the pilot returned to O'Hare to get the big C-130 Hercules ready for takeoff while Able Team continued to follow the sedan. How they would handle the coming ambush was undecided yet, so the team members were preparing for all contingencies as best they could.

"Okay, I have good news, and bad news," Schwarz said, removing the earphone. "Bear has a positive ID on our ape. His name is Davis Lovejoy Harrison. He's a freelance spy, merc, assassin, you name it, and a former member of the Royal British Special Air Service."

"The SAS?" Lyons asked, frowning.

Schwarz nodded. "Yeah."

Lyons shrugged. "Everybody has traitors."

"Ain't it the truth, brother," Schwarz agreed, remembering a particularly dark incident in the past of Stony Man.

"What's the bad news?" Blancanales asked, turning slightly in his seat.

"Phoenix Force has lost Harrison in Russia. They think he's heading for the…Kreel Islands?" Schwarz said the name as a question.

"Kuril," Lyons corrected. "Damn, that's a common jumping-off point for Japan, North Korea and Red China. If Harrison disappears in there, he's gone for good."

Once past Midway, the apartment buildings alongside 55 were taking on a pronounced disreputable appearance, with many of the windows boarded shut, the roofs obviously sagging from fire and damage. Dotting the dirty landscape were billboards empty of advertising, but covered with gang symbols.

"How solid is this ident?" Blancanales asked, gazing thoughtfully out a window.

"David got a confirm on his SAS tattoo from a Chinese airline pilot, and then Tucholka rolled over on the guy," Schwarz said with a grin.

"Ricky the Stone dropped a dime on a client?"

"Had to. Akira held his retirement fund ransom."

"Clever," Blancanales acknowledged. "Always hit 'em where it hurts."

"Agreed. Also, his description matches that of a known ape that assassinated a French minister. No fingerprints on file, but his general build matches that of

Professor Johnson, and according to MI-5, Harrison was trained to be a chameleon, a master of disguise. This is our boy, all right."

Swinging around a flatbed truck full of pressurized gas containers, Lyons couldn't help but notice the irony. A chameleon was after the Chameleon. Not good.

"Okay, Harrison steals the Chameleon, and Cascade sends a hitter to take it from him," Lyons said slowly, flexing his hands on the steering wheel. "But how did they know?"

"Harrison must have agreed to sell them the device, and let something about the location slip," Blancanales said, hazarding a guess.

"Then Woods got greedy and decided on a double-cross," Schwarz added. "Only, Harrison was already long gone to Russia."

Passing a section of the highway under construction, Lyons waited until the Cadillac was past the heavy steel plating covering the exposed guts of the road. "Sounds like Harrison is doing a double-dip," the Able Team leader growled.

"Selling the Chameleon to two people at once?" Blancanales said, rolling the idea around for a moment. "Yeah, makes sense. He's delivering the Chameleon to somebody in the Kuril Islands, and to Peter Woods."

"Well, he's not going to fly halfway around the world to meet them in person," Schwarz said, leaning forward to rest both forearms on the top of the front seat. "Must be planning on faxing them the blueprints and schematics…" The man stopped and shook his head. "No, no way. He wouldn't risk sending anything that sensitive openly. The NSA might stop it in midtransmission. Harrison must plan on using an encoded e-mail file, something like that."

"Then Cascade transfers half the funds to his numbered Swiss bank account," Blancanales said, frowning. "And Harrison e-mails them the key to open the file, and they send the other half of the money. Nice and safe, and everybody wins."

"Until the bombs start falling," Lyons stated, glancing at the clear blue sky. "Okay, new plan. Screw the ambush. We need to find the other end of that incoming telephone call. We're going to accept the transmission of the coded file from Harrison."

"That could be anywhere," Schwarz said, sitting back. "But we only have one place to start looking."

"The automobile plant," Lyons agreed, accelerating the Cadillac. "We're going to need to visit a hardware store before going into downtown Gary."

"Way ahead of you there, Carl. I'm already checking for the location of one near an exit," Blancanales said, tapping buttons on his cell phone. The tiny plasma screen began scrolling with pictures of street maps. "Okay, take the next exit and make a left."

"What kind of resources does Cascade have?" Schwarz asked, pulling out a 9 mm Beretta and checking the sound suppressor. "Any contacts in Russia or along the Pacific Rim?"

Maneuvering around a pothole, Lyons slipped into the right lane. "They're strictly Chicago based. Brognola listed them as having about two hundred guys. Rumor has it they run a local street gang called the

Bloodhawks to shake down the local merchants, jack cars and deal drugs."

"Size?"

"Unknown."

"Swell," he muttered. "Anybody undercover we should stay alert for and try not to shoot, DEA, FBI?"

"No," Blancanales stated coldly, tucking away his cell phone. "Or rather, nobody who's still alive."

A minute of silence filled the luxury car as the men absorbed that dire information.

"Nice folks," Schwarz said, holstering the piece. "Why haven't we paid them a visit before this?"

"Couldn't. Nobody knew where their headquarters was hidden until today," Lyons said, watching his rearview mirror.

A station wagon and a delivery van were coming hard and fast up 55, the two staying dangerously close. As the vehicles passed the Cadillac, he could see the station wagon was filled with grim-faced teenagers, openly holding machine pistols. Their clothing all bore the names of major corporations, their hair was a rainbow of different colors, some had earrings and others had silver studs in their lips or nostrils. The grim young faces glistened with jewelry. But the weapons in their hands were held correctly and shone with fresh oil.

The windows of the van were tinted a silvery sheen and impossible to see through.

"Heads up," Lyons warned, pulling his Atchisson autoshotgun onto the front seat. "Looks like reinforcements have arrived."

As the vehicles got closer to the black sedan, it

slowed to match the pace. Then a window was rolled down and the driver waved them back. Slowly, the station wagon and van moved into flanking positions behind the sedan and spread out to give combat room.

"Crew wagons," Schwarz stated, starting to remove the sticky tape from around an HE grenade. There was a canvas satchel on the floor mats filled with high explosives. "Think those are the Bloodhawks?"

"From their apparent age, I'd say yes," Blancanales said, hunching his shoulders to adjust the holster under his arm. "Gadgets, call Barbara and see if the state police have any info on rival gangs in the Gary area."

"Looking for somebody who doesn't like the Bloodhawks?" he asked with a half smile. "The enemy of my enemy is my friend, and all that?"

"Along with a hell of a diversion," Lyons answered tersely. "Get hard, people. The shit is about to hit the fan."

"And which one are we again?" Schwarz asked, inserting the earplug for his compact radio.

"Ask me later," Blancanales grunted, thumbing a 40 mm shell into the M-203 grenade launcher.

The White Pearl

"HE SAID that he was a meteorologist?"

"Yes."

"Was he carrying any electronic equipment?"

"No, sir. Just a suitcase." The first mate of the *White Pearl* paused, and then hurriedly added, "And a thermos of hot coffee from the galley. We sell them to the staff of the weather stations along the Kuril Islands."

From behind the thick scarf masking his face, David McCarter grunted in acknowledgment at that. Swinging out to sea, the single hovercraft had made good time going around the mountains, in spite of its double load of crew. Kurtzman had arranged for a fuel drop at an isolated pier of a fishing village. There had been nobody in sight, just drums of high-octane aviation fuel, spare ammunition, some new civilian clothing and several thousand dollars in worn notes of various denominations.

Catching the *White Pearl* at sea had been easy with Carmen Delahunt guiding them via a real-time picture relayed from an orbital spy satellite. At the sight of the heavily armed men wearing the uniforms of Russian special forces and riding in a hovercraft, the crew of the passenger liner quickly dropped the aft ramp.

The *White Pearl* was designed to carry cars and trucks like a common ferry. Phoenix Force easily sailed onto the vessel and immediately spread out to search for Harrison while McCarter went to talk to the first officer. The young sailor was visibly shaken from the recent deaths; after all, his vessel was basically an oceangoing bus. The remaining officers were armed with pistols to handle smugglers, or the occasional bad drunk, but there had never been trouble like this before on the *Pearl*. Civilians, military and criminals both Japanese and Russian wanted and needed the ship in constant operation. Violence against the crew had always been absolutely out of the question.

Until today.

Walking around a corner, Hawkins came into view holding his AK-105 assault rifle. He also had a scarf wrapped around the lower half of his face as if it were bitterly cold, even though the temperature was a balmy sixty-five degrees.

In truth, the scarf was there to hide the stumbling efforts of the team members trying to speak Russian. Their radios were set for wide-open, two-way communications, and Tokaido was translating what people said to Phoenix Force, then quickly telling the Stony Man commandos how to respond. The scarves also helped hide their throat mikes, and the thick wool hats completely covered their earplugs. It was a cumbersome matter, but interrogating civilians hadn't originally been part of the mission plan. Once before this three-way kind of conversation had been used in a mission in Norway. But it had failed miserably then. Hopefully, they would have better luck with it this time.

"Well?" McCarter softly subvocalized into his throat mike.

Delahunt whispered into his ear.

"Davai otshyot!" he barked out loud in Russian.

Hawkins slowly saluted. "Sir, the passenger was dropped off at Simushir Island," he said, mumbling slightly. "The purser says his suitcase was checked for contraband..." Hawkins paused to jerk his head out to sea as if something had caught his attention. In truth, he was buying time for Tokaido to tell him the next sentence to speak aloud. It was a dangerous game the team was playing, and if the crew got wise, they would instantly stop talking. There was no danger of violence against the five Stony Man commandos—they were far too well armed—but the flow of vital information would stop abruptly, and there was no race on

Earth who could refuse to talk better than a suspicious Russian.

"And?" McCarter demanded impatiently.

The first mate cast a furtive glance at the man, but said nothing.

"The pursuer says his suitcase was checked for contraband," Hawkins repeated, "but we found this hidden in the man's pockets." Putting a hand into his pocket, Hawkins pulled out a wad of bills.

Accepting the cash, McCarter inspected it, then shook it wordlessly at the first mate. The sailor curled a lip in disgust.

"Criminal swine," the first mate growled. "So it's smugglers again, eh? I shall have him placed in handcuffs and delivered to the authorities the moment we return to the peninsula!"

Standing behind McCarter, Encizo worked the arming bolt on his AK-105, and the eyes of the first mate went wide.

"Or do you wish to take him with you...for questioning?" he said slowly.

Listening to the translation in his ear, McCarter waved the trifling matter aside, and the first mate visibly relaxed at not being ordered to turn one of his own men over to the military for a summary execution.

"David," James whispered over the radio, "we also found the silent KGB gun stored with the dead people in the hold. And one of them was the missing flight attendant, Gwen Tyson."

Giving another nonverbal grunt, McCarter walked to the gunwale and looked at the expanse of ocean behind the *White Pearl*. The ice-blue water stretched to the horizon in every direction, with only a scattered few rocky islands rising from its shimmering surface. There were six of the volcanic mounds in sight, and two of them were live with steam and dark smoke rising from the ragged peaks.

Simushir Island was a medium-sized landmass, almost fifty miles long, and it had three volcanoes, two live and one dead. The place had been a secret Soviet submarine base in the cold war, but that was long abandoned. Now the main volcano, Urataman, was being used a dump for spent rods from nuclear reactors by Russia, and Minatom, the Russian Ministry for Nuclear Energy, was arranging to accept toxic rods from other countries, as well. Anything to make a profit for the cash-poor nation. The Russian economy was recovering fast, but it was a long way from being stable yet, and every ruble counted. Even if it meant permanently polluting an island with hard radiation.

No, McCarter realized, Harrison wouldn't have arranged for a rendezvous there. It was merely another relay point. He either had a boat waiting for him, or his customers picked him up personally. The radar on the hovercraft had shown no sign of a plane in the sky, but a seaplane could have hopped the waves and stayed low enough to keep off the screen. Or was it a submarine? If Cascade was the first customer, then who was the second? Iran? North Korea? Unity? The list was endless.

In a burst of anger, McCarter slammed a fist onto the polished mahogany railing. They were so bloody close! But catching Harrison was like trying to grab a fistful of quicksilver. Every move that brought them closer, only made him squirt free in some and unexpected direction. Goddamn, the fellow was good! Fucking traitor. A member of the SAS gone bad. McCarter couldn't wait to get his hands on him.

Whispering under his scarf, McCarter spun about.

"Stop your vessel and drop anchor," he barked at the startled first mate. "Right now!"

"Yes! Of course, sir, at once." The sailor rushed away to scamper up the stairs for the bridge.

"Okay, this whole thing might be a diversion," McCarter spoke softly into his throat mike. "So until we know for certain Harrison didn't pass off the…device to somebody on this vessel, we're going to tear the ship apart looking for…it."

"It's the size of a shoe box," Manning said over the radio, his voice faintly distorted by a crackle of static. "The device could be anywhere on this ship."

"Then stop wasting time talking to me," McCarter growled, touching his throat. "And get on it!"

Something very hard was thrust into the small of McCarter's back. Small and round and hard. From experience the Stony Man commando could tell it was a gun barrel.

"I do not know who you are, Yankee," a voice from behind said in heavily accented English. "But if you are special forces, then I am a horse's ass!"

Snorting in disdain, McCarter started to turn and the gun barrel was shoved harder against his spine. Just below the cover of his NATO body armor. Exactly where he was vulnerable.

"Do not try my patience," the voice commanded. "Drop your weapon now, or die."

CHAPTER SIXTEEN

Gary, Illinois

"I don't think it's going to work," Carl Lyons said as the sign for Gary came into view from around a curve on the highway.

"Agreed," Schwarz said, holding his M-16/M-203 with one hand and rolling down the rear window with the other. The polluted air streamed into the Cadillac, carrying with it the stink of garbage, industry and despair.

Reaching down, Lyons clicked off the safety of his shotgun. "Get ready. We'll go for their tires and then—"

"No, wait!" Blancanales cried, holding out a restraining arm. "The Comanches have arrived!"

As the black sedan began to slow and angled in for the off-ramp, a bright yellow convertible raced into view, driving up the ramp, its headlights flashing and horn blazing. The driver of the sedan frantically veered away from the incoming car and slammed against one of his own escort vehicles.

The station wagon looped out of the way as the van

skittered across the highway and crashed into the concrete retainer in the middle. Its side windows shattered in a flurry of green glass squares, and the van driver hit the brakes, fighting the vehicle to a shuddering stop.

But by now a pale blue convertible emerged from the off-ramp, the collection of teenagers inside opening fire on the sedan with an assortment of weapons. The black car was peppered with lead and steel, and its headlights blew out, but the windows stayed intact, showing that they were bulletproof.

All around Able Team, the local drivers knew danger when it arrived and were peeling away for the next exit, led by the calm taxicabs.

Fishtailing about, the yellow Oldsmobile cycled up its top to expose a hunched-over driver in a black leather jacket and a shirtless teenager carrying an old M-1 A U.S. Army flamethrower. Both of the teens wore beaded headbands, and their bodies were covered with countless tattoos in a mawkish version of shaman magic symbols. Lyons knew enough about the Plains Indian tribes to see the kids were mixing Apache with Blackfoot, Delaware with Choctaw, and some stuff that simply looked like made-up nonsense.

Hefting the M-16/M-203, Blancanales grunted in disdain. "Comanches, my ass," he growled. "If there is a single drop of Indian blood in the veins of any of these punks, then I'm a ballerina."

"At least you got the legs for it," Schwarz quipped, removing the 40 mm antipersonnel shell of steel slivers from the grenade launcher of his own M-203. The sedan had already proved it was bulletproof, so a change of tactics was in order. Reaching blindly into a canvas bag of ordnance, he pulled out a 40 mm HE shell and thumbed it into the open breech of the grenade launcher.

"Wait for it," Lyons warned, both hands tight on the steering wheel as a flurry of spent brass rained across the Cadillac from the dueling cars ahead of them. He was trying to maintain a safe distance, but shrapnel and lead were flying everywhere.

"And don't miss, brother," Blancanales added grimly.

"Just tell me when," Schwarz said, sighting his weapon out the window of the Cadillac, concentrating on aiming the assault rifle. He would only get one shot at this.

Accelerating, the battered van moved to cover the sedan. Shouting a war whoop, the standing teen in the yellow Olds raised his ungainly weapon and sent a burning stream of jellied gasoline straight toward the station wagon. But the wind drove it back, and the fire never reached its goal.

However, the pyrotechnic display had the effect of clearing all the other vehicles off the road. Brakes smoking and squealing, cars were squealing to frantic stops along the berm. One suicidal soul started driving backward down the highway, but kept slamming into the concrete divider wall.

Waving machine pistols, the teenagers in the station wagon started to shoot back when the blue convertible came streaking along 55, darting between the two, and cut loose with a raw-throated salvo of shotguns. Teens inside the station wagon were thrown back minus faces, their automatic weapons still chattering as dead hands convulsed on the triggers. The artificial wood siding was blown off the station wagon as hot lead punched out from inside the vehicle and the driver fought to maintain control of his rolling slaughterhouse.

Now the rest of the windows crashed out of the van, and a half-dozen M-16 assault rifles and a Thompson machine gun cut loose at the blue convertible, the thunderous rattle of the .45 Thompson audible over the chatter of the M-16 rifles. Two of the passengers took hits, one flopping sideways and losing his gun over the side. An Ingram machine pistol hit the rushing highway and exploded into pieces, clip, bullets, springs and assorted parts tumbling behind the speeding vehicles.

Dodging a pool of jellied fire on the asphalt from the badly aimed flamethrower, Lyons scowled at the sight of a civilian in a Honda Civic still on the roadway. The idiot behind the wheel of the economy compact seemed fascinated by the battle as if it were on television.

"Rosario!" he shouted over the rushing wind.

"On it," Blancanales replied, placing aside the assault rifle. Drawing his Colt .380 pistol, he leaned out the side window, steadied the sound-suppressed weapon with both hands and gently squeezed the trigger.

In a strident crash the entire rear window of the Honda shattered, and then the side mirror was blown completely off the car body. Jolted back to reality, the civilian started screaming curses as he went straight through a Police Only break in the concrete divider. With tires squealing, he emerged with the northbound traffic and started building speed.

Lyons nodded at the sight. Good enough. Now they had some proper combat room for the two street gangs to battle it out with each other. But when would the driver of the sedan make his move?

The four battling cars swerved all over the road in a total disregard of safety or sanity. Now the kid with the flamethrower fought to sweep the fiery rod across the van. A professional soldier would have known better than to even try. He would have killed the stream, aimed at the van and then triggered the spray once more. But the street punk wasted huge amounts of fuel as he fought to control the rushing inertia and recoil of the liquid-fueled weapon. Then he recoiled as the pressurized tank on his back was ruptured from a bullet. There was a brief rush of fire, and then the tank and flamethrower both were extinguished as the fuel supply was exhausted.

"Talk about timing," Schwarz snorted. Then he frowned and touched the receiver in his ear. "Hold it, our guy is finally making a call to his boss."

"Took him long enough," Blancanales snarled, as a sign flashed by showing that they were now leaving the city limits of Gary.

"Now it's our turn," Lyons growled, and twisted the wheel hard to charge straight for the black sedan.

As the heavy vehicle came close, Blancanales and Schwarz each unleashed their weapons in an orchestrated sweep. The tires blew, the windows shattered and the rear trunk filled up. Dropping his cell phone, the driver fought to control the sedan as Blancanales sent a thermite shell into the trunk, and Schwarz pumped a high-explosive round into the front seat.

The U.S. Army shells hit and detonated, the combined blast almost tearing the sedan apart. Then the gas tank ignited, flipping the armored vehicle to tumble along the highway, throwing off burning wreckage in every direction.

Down the road, the three battling vehicles seemed to not even notice the destruction of the sedan as they continued their high-velocity combat, blood and brass falling to the asphalt.

Softly in the distance came the howl of police cars.

"Good," Lyons said, slowing the Cadillac. "Okay, back we go. They're going to be busy here for quite a while."

"Yeah. Now Woods will be forced to send people out to check what's going on with the Bloodhawks, weakening his defenses at their headquarters."

"Primed for an invasion."

"But not for long."

"There's an exit two miles ahead," Schwarz said, checking his handheld computer. "We can cut west and reach the factory by coming in from the other side."

"First we find a hardware store," Blancanales corrected.

Schwarz frowned at that, then slowly smiled. Oh yeah, of course. How could he have forgotten?

The White Pearl

KEEPING HIS HANDS in plain sight, McCarter stayed very still on the deck of the ship as Carmen Delahunt whispered instructions over the radio in his ear. "Help is coming," she said calmly. "But stall for as long as you can!"

"Now listen to me," McCarter started slowly in Russian.

"Shut up!" the man behind him ordered, shoving the gun harder into his back. "Your friend with the little box is long gone, Mafia pig. This must be about drugs for you to dare pose as the military. Tell me, who is your contact for the cocaine and things will go easier for you."

"Now!" Delahunt said loudly.

Throwing himself to the side, McCarter did a shoulder roll and came up with his pistol out just in time to see a sailor fall limply to the deck with a revolver in his grip. As the cocked weapon hit, it discharged and blew a hole in the gunwale the size of a fist.

"Is he alive?" Hawkins asked, his AK-105 held backward in his hands, the stock forward.

McCarter frowned as excited members of the *White Pearl* crew started arriving from every direction at the sound the gunshot.

"Keep them back," McCarter subvocalized into his throat mike to the rest of Phoenix Force. "And Cal, get the hover ready to go. We may need to leave fast."

"On it, David," James replied over the radio, and the scarf-wrapped man sprinted away from the assembling crowd to head toward the hovercraft on the rear deck.

Manning and Encizo pushed the more curious of the passengers away from the man sprawled on the deck, while Tokaido reported their translated mutterings. But it wasn't necessary; McCarter knew the faces of frightened people when he saw them. For most, this was supposed to have been a pleasure cruise, breathing in the fresh salt air, watching the volcanoes and maybe, if they were lucky, spotting a pod of humpback whales in the water. Instead, they got half a dozen murders and an invasion of armed military forces.

"I'd ask for a bleeding refund," he muttered, kicking the smoking gun out of the twitching fingers. It clattered across the deck and over the side into the sea.

"I don't think he's dead," Hawkins stated, swinging

the AK-105 into its proper position. There was a small tuft of hair sticking to the wooden stock of the weapon.

Somebody in the crowd shouted a demand in Japanese, and Manning fired back a staccato burst of the same language and shut them down fast.

"Go back to your rooms!" Encizo ordered loudly. "This is military business! Go back now!"

As the passengers and crew started to move reluctantly away, McCarter knelt and turned over the unconscious man. It was the purser. Exploring the back of the man's head with gentle fingertips, McCarter saw it was only a scalp wound and nothing serious. Hawkins had moved fast, but not with lethal force, thank God. Searching the purser, McCarter found nothing of importance until discovering something flat taped to the small of his back. Cutting the man's shirt open, McCarter found a leather booklet securely held in place by crisscrossing strips of duct tape. The Stony Man commando ripped the item free and peeled off the tape to thumb open the booklet.

He already had a bad feeling what it might be, and his suspicions proved to be correct. The contents were in Russian, but the photo and government seal clearly showed the man's true occupation.

"The goddamn FSB," McCarter growled, slowly standing. "He's a member of the Russia FBI. Probably a plant to keep track of all the drug smuggling."

"And he came out of cover because of Harrison?" Hawkins snorted.

"No," Encizo said, over the radio. "Because we're not Russian special forces, and he knew it."

The FSB agent started to groan just then, so easing out his tranquilizer gun, Manning shot the man once in the side. The Moscow operative jerked slightly from the impact, then fell back.

"He's gone for hours," Manning stated, holstering the weapon. "What now, David?"

"Patch that wound," McCarter directed gruffly.

With James at the hovercraft, Encizo took over the job as medic and started applying a simple pressure bandage to the laceration.

"Our FSB friend here mentioned somebody leaving with the 'little box,'" McCarter stated, slinging his assault rifle over a shoulder. "He thought it had to be drugs because it was so small, but it must have been the Chameleon."

"That didn't have to be Harrison," Hawkins observed. "But either way, getting the unit back is our top priority."

"Then we get the dirty little traitor," McCarter said in a low voice of granite. His hands tightened on the strap of the AK-105 assault rifle, the knuckles turning white.

"Hey, David," Manning whispered, stepping closer.

McCarter angrily snapped his head at the man, then relaxed slightly. "No problem," he replied in a more normal voice. "Retrieving the unit comes first. It's all under control."

On the flying bridge, the first mate was using binoculars to try to get a better sight of what was happening on his ship, so Hawkins moved to block his view. "Okay," he said softly. "So we follow the Chameleon."

"Well, he's not on Simushir Island," Encizo commented, packing away his medical gear. The volcanic island was only a few hundred yards to the south of the anchored ship, and they could see completely across its wide flat landscape. Aside from the smoking volcano dominating the middle of the landmass, the emerald-green island was almost devoid of features.

"Hell, son, you couldn't hide a jackrabbit in the putting green," Hawkins drawled, "unless it went inside the volcano." The smoking peak choose the moment to rumble like distant thunder.

"Not likely," McCarter agreed, looking out to sea. "That leaves three islands in the immediate area."

"No, two," Manning countered. The middle island was only jagged black basalt rising straight up from the crystal-clear water. There wasn't enough flatland there to take a piss on, he knew, much less do anything else.

"We could split up and hit them both," Hawkins suggested. "Do a fast recon...aw, hell, we only have one hovercraft. Takes hours to row across the distance in a lifeboat."

"Maybe he was meeting with a sub or a seaplane?" Encizo suggested, watching a handful of crew members loitering close to the hovercraft. "Cal, company."

James jerked about and snapped off something in Russian. The sailors raggedly saluted and all but ran to the companionway and disappeared from sight.

"What the hell did you say?" Encizo asked, amused.

Across the ship, James shrugged. "Beats me. Ask Akira. But it sure lit a fire in their shorts, eh?"

"Got that right."

"Can the chatter," McCarter demanded, straightening the scarf around his mouth. "How's the sky?"

"Radar is clear," James stated from the hovercraft, bending over the small control board. "But then with the Chameleon, Harrison could have met with an aircraft carrier and we'd never know it unless we saw the thing."

"Enough. Let's move out," McCarter said, heading aft. "We've extended our welcome here far too long as it is."

Hawkins jerked a thumb at the unconscious man on the deck. "What about the feeb?" he asked, using the American slang for an FBI agent.

"Bring him along," McCarter said over the radio link without turning. "We can't leave him behind to talk to the crew. Once the *White Pearl* is back under way again, we'll drop him off on Simushir Island. When he comes to, he can walk to the weather station and call for help."

"And if there are any more FSB agents about," Encizo observed, "he'll act as a hostage and slow them down."

"The FSB, a kinder, gentler KGB," Hawkins said, slinging his weapon and lifting the man in a fireman's carry, the body draped across his shoulders.

"Weather station," Manning muttered, looking at the volcano. "Hey, David, think our boy may be there? Hiding in plain sight again?"

McCarter stopped and looked hard at the rumbling peak. The weather station was only a tiny white dot on the dark side of the steeply sloping mountain. There was a road, but it was invisible at this range, the trail little more than a cut in the hard basalt and raw stone. Not a single tree grew along the side of the volcano; it was as bare as the lunar landscape.

"Maybe," McCarter said thoughtfully, rubbing his nose with a fist.

"Nope, he's on Matua Island," James said over the radio. "Or, at least, the Chameleon is. Heads up, boys. I've been watching the radar screen for MiG fighters, and for a brief couple of seconds that northern island disappeared from the screen."

The entire island? "Glitch?" Hawkins demanded, striding faster toward the hovercraft.

"Negative on that. Everything registers A-okay. We are fully operational and running smooth."

"Son of a bitch was testing the unit," McCarter said, then the truth hit him like a punch from the dark. "Bloody hell, no! The buyer was testing the unit!"

Lurching forward into a full run, McCarter switched frequencies on his radio. "Stone House, this is Firebird. We have a possible location on Harrison. Repeat, we have a possible location. It's Matua Island. Repeat, Matua. We are in pursuit. Tell Lyons the balloon has gone up! Firebird out!"

"What about our guy?" Hawkins asked, shrugging the man on his shoulders.

"Leave him," McCarter stated. "By the time he wakes, it'll all be over."

"One way or another," Manning agreed, heading for the hovercraft.

CHAPTER SEVENTEEN

Gary, Illinois

The dimly lit hallway was filthy, trash strewed about and a dead rat lying in a niche that was supposed to be holding a fire extinguisher. Graffiti covered the walls, and most of the ceiling panels were gone, exposing the metal framework designed to support the foam squares. The original ceiling beyond the framework was cracked plaster, veined with insulated wiring and an empty light socket.

With three armed men in front of him and four behind, Peter Woods strode along the dirty hallway, glancing impatiently at his watch. What the hell was going on? Why hadn't anybody reported in yet? Biggest deal of his life, going to turn the world upside down, and the punks were probably off getting laid or fighting with some rival gang. Damn fools.

Surrounded by the Magnificent Seven, Woods turned at an intersection and entered what once would have been the secretarial pool of the factory complex. A skylight admitted milky light, softening the splintery remains of the broken furniture and smashed typewriters. Pausing to light a slim panatela cigar, Woods drew in the dark smoke, then scowled at the shadows in the far corner.

"Who the fuck is that?" he demanded, pointing at a pile of rags partially hidden under a mailing table.

Tall and wide, Brian Ledbetter pulled a piece and rushed the table. Thumbing back the hammer, he kicked over the table and the rags came to life, raising a pair of skinny arms.

"Please, I ain't hurting nothing," the old man croaked, trying to get farther into the corner.

"Here now, that's okay. Stay calm, old-timer," Ledbetter said gently, lowering the muzzle of his gun. "There's barbed wire all around this place. How did you get inside?"

The old man shook a scrawny finger to the left. "There's an old coal chute—" he started to explain.

Raising a hand, Ledbetter cut him off. "Sure, I left it open. Just wanted to know, thanks." Firing from the hip, he pumped three rounds into the rags, and the old man toppled over without a sound.

"Tony, Gary, toss it outside," Ledbetter ordered, holstering the piece.

"No, leave it," Woods said around the cigar in his mouth.

The leader of the Magnificent Seven shrugged in response, and the group started along the next corridor. Halfway down, Woods stopped and slipped a magnetic card into a crack in the wall. There was a subdued click, the low hiss of hydraulics working, and a section of the opposite wall disengaged to swing aside and bright lights filled the ramshackle hallway.

Stepping into the light, the group spread out so that Peter Woods could lead the way now. Striding past a sandbag nest containing armed guards and .50-caliber machine gun, Woods gave the eye to a group of Cascade soldiers sitting at a table cleaning assault rifles, and then pushed his way through a revolving door. The glass in the door had been replaced with Plexiglas and rubbed with sandpaper to make it almost opaque. Any cops trying to bust the place wouldn't be able to see what they were heading into by going through the door, giving Cascade valuable time to erect its interior defenses.

Past the door, cool air blew briskly from the ceiling vents to carry away the stink of the abandoned factory outside. In here, the raised floor was spotlessly clean, the ceiling intact and the area well lit with fluorescent ceiling lights. A dozen people were at consoles operating controls, and hulking machines larger than refrigerators formed neat lines along the flooring. A steady hum pervaded the cool air, along with the faint aroma of ozone, from the operating Cray supercomputer.

"Are you ready?" Woods asked, looking proudly at the mainframe. It was an older model, slow and feeble compared to the massive Cray IV supercomputers used at his legitimate business offices in the downtown Loop of Chicago. But this machine was the heart of a very profitable Internet pornography business, stealing content from one Web site to sell it to another, and occasionally hacking into banks for a little debit-card fraud. The more money Cascade generated to finance its military operations, the fewer paper trails there were leading back to him. The old Cray more than served the needs of his covert organization, and had the added benefit of being unknown to exist. Even the Feds couldn't try to stop what they didn't know about.

Which was why the location of this base was such a closely guarded secret. Peter Woods owned all of the land in this section of Gary, and nobody would ever get permission from the city to start urban renewal. The sprawling jungle of the industrial slum was merely another layer of protective camouflage for Cascade.

"Are we ready? Absolutely, sir," the chief technician said, giving a crisp salute. "Once we get the plans for the jamming unit, we'll have it bombed across the Internet in five minutes."

"All general recipients?" Woods asked, clasping both hands behind his back.

"Mostly, yes sir," the chief technician said slowly. "We tried to get some of the more radical Arab groups to buy the plans—"

"Buy?" Woods snapped, yanking the cigar from his mouth. "Buy? You were supposed to convince them it was a gift from American sympathizers!"

The chief technician swallowed hard. "Yes, Mr. Woods, I know. But quite a few of the terrorist groups thought the offer sounded too good to be true, and wouldn't have anything to do with it. So I started offering the jamming unit for sale, and the numbers went back to where they were supposed to be."

Puffing on his cigar for a few minutes, Woods said nothing.

"We need maximum distribution to elicit total chaos in the Middle East," the man nervously added.

In exaggerated slowness, Woods removed the cigar. "Admirable," he said at last. "Smart move. Well done."

"Th-thank you, sir."

"Once we get it out, what kind of a response time can we expect from the NSA?" Woods demanded, blowing a gray ring at an air vent. He knew the smoke was bad for the Cray, but it was his machine, and he did what he liked with his property.

"Ten minutes, sir. Two if they know it's coming."

Woods tilted his head, so that the rising smoke obscured his features. "Do they know it's coming, son?" he asked in a deceptively gentle voice.

The chief technician went pale. "Sir, no sir!"

"Good," Woods said, putting the cigar back. Walking among the humming servers, Woods looked at the video monitors showing different locations around the factory. Most of the screens were devoid of life, alleyways, empty rooftops and such. One showed a hooker working the street corner, and another displayed a dealer conducting business at a traffic light. Cars would stop, he'd approach, make the sale and the car would drive on again. Total elapse time, twenty seconds. But it wasn't drugs. Woods had nothing to do with that shit. He sold guns. To old men, children, gangbangers, housewives, cheerleaders, hell, he gave guns away from free to homeless families to protect them from the predators of the night! What would the hijackers on 9/11 have done if the all of the passengers on board those planes had been armed? Nothing. That's what would have happened, instead of the biggest disaster in the history of the nation. Guns made America, and guns made America strong. The disarming of this once great nation was a Communist plot to weaken democracy, and he would never let it happen. Never! No matter what the cost was in dollars, or human life.

"The right to be armed is the right to be free," Woods muttered, then turned to face the waiting technicians. "It's a glorious day, gentlemen! War is what this country needs to get back on its feet. We're too fat, too rich, too lazy! Combat makes us leaner, smarter, faster!"

"Butter will make us fat, guns make us strong, eh, sir?" The chief technician chuckled in agreement.

With a guttural snarl, Woods lunged forward and punched the chief technician in the stomach. The other people in the computer room could only gasp as the chief technician dropped over and fell to his knees, gagging and dry heaving for breath.

"How dare you quote Hermann Göring to me!" Peter Woods snarled, raising his fist as if to strike again. "My grandfather died fighting Hitler!"

"But, sir, I…" the chief technician wheezed.

Turning red, Woods advanced to tower over the cringing man. "Shut up!" he roared. "If you ever cross the line like that again, I'll turn you over to our turkey doctor!"

Raw fear contorting his features, the chief technician

stammered out an apology, but Woods turned his back on the man.

"You there!" Woods shouted, pointing at another technician.

"Sir?" the middle-aged man asked, going pale behind his glasses.

"Can you handle the Cray, yes or no?"

The hacker cast a furtive look at the chief technician on the floor. "Yes, sir," he said with growing confidence. "Easy as pie."

"Good. You're in charge."

"Thank you, sir!"

"Don't fail me," Woods growled menacingly, as a red light flashed above the revolving door.

A few seconds later, the frosted panels swung aside and Brian Ledbetter walked into the room. "I heard shouting," he said, an automatic held steady in his fist.

"Nothing important," Woods replied, walking past the former chief technician. "Where's Mannix?"

"Checking on the walkways between the buildings, making sure they're all guarded. Keep the boys on their toes."

"Good. How soon will we be ready?"

"We're ready now," Ledbetter said, sliding the weapon away. "Harrison and his men will have a hard time getting in here, sir."

Woods scowled. "Men? What are you talking about. The British bastard always works alone."

"Well, the way I see it," Ledbetter said, spreading his hands, "our boy is no fool. Somewhere along the way

Harrison could have gotten some muscle to back him up. Say, ten, maybe fifteen guys tops."

"That many? And our alarms are useless against the unit he carries."

"No problem. I have Yang walking the perimeter with his boys," Ledbetter said.

"Call them back."

"Sir?"

"We should let Harrison and his associates inside the factory," Woods said calmly, removing the cigar to inspect the glowing red end. "Then we flood the building with poison gas, and after they stop twitching, we get the jamming unit without firing a shot."

"Now where's the fun in that?" Ledbetter asked, twisting his lips into a hard grin.

"We're not here for a good time," Woods growled, staring at the clock on the wall. "We're here to save a nation from itself. We're patriots! Remember that."

Firebase One

IN SPITE of the armed guards, Harrison approved of his new environment. The air was crisp and clean in the elevator, completely lacking any trace of the sulfur from outside spewed forth by all of the neighboring volcanoes.

Arriving at the western end of the island of Matua, Harrison hadn't been startled when armed men rose from the sandy beach wearing camouflage fatigues. After he exchanged passwords with them, the guards took Harrison under escort, then pushed his borrowed dinghy back into the water. Once it was far enough away from shore, the Japanese terrorists shot numerous holes in the thin hull, sending the vessel to the bottom of the bay. That seemed to carry an ominous tone to Harrison, until he realized it was simply done to mask his location from any possible observers. Very wise.

A small cave in the side of a low hill led to a set of steel doors painted the same color as the surrounding rock. Past the door, an elderly man smoking a cigarette and wearing a white lab coat accepted the Chameleon from Harrison, along with a CD containing the engineering blueprints, electrical schematics for the device. This was as arranged in his earlier communications with Yangida Fukoka, the man in charge of this cell of Nucleus, the infamous Japanese terrorist group.

As the nameless scientist rushed away with the device and disk, Harrison tried to hide a frown of disapproval. Not for the terrorists, but for himself. Now that he had seen their hidden fortress, Harrison wished he had asked for more money. This base had to have cost millions to build in secret! And right under the noses of the damn Russians, too.

"This way, noble sir," the larger guard said in halting English. "Director Fukoka wishes to see you personally."

"*Hai! Domo,*" Harrison replied in flawless Japanese, and gestured the guards onward.

The surprised men exchanged glances and then started down the clean white corridor and into the central elevator of a bank of five. As the doors closed, Harrison hid a smile. Five elevators for an organization of only a few hundred people? Bullshit. Most of the lifts were probably dummies. The central elevator and the

wings would be the easiest for hurrying people to remember, so those were probably the only ones that actually worked. The others would be death traps for any
invaders. Once again, his respect for Nucleus went up,
as did his apprehension. The group was known for keeping its word to weapon dealers. That was a vital prereq-
uisite in their line of work, or else soon they would find
it impossible to obtain any of the supplies and materials needed for their agenda. But the Chameleon was a
one-time offer. Would they still play cricket?

Casting a furtive glance at his escorts, Harrison nervously checked the trick cigarette lighter in his pocket,
his watch and collar. They had taken his gun on the
beach, but stopped at that. It was their first and only mistake so far. He was still well armed, and more than capable of fighting his way free of the underground
firebase.

As the elevator doors opened, a muted voice announced the base status was green and that all launch systems were go. Harrison filed away the information with
a placid expression. He had already deduced that the
Japanese terrorists wanted the Chameleon for missiles.
It was the most logical way to utilize the jamming field.

Their footsteps rang loudly on the terrazzo flooring,
but the noise drew no attention. Nobody else was in
sight, as if the passageways had been cleared for his
coming. The ventilators gave a soft hum as they pushed
clean air past filtration screens, and just for a moment
there came the muffled cry of a man in terrible pain. The
guards gave the incident no attention, so Harrison forced
himself to do the same. Sympathy for others was con-

sidered a weakness to many who followed the old bush-ido code of the warrior. Could the cry have been fake, a test of his resolve? There was no way of knowing, but the man decided to stay alert for further tricks, and sur-reptitiously moved his cigarette lighter from his shirt to a pants pocket where it could be reached faster.

Suddenly, the lights flickered. The guards instantly drew their side arms and backed away from Harrison, but he merely smiled at the actions. The scientist was merely testing the unit to make sure it was working properly. A logical precaution.

As the rippling effect faded away and the lights re-turned to full brightness, Harrison waved the guards on. They slowly holstered their weapons and started along the hallway once more, but now maintained a healthy distance from Harrison, as if he had personally generated the disrupting effect of the jamming field.

There were few doors along the way, all of them made of plain steel with very advanced electronic palm locks set into the wall alongside. Harrison allowed him-self to chuckle at that. Trust the Japanese to use only the latest technology. Were the terrorists trying to impress him with their level of technology? That was foolish. What did a terrorist really need aside from a fast car and a good throwing arm? Silly buggers were always mak-ing things more complex than they had to be.

However, as they progressed, Harrison noticed that the hallway was reinforced every few meters by thick metal beams. Could the earthquakes from the neighbor-ing volcanoes really be that bad? Or was this base more of a bomb shelter than a firebase? Exactly what sort of missiles was Fukoka planning on launching, and against whom? England, perhaps? The former SAS agent felt a rush of concern for his homeland, and fought to keep the expression from his face. Ice. He was ice. Remember that. The Japanese hated uncontrolled displays of emotions. They considered it a sign of weakness, and that could get him killed down here. A weak man couldn't be trusted to keep his mouth shut.

At the end of the long passageway, the smaller guard stepped aside and drew his weapon, while the larger man placed a bare hand on a touch plate set into the wall, then he put an eye to a retinal scanner and finally spoke something in Japanese to a voice lock. Harrison was impressed. Triple security, eh? This had to be the command center. So he was going to meet the boss, and wasn't being escorted to a small cell to be shot in the back of the head. Or at least, not yet he wasn't.

The door gave an answering tone, and heavy thuds sounded as massive locks disengaged. Ponderously, the door swung aside on thick hinges to reveal it was a truncated cone of different metals and materials. The guards gestured him in, and Harrison took the lead. As he stepped through the opening, he noticed several layers of lead and cadmium among the armor plating of the portal. These boys were prepared for atomic radiation. But were they launching nukes at somebody, or preparing for incoming bombs? Either way, it was chilling knowledge.

Standing still while the door cycled shut behind him, Harrison looked around the command center with unfeigned interest. Few outsiders had ever seen this room, and fewer still lived to tell the tale.

The next room was really an antechamber, with a thick Plexiglas wall restricting access. Behind the transparent barrier were rows of computer and monitoring stations staffed by grimly silent Japanese men and women. The far wall was a large plasma-screen display of the world showing the current weather patterns across all of the major continents and oceans. Cryptic symbols scrolled along the bottom of the screen, and as he watched the weather map faded away to be replaced by detailed maps of four large cities. The roads and buildings may have been recognizable to somebody from the locations, but to Harrison they were merely random patterns. At least, none of them were downtown London.

Standing in front of the display was a slim man with ebony hair and wearing an extraordinarily good suit. His hands were clasped behind his back, with a gold Rolex watch on the left wrist, and a blue tattoo on the back of the right hand, three interlocking circles.

As the man turned, he spoke to one of the people at a computer station. There came a subdued click, and the Plexiglas barrier rose into the ceiling with the soft sigh of working hydraulics.

"Good evening, Major Fukoka," Harrison said, giving the polite half bow of equal partners in a business deal who weren't close friends.

The heavily scarred terrorist frowned at the precise gesture of courtesy and reluctantly returned it.

"Good evening, Mr. Harrison," the major said in polished tones. "I trust your journey was uneventful."

"It was successful, which is much more important," Harrison said, pushing back a lock of hair moved onto his face from the constant warm breeze blowing from the air vents. Time to go on the offensive and show his strength.

"Although, I must admit that I am curious as to how you managed to transport nuclear warheads here for your missiles," Harrison added, tilting his head. "This close to the big three, I wouldn't have thought such a thing impossible." The big three in that part of the world meant Japan, China and Russia. Korea was a poor nation without much in its favor but raw hatred and stolen technology.

Frowning slightly, Fukoka studied the other man for a moment before answering.

"You are correct, it is impossible," the major replied, looking over a shoulder at the computerized wall map. "The North Americans with their Keyhole and Watchdog satellites closely monitor all suspicious radiation. So we have gone a different route."

Politely, Harrison waited for the director to continue, but Fukoka merely watched him back. The Briton sensed a test of some sort again. Damn Japanese were always playing brinkmanship. Hmm, if the missiles weren't armed with nukes, what else was there? Germ warfare was too easily controlled. Conventional explosives would do pitiful damage without pinpoint accuracy, which would be impossible without radar guidance. And the destructive power of a dirty bomb was minimal.

"So you have them," Harrison said, crossing his arms. "A gas-vapor bomb."

"The proper designation is FAE, a fuel-air explosive," Fukoka corrected. "But, yes, you have guessed correctly. We have them in abundance. The U.S. Marines used the devices extensively in Vietnam to clear away the jungle and make instant landing bases for their gunship helicopters. Hundreds were recovered during the Tet Offensive, and we acquired most of them. Since then, our people have been steadily developing them to new levels of power and efficiency."

"Efficiency is the key."

"That is correct."

As no further information on the subject was coming, Harrison changed topics. "So those are your targets," he said carefully. "Interesting choices."

"Obvious ones," Fukoka said, arching an eyebrow. "Can you identify the cities?"

Another test? Maybe. Or more likely a test of his stupidity. "No," he said honestly. "I cannot."

"Good, then you live," the major said casually.

Walking across the bunker, Fukoka went to a wall safe, opened the steel door and extracted a small leather case.

"Dr. Tetsuto?" the major said loudly, closing the safe and twirling the dial.

There was a crackle of static from the ceiling. "Yes, Major Fukoka?"

"Is the merchandise legitimate?"

"Merchandise? Oh, the unit. Yes, yes, the unit is just as promised. My staff is duplicating it right now. We should be done in an hour."

"One hour?"

"It is all off-the-shelf technology," Dr. Tetsuto explained, exhaling noisily. "Only the configuration is unique. Brilliant, actually." There was a pause as there came the sound of crinkling plastic wrap, followed by the striking of a match.

"Do you wish to observe?" Tetsuto said, puffing.

"Yes, but time does not permit," Fukoka replied, looking at Harrison standing across the room. "Please continue with your work, Doctor."

"Of course." There was a crackle as the speaker in the ceiling was turned off.

Crossing the control room, the major passed the case to Harrison, who accepted it with a quarter bow of respect between friends. This gesture, Fukoka insultingly didn't return.

"You may leave now," Fukoka said. "Since you have kept your part of the deal, I shall keep mine."

"*Domo.* Perhaps we can do business again some time." Harrison smiled, savoring the deliciously heavy feel of the bag. He wanted desperately to look inside, but that would have been a deadly insult to the Japanese. They may be terrorists, but they still carried the onus of their rigid society.

"That possibility is why you are still alive," Fukoka replied curtly. "My distaste for spies is intense." He turned away. "Guards!"

Both of the armed men gave crisp salutes. "Sir!"

"Escort our guest to the western tunnel. See him safely off the island, and then monitor his journey to make sure he does not try to come back."

As the guards started the process of opening the blast-proof door, Harrison felt his face burn red with the accusation, but controlled his temper. Tests, the damn

Japanese were always testing your resolve, your intelligence, your control.... Bah, the Americans were much easier to deal with. They paid in cash and asked only a speedy delivery. Fukoka would go insane when he learned of the sale to Cascade. How very pleasant. Harrison hid a smile from his face.

"It was a pleasure doing business with you, Major," Harrison said, walking out of the room without looking back.

Major Fukoka raised an eyebrow at the gesture, and started to reach for the .40 Magnum Fabrique National inside his suit, but stayed his hand. Now wasn't the time or the place. Later he would deal with the offensive little Briton at a more private location.

As the armored door boomed shut and locked, the major walked back to the wall display and waited. Now the cryptic symbols scrolling along the bottom melted into proper Japanese showing the target zones: Beijing, Moscow, London, Washington, D.C.

It was a pity that all four of the missiles would have to be launched at the same time to disguise their firing as a volcanic eruption on Matua. Moscow would be hit first and then the hated Chinese. Unfortunately, because of the sheer distance to be traveled, the British capital would be warned by then, and if wise heads prevailed they might just gain that extra time to evacuate some of their parliament before the Chameleon-masked ICBM detonated above the city.

Yet, if only one missile got through to its target, that would justify the enormous expense of the entire project. The estimated death toll for Moscow alone was a million, for Beijing, two times that number. London twice that, and Washington the same.

Fukoka smiled at the thought. And that would only herald the beginning of the destruction. Afterward, the real firestorm would commence. With their capitals destroyed, the superpowers would turn on one another, and in the aftermath Japan alone would remain as undamaged and mighty. The plan couldn't fail.

He only hoped that the spy was on his way to one of the targets. Glancing at the clock on the wall, the terrorist leader frowned darkly. Ah, there wasn't enough time for him to even reach Tokyo, much less Beijing or Moscow. Pity. There wasn't much time remaining before the missiles launched and the rulers of the old world would perish in the fiery weapons of their own foolish creation!

Nothing could wrong now, Fukoka thought, chuckling inside. Only forty-five minutes remained until the end of the world.

CHAPTER EIGHTEEN

Illinois

As Able Team drove past a rusting sign that marked the boundary for Gary, Blancanales shook his head in embarrassment.

"Christ," he muttered. "And this was once the jewel of Illinois."

"Really? Well, I'm having flashbacks to Beirut," Schwarz said, looking sadly out the side window of the Cadillac.

Dodging potholes with the sure ease of a big-city dweller, Lyons merely grunted in agreement. How the mighty of commerce had fallen. Forty years ago, Gary, Indiana, had become famous because of a Broadway tune singing its praises back in 1905. But the city crossed the state line, and there was Gary, Illinois, and nobody sang the praise of either city anymore. Fifty years ago it would have been called a ghetto, twenty years ago, a slum. The new politically correct term was "brownscape." But giving it a fancy name didn't remove the stink of the hopeless or the reek of poverty.

Once the home for countless factories pouring out the wealth of the Midwest, the ruins of Gary now spread across the landscape like a pus-oozing sore on the face of a beautiful woman. The crumbling city was hated and forgotten. But not useless. It was the perfect hiding ground for the Republican Army of Cascade.

Occasionally checking the street map shown on the glowing personal computer on the nearby seat, Lyons drove the rented Cadillac quickly through downtown Gary. Nobody on the sidewalks or in the few other cars on the street seemed to be paying the brand-new Cadillac any attention whatsoever.

"Told you it would work," Blancanales boasted. "Camouflage comes in a lot of different manners."

"I guess so," Lyons acknowledged.

Before entering Gary, the team had stopped at a strip mall. First and foremost, they bought some old clothing at a Goodwill store. What they were wearing would pass unnoticed at O'Hare, but would mark them as narcs in Gary. Now properly attired in old shirts and denim work pants, they bought supplies at a small hardware store. Then driving behind the mall for some privacy, they got to work on the Cadillac. While Schwarz bent the radio antenna, smashed a headlight, dented the body and kicked off the hubcaps, Blancanales splashed orange primer randomly onto the gleaming Cadillac, and Lyons liberally applied strips of duct tape here and there. After about ten minutes, their rented Cadillac looked as if it were twenty years old and falling apart from rust, even though it was in perfect mechanical shape.

Back on the streets, the junked car melded with the rest of the sparse traffic.

Endless blocks of crumbling buildings, polluted water, fallen masonry, weeds, rust and decay spread outward in every direction. The air was redolent and thick with chemicals from the refineries, a reeking miasma of dying machinery. Rusting water towers dotted the ghetto, the metal support girders starting to bend as if they were kneeling down to feed like beasts upon the carrion of the dead city below.

"Beirut is beginning to look pretty good," Blancanales said softly, running a hand through his hair.

Tucking his portable radio into a cushioned holster under his denim jacket, Schwarz froze and adjusted the controls. "Roger, confirmed," he reported into his throat mike.

"What?" Lyons asked.

"David found Davis Harrison in the Kuril Islands," Schwarz said, touching the radio in his ear. "The buy has already gone down."

Slowing for a stop sign, Lyons noticed that nobody else was pausing, so he kept the Cadillac moving. "Which means Harrison can call Woods at any moment to sell them the duplicate plans," he concluded, going around an abandoned car left in the middle of the street.

"That would almost definitely tip off Woods that the thing at the airport was a trick to reveal his whereabouts, and he'll vanish," Blancanales added, frowning.

"Without the plans for the Chameleon?" Schwarz retorted. "No way."

"Way," Blancanales replied without humor. "Believe me, he'll run, fast and far."

"Gadgets, ask Bear to monitor the phone lines for an incoming call from the Pacific Rim," Lyons ordered. "If Harrison calls, kill the local phone service."

"No good, Carl. He might be using a cell phone," Schwarz explained, "and routing the call through Australia, France, New Jersey, anywhere he wants to. It's impossible for even Bear and his team to check the entire world."

"And if the phones die now, Cascade will know we're wise, and run. Then merely contact Harrison later and get the plans then."

"I was hoping this was almost over, and now it's just starting again," Lyons said, hitting the accelerator. "Okay, then, we have no choice. We find the headquarters for Cascade, get inside and capture Woods alive so that we'll be on the other end of that phone call."

"Then we clean house," Blancanales said, "and put Cascade out of business for good."

"Better stay sharp," Schwarz warned, working the bolt on his own M-16/M-203. "Woods has millions to spare, so Cascade is going to be well armed with everything money can buy. And that's a lot."

"But not everything," Blancanales added, spotting an American flag fluttering from the top of a pole above a small post office that resembled a fortified bunker. There was barbed wire coiling along the edge of the roof, and the windows were covered with plywood, but a sign on the front door said it was open for business, and there was a line of people inside holding packages. "Some things aren't for sale."

"Amen to that."

Braking at a red light, Lyons noticed the teenager coming toward the Cadillac. The kid's satin jacket was flapping open, and the checkered grip of an automatic pistol was jutting from his wide leather belt.

"Get out of the car!" the kid snarled, pulling out a Glock 17 pistol. "And give me your... Oh, shit!"

The cry came as Able Team swung a collection of M-16/M-203 assault rifle combos toward the teenager. At the sight, he dropped the Glock and raised both trembling hands.

"Joking, man." He attempted a grin. "Hey, it was only a joke, like, ya know?"

Accelerating slowly, Lyons left the would-be carjacker behind. As the Cadillac started to take a corner, the kid grabbed the fallen Glock and began to run for his life.

"Think he was a member of Cascade?" Schwarz asked with a straight face.

"Knowing their idiot philosophy about life," Lyons said, returning his attention to the road, "that could have been Woods himself."

Now the buildings grew in size and height, some of them covering an entire block. Chain-link fences lined most blocks, some intact and others sagging to the ground. Graffiti-covered concrete rails blocked the sidewalks and driveways of hulking factories, empty steel mills and burned-out warehouses. A scattering of homeless people meandered about, pushing shopping carts full of items ripped from the crumbling buildings: copper pipes, light switches, anything that might bring a dollar from the junk dealers and scrap yards. Several buildings were sealed off behind EPA violation stickers, and not even the swaggering street gangs dared to cross those dire warnings and risk early death from toxic-waste poisoning.

"This is it," Blancanales said, checking the personal computer in his palm. "The phone that the guy at the airport called was from this area."

Both sides of the street were lined with a complex of brick buildings bridged together above the street by conveyor belts, raised walkways and pipes of a hundred different sizes coming and going in controlled chaos. Weeds grew everywhere on the ground, the cracked asphalt rising and buckling from the harsh Illinois winters and no repair work.

"Do we know which building?" Lyons asked, reducing speed to a crawl as if looking for a parking spot.

"Hell, no. Officially, the building doesn't even exist, much less have services."

The Able Team leader grunted at that. "Good. Now all we need is a soft entry inside," he reminded, feeling the pressure of time. "Blowing down the front door is our court of last appeal."

The cracked sidewalks were closed off with wire fencing, but the curbs were empty. However, broken glass was everywhere, the tiny green cubes of automobile safety glass mixing with the brown shards of busted beer bottles. Potholes gaped in the ground like blast craters, one with a small oak tree growing from the windblown dirt accumulated at the bottom.

Yellow newspapers, corroded beer cans, cardboard fast-food containers and general detritus abounded. The front stoop of one building had a slope of green glass, covering the front steps. Weathered and peeling, the door was badly battered with holes at the bottom too small for even a child, but perfect for rats. Near a swaying guard kiosk, a dead dog was being pecked at by crows, and a man in stained and tattered clothes shuffled along in the street.

Two blocks down the street, a blond woman lifted her skirt at a slowly passing car. The grinning driver pulled to the corner, and the busty whore bent in through the passenger-side window to talk to the occupants and give Able Team an impromptu view of her dubious charms. A deal was obvious made, because she climbed into the car, the driver already loosening his seat belt.

Looking carefully at the ground underneath the fencing, Blancanales couldn't find any sign of rust flakes. Yet the wire fence was streaked with patches of dull red. "They either vacuum the sidewalk at night, or else that rust is fake," he said.

"Primer looks a lot like rust," Schwarz added thoughtfully, pulling out an EM scanner from the canvas bag at his side.

"No active scans," Lyons warned. "They might have detectors, passive scan only."

"Check," Schwarz said, tucking away the scanner.

Driving around a corner, Lyons braked to a halt and tried to get a feel for the area, but he was coming up with nothing. The Stony Man commando knew the terrorist group Cascade was hidden among the abandoned structures, but where? Could the trace have been wrong? Kurtzman was only human, and mistakes did happen.

In the rear seat, Schwarz pulled out a small box with a shotgun microphone attached to it with a springy cable. Placing a booster into his ear, he turned on the amplifier, thumbed the switch and began moving the ultrasensitive microphone about. A parabolic dish mike was the preferred method to do this, but once again they were hampered by the need to stay covert. At least until they found the bastards—then the kid gloves come off.

"Anything?" Blancanales asked hopefully.

"Water dripping, rats fighting over something, a low steady hiss, could be anything," Schwarz reported, his eyes closed tight to aid in concentrating. "No voices or machinery."

Sliding the Caddy into gear, Lyons drove along the complex of decaying buildings. The once proud factory stretched for blocks before them like forgotten ruins.

"Sweet Jesus, it'll take us weeks to scan this much," Blancanales muttered, squinting at the piles of destruction. There was a pair of military binoculars in his equipment bag, but they night as well set off flares as use something like that out in the open.

"Hold it," Lyons said abruptly, looking in his rearview mirror. "She's back."

"Who?"

"The whore."

"So soon?" Blancanales demanded suspiciously.

"Too soon," Lyons agreed.

Schwarz swung his microphone in that direction, but there was no conversation. The whore was alone in the vehicle, and now behind the wheel. Driving along a relatively clear section of roadway, she parked the vehicle near a gate and walked away, swinging her hips to secret music. A few moments later, the graffiti-covered louvered door of the factory loading dock rolled silently up and a bald man in a black turtleneck with an automatic weapon in his hand walked out of Building 14. Going to the gate, he paused and it opened smoothly.

"No squeaks or rubbing," Schwarz said. "The track is well greased."

Moving casually, the bald man went to the car, started it up and drove it through the gate and up a sloped ramp and into the loading dock. The gate slid closed all by itself.

"That must be it, Building 14," Schwarz said, turning the volume up to maximum. But after a few minutes, he turned it off and removed the booster plug from his ear. "Nothing, no noise at all. Sons of bitches must have it soundproofed."

"It's a slick ambush," Blancanales grudgingly admitted in professional admiration. "Anybody nosing around, the whore offers them the deal of a lifetime. If they say no, then they're cops, and the place shuts down. If the poor guy says sure, she takes him someplace secluded, cuts his throat and drives back in the car. They deliver it to their chop shop and turn it into cash."

"Too slick for some gangbangers or crack dealers,"

Lyons said in agreement, checking the .357 Magnum Colt Python under his jacket. "That's got to be Cascade. Let's go find a back door."

"Lead the way, dude," Schwarz said, checking the sound suppressor on his 9 mm Beretta.

Driving around the block, Lyons noticed a small hole in the wire fence. Pulling the Cadillac to the curb, he parked it behind some sort of machinery composed mostly of rusted heavy gears. Climbing out, Able Team opened the trunk and draped themselves with additional equipment and weapon bags.

Heading for the gap in the fence, Schwarz ran a passive EM scan to make sure the opening wasn't rigged with proximity sensors. When he gave a nod, Lyons slipped through, his Atchisson autoshotgun leading the way. Blancanales was next with his M-16/M-203, and Schwarz covered the rear, the EM scanner in one hand and the Beretta in the other.

The wind moaned softly among the buildings and machinery, and the Able Team commandos jerked their weapons about as a piece of newspaper fluttered past them carried along by the breeze.

Staying alert for infrared eyes on the ground or video cameras hidden in the shadows, Able Team moved quickly around the brick buildings, easing along a narrow alleyway filled with wooden shipping pallets of the kind used to haul cargo on trucks.

Lyons smiled at the sight. Bingo. This was a mistake. When these factories were in operation, wooden pallets were used. These sort of plastic pallets had only been around for about ten or twelve years. Far too modern and much too valuable to be found tossed casually aside.

Blancanales nodded at his friend at the sight of the pallets, and the team became more alert. Kurtzman had been correct; this was the headquarters for Cascade. The enemy was only yards away, protected by a maze of ruins.

"Coal chute over there," Schwarz whispered into his throat mike. "Always a good way to gain entrance."

With Blancanales giving cover, Lyons went closer and lifted the heavy iron lid. The old hinges didn't make a sound, and he gently lowered the iron hatch carefully back into place.

"Reeks of WD-40 oil," he announced softly.

"No reading on any sensors or trips," Schwarz said, scrutinizing the scanner in his hand.

"It's a trap," Lyons said with some satisfaction. This was the first hard evidence that they were on the right track.

"Fire escape ladder over there," Blancanales suggested, jerking his weapon in that direction.

"Seems okay," Schwarz said, waving his scanner at the ladder. Approaching warily, Lyons shouldered his weapon and took hold of the bottom of the escape ladder. Giving it an easy tug, he wasn't surprised when the extendable ladder slid down silently on well-greased tracks. Then the team froze at hearing the sound of footsteps approaching. Two, no, three people. Moving fast, Lyons and Blancanales swung their weapons into play, but stepped aside to leave a clear field of vision. Schwarz stayed in the middle and drew his pistol.

"Okay, who's catching the clap from Arnette this time?" somebody said, laughing, walking into the alley.

Leveling the Beretta, Schwarz wasted a precious second acquiring the targets as they came into view: three teenagers dressed in black jeans and black leather dusters like something from an Italian Western. Two of the young men held Tech-9 machine pistols, and the third had the checkered butt of a huge revolver sticking backward out of his belt.

At the sight of Able Team, the teenagers clawed for their weapons. But before they could fire, there came three fast chugs, the sounds coming so close together they almost seemed to be like a single hard cough.

Moaning in pain, the youths doubled over, dropping their weapons and grabbing their bloody stomachs. Tracking the bodies with their own weapons, Lyons and Blancanales watched coldly as Schwarz leveled his Beretta and fired three more times, ending the suffering of the youths now that the weapons were gone. One of his earliest lessons in combat had been that dying enemy gunners often convulsed wildly, their spasming fingers tightening on triggers and blindly firing weapons even as they died.

As Schwarz reloaded the Beretta, neither Lyons or Blancanales complimented their friend on his speed and marksmanship. These young people had chosen the wrong path, and they paid the ultimate price. Schwarz had merely done what he had to do for survival.

Leaving the bodies where they lay, Able Team swiftly climbed to the roof of the factory. Now with a panoramic view of the abandoned complex, they could see the whore was back on the distant corner, wiggling her hips and chewing gum as she walked the perimeter of the hidden base.

The roofs of the adjoining buildings were deserted, some of the more distant structures starting to sag as the harsh Midwestern winters weakened the wooden supports underneath. Bird nests abounded, and there was a surprising amount of hubcaps and plastic Frisbees.

Staying in the middle of the roof where he couldn't be seen from the street below, Schwarz aimed his shotgun mike at the nearby buildings and fiddled with the controls.

"Nothing," he said in disgust. Then added, "No, wait. Ah!" Walking across the roof, he swung the mike back and forth until it was pointing at a ventilator fan, the galvanized tin slowly rotating in the gentle breeze from the garbage-filled river.

"Okay, it's gone now," he said. "Somebody must have been walking past an air vent and I caught a piece of their conversation."

"Anything useful?" Lyons asked tensely.

"Something about a vault door. I didn't hear all of it."

"Damn."

In the middle of the roof was a skylight, a small satellite dish aiming at the blue sky above bolted to the frame and protected by coils of concertina wire. The sharp edge of the military razor wire glistened in the pale sunlight.

Shouldering his weapon, Blancanales knelt on the roof and checked the area for traps. When he was satisfied that it was clear, he pulled out a pair of cutters and carefully snipped through the concertina wire. As one coil parted, it lashed out backward. He ducked, and the razor strand came so close that he saw his own reflection in the metal for a split second.

"That was a near thing." He exhaled deeply, pocketing the cutters.

Reaching out a hand, Lyons touched the man's cheek and came back with a finger dripping red.

"Closer than you think, Rosario," he commented, wiping his hand clean.

As Blancanales opened a medical kit to slap on a bandage, Schwarz pressed his mike to the glass of the skylight. Turning the volume to maximum, he heard nothing unusual.

"Clear," he reported, pocketing the device.

Running the tip of a knife along the edges of a pane of glass, Lyons cut away the hard putty, then used a piece of duct tape to lift the square of glass out of its recess in the frame. Peering down, he saw only a filthy room, then he went stiff at a familiar smell.

"Fresh corpse," Lyons whispered. "I'd guess it was only a couple of hours old. Can't mistake that reek of pennies and shit."

The others knew the phrase. Fresh blood smelled like copper pennies, and almost every corpse relieved its bowels as the muscles eased into death. Pennies and feces, the telltale aroma of violent death.

"Why would they leave a body there?" Schwarz asked, frowning. "Unless somebody pissed off the boss."

"More likely it's bait in a trap," Lyons countered, rocking back on his heels. "What cop would pass by a corpse without investigating?"

"So these boys are expecting trouble."

"Let's find out," Schwarz said, lowering his microphone through the hole in the skylight all the way to the end of its wire.

Listening closely, he thumbed the volume and the gain about, his face taking on a hard expression.

"Sounds like the hissing of a hydraulic power line. But nothing in this factory works anymore," Schwarz said, puzzled, then he frowned deeply. "Ah, hell, you guys thinking what I'm thinking?"

"They have an armored door guarding the entrance to their base," Lyons answered, rocking back on his heels. "Then we can't go in this way. We don't have the explosives to blow open a bank vault door."

"Nowhere near enough," Schwarz confirmed, tucking away his equipment again. "Hand grenades and 40 mm shells aren't going to dent a door that needs hydraulics to move."

"Meanwhile, Cascade springs whatever trap they have set near the dead guy." Lyons frowned as he stood. "Claymore mines, poison gas, whatever."

"That is, unless we get them to open it for us," Blancanales said, looking at his teammates.

"Got a plan?" Lyons asked, noticing the scrutiny.

"Yes. You've got a hot date." Blancanales smiled, pulling out his wallet. Withdrawing a sheaf of cash, he offered it to Lyons. "We'll cover you from up here."

A date? Taking the cash, Lyons looked sideways at the street below. The scantily dressed whore was still standing on the corner, watching and waving at every car that passed.

"I just hope that isn't Arnette," he said, tucking the money away and starting for the fire escape.

Three men against two hundred were bad odds, but Lyons could hear the clock ticking, and if this trick didn't work, Able Team would have no choice but to go straight in with guns blazing, which was tantamount to suicide. But that did give him an idea. Maybe there was a way to balance the odds slightly more in their favor.

Climbing down the ladder, Lyons pulled out his cell phone and hit a memorized number. The call was answered in the middle of the first ring.

"I have a job for you," Lyons said, starting briskly through the alley.

CHAPTER NINETEEN

Matua Island

The opal-blue water of the caldera was clear all the way to the sandy bottom. Shoals of colorful fish swam among a waving aquatic forest of kelp. A volcanic sink-hole that had flooded a hundred years ago, the caldera of the island was shaped like a giant capital letter *G*, and the gentle ocean waves rolled in through the mouth to wash over a natural barrier of coral.

Skimming along the bay was a speedboat with the two armed guards of Nucleus sitting at the front of the craft. Sprawled on a cushioned bench at the rear of the speedboat, Davis Harrison clicked shut a handcuff around the handle of a briefcase, the money locked safely inside. This job was nearly done; all that was left was to call Cascade and send them the duplicate files on the Chameleon, collect another fee and then go on vacation somewhere for a while. Australia maybe, lots of pretty women at their topless beaches, decent beer and some of the best T-bone steaks in the world.

"Avanti!" Harrison called out in Italian, knowing it would annoy the Japanese men. "Go faster! I have a hot date waiting for me in Melbourne!"

The guard steering the speedboat didn't turn, but the other man did, his face grim and disapproving.

Harrison laughed at the dour expression and lolled a hand over the low gunwale. The Pacific Ocean water was particularly warm in this region from a young submerged volcano just to east of Matua. The rumbling lava cone was so new it hadn't even been named yet. But that didn't seem to bother the huge schools of fish flocking in to gorge themselves on the almost invisible tiny sea shrimp who also sought the warmth of the volcano. Distorted rainbows of living colors moved under the speedboat as it started around the point of the caldera, the fish parting before the craft and closing ranks in its turbulent wake.

Basking in the brief joy of a successful job, Harrison threw his head back and closed his eyes to savor the warmth of the sun. Once back on Simushir Island, he'd catch the *White Pearl* on its return trip and sail away to Japan. He would call Cascade there…but why wait? Pulling out his cell phone, Harrison turned it on and waited for the screen to light.

"Stop that at once!" the second guard snapped, drawing a pistol.

Harrison froze at the sight, then slowly spread his fingers wide to show they weren't activating the phone.

"Something wrong?" he asked.

"No calls," the terrorist commanded, motioning with the pistol. "Satellites could track it here. Toss it over the side."

Harrison felt his stomach tighten. The programmed

number on the phone was his only link to Cascade in America. If he lost it, the deal was dead and he would be out almost a million dollars.

"Look, it's off," Harrison said, turning the phone toward the guard. "I'll just tuck it away. No problem."

The guard stood and clicked back the hammer on his pistol. "Then you'll just call once on Simushir," he stated with a growl. "It goes over the side right now, or you die."

Heavily a heavy sigh, Harrison looked at the cell phone and started to reach past the gunwale of the speedboat as a diversion to cover his left hand coming out his pocket with his cigarette lighter. The device hissed twice, and the guard reeled back, the tiny poison darts buried deep in his throat.

With an inarticulate cry, the pilot spun and caught two more darts in his face, one of them going directly into an eye, bursting the sack. Even as the neurotoxin galvanized his muscles, the screaming man managed to pull a pistol and fire three times, hitting nothing before limply falling facedown onto the deck.

Tucking the precious cell phone away, Harrison advanced upon the dead men and fired twice more just to make sure they weren't faking. Pocketing the lighter, he hauled them to the rear of the speedboat and took over the helm. The boat had started veering out to sea with nobody at the wheel, and he began to head it eastward and back toward Simushir. Then he smiled and changed course to due south, checking the compass on the control panel and the fuel gauge. Yes, there was just enough. Excellent. To hell with Simushir Island. He'd go directly to Japan! There was a breeding ground for great white sharks along the way. He could toss the bodies overboard there and they'd never be found. With any luck, their organization might think the men had killed him and taken the money for themselves. Hmm, it was just possible he could get a replacement payment from Major Fukoka for the Chameleon. That would make three fees for the same item!

Speaking of which… As the speedboat surged forward, Harrison pulled out the cell phone. No calls, eh? Watch this! He hit several buttons in the proper sequence, the scrambled number for Cascade was activated and the first of the relay phones started ringing.

Stony Man Farm, Virginia

"THERE'S AN OUTGOING cell-phone call from the vicinity of Matua Island," Akira Tokaido announced calmly, his hands flowing across his silent keyboard. "It's mobile. Probably a boat or plane. I'm trying for a trace."

"Carmen, is the dummy ready?" Kurtzman snapped anxiously, wheeling his chair closer.

Masked by the VR helmet, the woman waved a gloved hand. "All set to go," she said. "Just tell me when."

"Davis Harrison is calling a farmhouse outside of Dublin, Ireland," Tokaido announced, both eyes firmly closed. The headphones he wore jumped from the rock music playing. "Ah, a former IRA bomb factory. Clever boy. Okay, the second relay has started…it's a mining company in Tombouctou…."

"In the eastern mountain range?" Kurtzman asked.

Tokaido merely nodded, concentrating on his task.

"I'll bet it's the hideout for those bandits raiding caravans in the area," Kurtzman muttered, thumping a hand on the armrest of his wheelchair. "The son on a bitch is giving us his goddamn résumé. He probably hid a relay box every place he's ever done a job."

"We're in Cairo now," Tokaido said, staring to frown. "The signal is splitting…one call is going to Langley, Virginia. I'll ignore that one. It's a fake. Aha! He's going on a ground line now, across the transatlantic cable. I can kill the call now if you want."

"Carmen?" Kurtzman asked a ton of questions in his voice.

"Just tell me when," she repeated calmly.

"And we're in Nova Scotia! A lighthouse off the northern shore…now, that one I know. It's an SAS safehouse! David has mentioned it from time to time."

"Get ready, I'm betting this is the last leg," Kurtzman said. "He'll want the call traced back to his old agency, a little political revenge for the SAS kicking him out."

Tokaido leaned forward over his console. "We've gone cellular…back on landlines…damn, this guy is good… switching through Texas…cellular again…Illinois!"

"Now!" Kurtzman shouted, pointing across the room.

Without a word, Delahunt flipped a switch.

"Did it work?" Kurtzman demanded.

"Unknown," Delahunt said, removing her helmet. "The timing had to be perfect, so either Cascade just got the design plans on how to make a Sony PlayStation, or the schematics for the Chameleon. There's no way to tell."

"Inform Able Team the ball may be in play," Kurtzman directed her, then turned. "Akira, good job. Now give Phoenix Force the location of Harrison. It's their job now."

"Does Barbara or Hal want him alive anymore?" Tokaido asked, stroking his keyboard once more with the skill of a concert pianist.

Turning his chair around, Kurtzman snorted at that. "For the moment."

Near Matua Island

AT THE BOW of the hovercraft, Hawkins was watching the horizon of the ocean with a pair of binoculars. Line of sight in the open sea was seven miles, but the volcano peak of Matua rose high enough to be visible for well past a hundred miles.

"Alert," Akira Tokaido said over the radio in his ear. "Somebody has just placed a cell-phone call to Cascade in your immediate area."

"At sea?" McCarter demanded, touching his throat. "Where?"

"Just east of you. Roughly four miles."

"Move!" McCarter roared, pointing to the right.

Holding the joystick tight, James shoved the throttle all the way and the hovercraft rocketed forward, flashing above the ocean waves.

"Anything on radar?" Encizo asked, swaying to the bouncing motion of the speeding craft. Opening the breech of the grenade launcher mounted beneath his AK-105, he slid out the antipersonnel round of steel slivers. Designed by the DEA to blow off door locks so they could instantly enter drug labs, what the thundering barrage of metal fléchettes did to human flesh had to be seen to be believed. Tucking the AP shell in a pocket, he thumbed in a stun bag round and closed the breech with a solid snap. They still wanted to take Harrison alive. If only for a little while, until they knew who had the Chameleon and what they planned on doing with it.

Craning his neck, James did a fast check. "Not yet. Radar screen is clear."

Tense minutes passed, and then James sharply whistled, gesturing to the southeast.

Swinging his binoculars that way, Hawkins saw it was a small speedboat with a slim, pale man at the wheel.

"It's Harrison!" he called out.

McCarter growled and raised his AK-105, then lowered it again. The speedboat was far outside the range of the assault rifle. Swinging up the Barrett, Manning braced himself and worked the bolt, levering in a cartridge.

"We want him alive," McCarter reminded brusquely, sounding almost sorry he had to say it.

"That was the plan, David," Manning growled and stroked the trigger.

As the Barrett boomed, Hawkins watched the speedboat closely. The first shot seemed to have hit nothing, but firing from a bouncing platform at a bouncing target was damn near impossible at this distance. However, Hawkins saw Harrison snap his head around as the noise of the Barrett reached him a second later. The man dropped his jaw at the sight of the oncoming hovercraft filled with armed men.

His own hands aching to fire, Hawkins barely restrained himself as Harrison shoved the throttle of the speedboat all the way. The nimble craft leaped forward, almost doubling its speed.

Levering in another round, Manning fired again, and this time, a huge chunk of the wooden gunwale exploded off the speedboat. Incredibly, Harrison left the helm and rushed to the rear of the craft. The reason why was made clear in just a moment as he tossed two bodies overboard. Oddly, he had a briefcase handcuffed to his wrist, but it was clearly too slim to hold the Chameleon unless he had totally disassembled the jamming unit.

As the lightened speedboat increased its speed again, Harrison raced back to the helm and swung directly away from Phoenix Force, heading out to the open sea.

At first, the distance between the two crafts stayed the same, then the gap slowly began to widen. McCarter bitterly cursed at the sight. The hovercraft was a lot faster than the speedboat, but it was also carrying tremendously more weight. The chase had started equal, but now it was all in favor of Harrison.

"He's getting away," Enzico pointed out, firing his assault rifle, even though he knew the rounds couldn't reach.

"If he does, we'll never find him again," McCarter stated, switching his grip from the assault rifle to the 40 mm grenade launcher mounted under the main barrel. "Okay, we have no choice. Dead is better than escaped. Take him out!"

Expecting that order, the team raised their weapons and cut loose, the combined chatter of the Kalashnikovs almost equaling the strident boom of the unleashed Barrett. Harrison ducked just in time as the back of his chair was blown apart. Then something splashed into the waves just off his bow and exploded, pelting hot salt water across the speeding vessel.

More 40 mm grenades rained down around the boat as the team got the range of their moving target. Then the Barrett spoke once more and the cowling was slammed off the aft engine assembly. With a gurgling sputter, the twin gasoline motors stopped working, only to whoof into orange flames.

As the powerless speedboat began to coast to a stop, a dripping-wet Harrison popped into view with two handguns, firing both together. McCarter emptied a clip at the man, but only the last few rounds finding their target as the hovercraft finally got into range. Blood exploded from Harrison's left shoulder, and he spun about to drop out of sight again.

Still racing closer, James sharply angled the hovercraft aside as a wheezing Harrison appeared with a flare gun held in both hands. The sizzling charge rocketed past the hovercraft, missing the engine by only a foot. Phoenix Force answered with their Kalashnikovs, the lead chewing up the speedboat from stem to stern. Incredibly, their quarry popped up once more with two weapons in his grip, the briefcase dangling from his wrist now with a sheet of paper sticking out of the side showing it had just been opened and hastily closed. As the flare gun flashed in discharge, he dropped it and held the larger pistol with both hands before working the trigger. There came the deep, strident boom of a rifle.

As the flare streaked by harmlessly, something punched hard through the rubber skirt of the hovercraft, and there came the horrible high-pitched scream of a turbine shattering, the blades breaking into countless pieces.

Dropping his rifle, a cursing James grabbed the joystick with both arms, trying to bring the wildly veering hovercraft back under control by brute force.

Forcing his chattering assault rifle to stay on the speedboat, McCarter scowled as he shot numerous holes in the hull at the waterline. What kind of bleeding weapon was that? The man was holding a pistol, not some sort a bloody hunting rifle! Then McCarter noticed Harrison working the bolt on the pistol to ram in another huge brass cartridge. A bolt-action pistol?

"That's a Wichita Thunderbolt!" Hawkins shouted over his chattering weapon. "Fires a .575 Magnum rifle round!"

"We noticed!" McCarter told him, sending another 40 mm round toward the listing speedboat.

Grinning in triumph, Harrison raised the bizarre weapon again as the bow of the craft violently exploded from the incoming grenade. Thrown sideways, he lost the Wichita and it went flying.

Desperately throwing himself after the weapon, Harrison tried for a save, but it went over the side and vanished into the ocean.

With a roar, the burning engines blew apart, spreading the flames across the listing vessel. Suddenly, the hovercraft leveled out and darted forward. McCarter and Hawkins stitched Harrison across the bloody shirt and the man staggered, but didn't go down. He was wearing body armor!

Diving for the deck, Harrison came up again with a revolver and the flare gun in his red-streaked fists. Shifting his aim, Encizo fired, and the stun bag hit Harrison directly in the face. Blood and teeth went airborne as he went backward over the side and splashed into the water.

It took James a few moments to guide the hovercraft around the burning speedboat, and as it got clear the Phoenix Force commandos discharged everything they had into the murky water. A red stain appeared and began to spread outward. Ruthlessly, Manning lowered the barrel of the Barrett and put a couple of deafening rounds smack through the middle of the crimson fog.

Using his body weight to control the joystick, James maneuvered the damaged hovercraft in a circle around the area, as the rest of the team randomly shot into the ocean. Encizo pulled the pin of a grenade, but McCarter stopped him.

"Don't waste it," he said as the red stain continued to expand. "He's dead. Look."

"The cavalry arrives," Manning stated, shouldering his weapon. A couple of shark fins were cutting through the waves nearby, the deadly killers obviously attracted by the smell of fresh blood in the water.

"Now let's find the buyer on Matua," McCarter said.

Very carefully, Encizo reinserted the pin into his grenade.

"Well, whoever they are," Hawkins said, slapping in a fresh clip, "they can't possibly be as much trouble as this guy."

"Let's go find out," James said, turning the off-balance hovercraft directly toward Matua Island.

CHAPTER TWENTY

Cascade Headquarters

Drumming her blue fingernails on the steering wheel of the Cadillac, the angry whore looked down at Carl Lyons crouched under the dashboard.

"Okay, we're here, asshole," she snapped. "Now what? If this is a robbery—"

"Can it! Act normal and you stay alive," Lyons ordered, nudging her nylon-clad thigh with the muzzle of the Colt Python.

Flipping a wave of platinum hair over a bare shoulder, the busty whore sneered in reply, then put on a neutral face as the doors to the loading dock of Building 14 began to lift open.

"They're going to bust you apart," Arnette muttered out of the side of her mouth. "And I'll piss myself laughing to death."

Lyons just gestured with his Colt Python for her to keep driving. Shifting into gear, the woman pressed her sandal on the accelerator.

"Tony Stark, this is the Professor," Schwarz whispered in Lyons's ear over the radio. "Bear just reported that Cascade got a call from Harrison. They tried for a switch, but don't know if Woods has the goods or a dummy. The ball could be in play."

Lyons frowned. That meant that Woods now knew the airport had been a trick, and that somebody was coming his way after the Chameleon. Damn. No time for finesse anymore.

"Roger, Professor. Looks like it's balls to the wall. We'll meet at the graveyard."

"Confirm. Out."

"Whadya say?" Arnette drawled, raising an eyebrow.

"Just keep your hand away from the emergency brake," Lyons warned, cocking back the hammer on the massive revolver. "A sudden stop might make me accidentally blow off your tits."

Her eyes flashed alive with fear, and Arnette made no reply, but she quickly placed her left hand back on the steering wheel where it was in plain sight.

"Laughing," she said again softly. "I'll be laughing all the way to your fucking grave."

Lyons started to answer when the hum of the radio in his ear became crackling static. Bear was on time as usual. Feeling the electric surge of adrenaline, the Able Team leader turned off the radio and removed the earplug. Radios would be useless in Gary until further notice. How long it took Woods and Cascade to figure that out depended on a lot of things, first and foremost being how fast Lyons could breach the main building.

Driving past the wire fence, the big Caddy jounced

over the cracked concrete of the access ramp making certain ample portions of Arnette's anatomy bounce in a most distracting manner before it stopped. As she braked to a halt, the loading-dock door rumbled shut behind them with a hard clang of metal on metal.

"You're ours now, idiot," Arnette muttered. "You'll never leave this building alive with one red cent."

"And who says it's a robbery?" Lyons asked, watching the windows for moving shadows.

Confusion crossed the woman's face, and under its softening effects, for the first time Lyons caught a fleeting glimpse of the great beauty that had once been her wealth in youth, before the savage street took it away. As a former cop, the first thing he had noticed were the needle marks on her arms and thighs. It's why she wore sandals, to shoot out between her toes, because her arms and legs were too tender to take the needle anymore. Smack, probably. It didn't matter. It was all a one-way trip to oblivion.

"Just leave the damn engine running," Lyons warned, getting ready.

"Hey, Arnette!" a male voice called out. "Busy day, huh, baby?"

Drumming her nails on the wheel with hard clicks, Arnette stayed motionless and stared straight ahead.

A bald man appeared at the window wearing a black turtleneck and a tan leather rig supporting an Uzi submachine gun.

"Something wrong, honey?" he asked with a lopsided grin. "Yang isn't really that mad at you for giving him a dose. Hey, shit happens."

Arnette flicked her eyes to the right. The bald man followed the look and stepped back in shock at the sight of Lyons pushing aside a dirty blanket.

"Sweet Jesus!" he cried, digging for the Uzi.

Lyons fired once, the Magnum slug from the .357 Colt Python blowing away half the bald head. Even as the body dropped from sight, Arnette started screaming obscenities at the top of her lungs, and beat frantically at the stinging residue of the muzzle flash across her skimpy clothing.

Having already jimmied the lock, Lyons kicked open the passenger-side door and dived out, firing fast at two more men moving his way. They fell back into forever, one of them dropping a sawed-off shotgun. Spinning fast, Lyons saw six more people across the garage, some of them going for weapons, others just standing there with their mouths hanging open.

"Freeze! This is the FBI!" he shouted, swinging up the Atchisson autoshotgun.

Now everybody went for a gun, and Lyons cut loose, the deafening roar of the superfire blowing a hellstorm of hot death. Literally chewed to pieces, the members of Cascade died on the spot, the tools on the pegboard behind them clanging loudly as they danced from the ricochets and penetrating rounds.

"You're a feeb?" Arnette shrieked, using the street term for the FBI as she got out of the Cadillac.

As Lyons dropped the clip to reload, Arnette reached inside her blouse, pulled out a Remington .32. With no choice, Lyons threw the shotgun at her and went for his Colt. She ducked the flying shotgun and fired, the round hitting Lyons smack in the chest. He grunted as his NATO-issue body armor took the impact, then he fired back.

Walking briskly across the bloody garage, the Able Team leader checked her pulse, but it was useless.

"Dumb move, Arnette," he said softly, reclaiming the shotgun. "Real dumb."

Reloading quickly, Lyons checked the rest of the loading dock and found nobody else around. But he did spot a Mack truck with a Rolls-Royce Caprice in the back. Had to be Peter Woods's private wheels, he decided.

Shooting out all four tires on the Rolls with his Colt, Lyons then hurried back to the main garage and went up the catwalk to the overpass. Stepping outside, he felt incredibly exposed, and bent low to try to stay behind the iron safety railing as he raced between the two buildings.

Reaching the other side, he threw himself hard against he brick wall and searched for any reaction from the street below. There was no movement in the ruins, but certainly somebody had heard the Atchisson in operation. Okay, if not outside, then they were coming his way inside.

Just then voices sounded from behind the access door. Whirling, Lyons brought up his weapon just as the door swung aside.

"Who the fuck are you?" a bald man demanded, cocking back the hammer on his 9 mm HK pistol.

Were they all bald? Lyons fired from the hip, the Atchisson sending a grisly spray of the man backward into the arms of the Cascade members behind him. Releasing the autoshotgun to swing on its strap, the Able Team leader unlimbered the Colt and stepped into the building, firing at anybody with a weapon. Two more bald men died, one managing to get off a burst from an M-16 assault rifle before joining his brethren in eternity.

Grabbing his leg, Lyons cursed at the numbness spreading outward from the bloody area. There was no spurting, which meant the bullet hadn't hit an artery, so that was good. Gingerly probing the muscle, he found it was only a flesh wound and nothing serious. Good enough.

Using a pocketknife, he slit open the leg of his pants and slapped on a military field dressing, the adhesive edging sticking to his skin in spite of the slippery blood. Good enough for now.

Limply slightly, he moved onward, sweeping through the old factory, ducking under conveyor belts thick with dust, and rusty machinery, searching for the smell of death that would lead him directly to the hidden entrance of the Cascade base.

IN THE AIR-CONDITIONED computer room, the technicians were busy at the consoles preparing the huge, humming Cray for its next task. Behind a soundproofed door, Peter Woods sat in a small office and watched the men at their tasks while skimming through the thick sheaf of printouts spread out on the desk.

He hated to admit it, but Harrison had come through as promised. The schematics seemed very complex to Woods, but he was no scientist. This was it, the key to the future! The ultimate stealth shield. By God, with this in the hands of the enemies of democracy, war in the Middle East was assured, and then Congress would be forced to unleash the military might of the nation, and America would finally rise to its proper position as the ruler of the world. Millions would die, of course, but billions would be freed from starvation and slavery. It was a more than fair exchange in his opinion.

Standing near a bubbling coffeemaker, Tommy Mannix was leaning against the concrete wall and talking on the phone.

"Yeah, okay, thanks," Mannix said, and replaced the phone on the wall. "We might have some trouble. Brian just reported gunfire from the loading dock. He's going over to check it out."

"Probably just another bum," Woods rumbled, running his fingers along the pages of electronic circuitry. History was in his hands. The new history of a better world. "Any word from the Bloodhawks yet?"

"Not since they first got hit by the Comanches, no, sir."

"Hmm, well, tell Brian to stay where he is. Have Yang and his brothers check it out the loading dock. They're walking the perimeter today."

"Can't. They don't answer their radio."

Woods snapped up his head at that. "Yang doesn't answer?" he said, speaking each word individually. "That anal-retentive nancy would report if he was having brain surgery. How long has it been since they last called?"

Mannix shrugged. "Not long. About fifteen, twenty minutes," he replied confidently. "Chief, we got 120 guys here today, along with me and the Magnificent Seven. Let the Comanches come if they want. We'll mop the floor with the little bastards. It'll be Custer's Last Stand all over again."

"General George Armstrong Custer lost that battle, Tommy," Woods stated. "Are the phones operating?"

"Sure, no problem there."

Chewing a lip, Woods looked at the papers in his hands, then stuffed them into a waterproof folder and sealed it tight.

"I don't like this," he said, standing upright and tucking the folder under an arm. "Send out two armed recon teams to sweep the exterior perimeter for strangers. And call a red alert using the house phone. I want this whole building sealed and ready for combat. Get some people on the roof with LAW rockets and Stingers."

"Just because there's trouble with our radios?" Mannix chided, crossing his arms. "Come on, Chief. Sure, the timing seems a little odd, but—"

"And what about the gunshots in the garage?" Woods interrupted.

"Hell, we don't even know there were any, yet."

"I'm betting there was gunfire," Woods replied. "Actually, Tommy, I think we're already surrounded and the Feds are getting ready to come in."

"The Feds? What makes you think so?"

"This!" Woods roared, shaking the computer printout. "Because if I just bought a million bucks' worth of mil tech, then those flickering lights at the airport were a trick to make us reveal our headquarters."

Furrowing his brow, Mannix thought that over for a minute. "No way," he decided. "Not even the FBI could get the authorization to mess with the power at a major airport."

"On that point we fully agree," Woods growled, picking up the private phone on his desk and hitting a red button.

"Sir?" a man answered.

"How soon can we send the plans for the Chameleon over the Internet?"

"Whenever you wish, sir. We've just finished the decoding process so it can be read by everybody."

The jingling of the cell phone in the pocket of his sports coat interrupted Woods just then. Pulling out the phone, he flipped back the cover and thumbed the accept button.

"Yes?" he demanded, but there was only a hiss of static and then a click.

More irritated than suspicious, Woods scowled at the device, and on impulse hit redial. But the screen stayed blank. The return call had been blocked.

"Who was it?" Mannix asked.

"Nobody," Woods muttered.

"But wasn't Harrison the only person who knew that unlisted number?" the chief of security for Cascade asked pointedly.

Ice exploded in Woods's stomach at the stark realization that Mannix was right. Dropping the cell phone, he grabbed the receiver for the house phone again.

"We're under attack! Send the files!" he shouted just as the lights went out and the room became pitch-black.

"Son of a bitch," Mannix muttered, and then came the sound of flicking. A moment later, there was a flicker of light as the man got a butane lighter working. "We blow a fuse or something?"

Saying nothing, Woods opened a drawer in his desk

and pulled out a Sam Browne gunbelt. His father's initials were branded into the thick leather, and the buckle was proudly notched with the three dozen men the Texas Ranger had shot down in the line of duty, before an near-sighted storekeeper had accidentally shot the man in the back during a robbery. Watching his father slowly die in the hospital had been a life-changing moment for ten-year-old Peter Woods, gaining the knowledge that heroes died, and only the rich and the strong could survive in a world of betrayal. Cascade was born that day, and now his dream was in danger of dying stillborn. Unacceptable.

With a loud clack, bright lights flooded the office from the corner of the ceiling as the battery-powered emergency lights come on automatically.

There was a knock on the door, and it swung open to show Frank Wojtowicz, one of the Magnificent Seven. The big man was wearing an unlaced flak jacket and carrying an M-16 assault rifle. The bayonet on the end shone mirror sharp in the harsh glow of the emergency lighting.

"Report," Mannix snapped, tucking away his lighter.

"We lost all power from the city grid," Wojtowicz answered.

"Orders, sir?" Mannix asked, turning.

"Switch to the backup generator," Woods demanded gruffly.

"Already on it, Chief," Wojtowicz replied. "I sent one of the hackers down to the basement with a flashlight. We should be back on-line in just a couple of minutes."

"Send somebody to keep him company," Mannix said. "We may have intruders."

Bringing the M-16 to his chest in a salute, Wojtowicz nodded in acknowledgment and left, closing the door.

"With the power dead, we can't send the plans over the Internet," Woods said in a deceptively calm tone. "That cell-phone call must have been to make sure I was here, before they pulled the plug."

"But we'll have power back soon enough," Mannix said.

"That was just the opening shot." Lifting the house phone, Woods punched for an outside line and got only silence.

"As expected, the land phone lines are cut, and the radio is jammed," he said, replacing the receiver. Woods was trying hard to control his temper; this wasn't the time to go on a rampage. A million dollars' worth of computers reduced to paperweights because some clerk pulled a plug.

"We can use a cell phone," Mannix offered, pulling out a small model. "Here you go."

"Go ahead and try," Woods muttered.

The man worked his phone for a few minutes, then tucked it away. "Dead," he said grimly. "You're right, it's the Feds. Who else could kill the city power and block all cell phones and the landlines?"

"Navy SEALs, CIA hit team, Delta Force, the secret police, lots of people," Woods said, checking the clip in the Colt .45 pistol.

Mannix threw a glance at the door to make sure it was closed. "Are there really secret police? I know we tell the members that," he said slowly, lowering his arms. "But I thought it was just bullshit to keep them in line."

"It was until today," Woods replied. "However, we've always been too small for them to bother with."

"Not anymore, Chief."

"No, Tommy, not anymore."

Just then the lights returned and the banks of computers in the next room revved back to their usual humming state. With a click, the emergency lights turned themselves off and began recharging their batteries again.

Holstering his weapon, Woods lifted the receiver on the desk. "Security desk," he said, and there came a fast series of clicks.

"Yes, sir?" Brian Ledbetter answered.

"Anything on the video cameras?" Woods demanded.

There was a pause. "They're still down, sir," Ledbetter replied. "Should be back at any second."

Without comment, Woods replaced the receiver.

"They're coming," he stated. "Very well, this is our day to be tested in the fires of war."

"Good! Let them come!" Mannix snarled, going to the wall locker. "We have more than enough firepower and troops!"

Yanking aside the door, he pulled out an M-60 machine gun, and a slung a canvas bag of coiled ammunition belts over a shoulder.

"To fight the whole army? Don't be a fool, Tommy," the leader of Cascade said, glancing at a locked box set on his desk. Inside that were the controls for the self-destruct charges, the poison gas and several other devices that his security team knew nothing about.

In brutal logic Woods knew that the wisest course would be to release the poison gas right now and flood the building. But Mannix wouldn't allow him to do that without giving the others a chance to get to safety first. Fine, if the man wanted to be a hero, so be it. Woods didn't like running, but he hated losing more.

"It seems you can have that fight, Tommy," Woods said grimly, inserting a key into the lock and twisting left, then right, then left once more. The safety disengaged and the thick metal lid of the box lifted up to reveal a set of glowing buttons and a single dial.

Mannix narrowed his eyes at the sight, until Woods closed the lid and tossed him the key. Still holding the M-60 machine gun, Mannix made the catch.

"Left, right, left again," Woods reminded, tapping the box. "Then hit the green button. Tap it twice and you've got ten minutes, three times gives you fifteen. Your call. But don't dawdle, or you're dead."

"No problem," Mannix said, pocketing the key.

"I'll take the plans and head for the tunnel," Woods said, sliding the folder under his arm again. "Use the house phones to direct a recall of our people into the vault. You and the Seven stand guard at the door until the last man is safely inside. Then set the self-destruct charges and meet me down in the tunnel."

"Now you're talking." Mannix grinned, swinging up the breech mechanism to insert a belt of armor-piercing cartridges. "Afterward, the Feds can sift through the rubble for ten years trying to figure out if we escaped or died in the blast."

You mean, whether or not, *I* lived, Woods corrected privately. They'll know for sure about you, hero.

"Exactly, my friend." Peter Woods smiled coldly.

CHAPTER TWENTY-ONE

Matua Island

Approaching Matua Island, James fought the trembling hovercraft over the cresting waves of the surf while the rest of Phoenix Force swept the island with binoculars to try to locate the departure point of the speedboat. Fast and small, the craft was little more than a launch, suitable for ferrying people, but not for very long distances.

"It had to come from something else," McCarter grumbled, adjusting the focus on the binoculars. "A yacht, a seaplane, a base maybe. No way it motored here from the mainland."

There was nothing in sight except fields of grass, hills of wildflowers, evergreen trees, grooves of bamboo and the central volcano, Sarychev Peak. Steam was coming from the craggy top, but that had been happening for a long time. According to Carmen Delahunt, Sarychev hadn't erupted since 1986.

Not today, Lord, McCarter silently prayed, tucking away the binoculars. Please, not today.

Driving the hovercraft out of the ocean and onto the white sandy beach, James eased the physical tension in his shoulders as controlling the machine got noticeably easier. Its operation was a lot smoother with solid ground beneath the three remaining turbines.

"Wichita Thunderbolt, my ass," James muttered, flexing his tired hands.

Seals barked loudly in annoyance as the hovercraft swept by, throwing out a stinging wind of sand. Most of the seals scattered at their approach, the females barking defiantly as their pups scampered behind them for safety. The males snorted challenges and ran away, trying to lure this strange new enemy away from their families.

"These animals are terrified of people," McCarter said in some satisfaction. "But this island is supposed to be deserted. Not even a weather station here."

"Fear like that takes time," Encizo rationalized. "Sounds more like a permanent camp than merely a layover."

"If that's true," Manning said, squinting into the distance, "why would they have Harrison deliver the Chameleon right to their doorstep?" Frowning, the man continued in a rush of words, "Aw shit, they're planning on using the jamming field immediately!"

"But for what?" McCarter demanded, swaying to the motion of the hovercraft as it went around another colony of seals. "What are they planning to do with it, and who are they?"

"Doesn't matter," Hawkins said, craning his neck to look over the lush island. "If the buyers are here, then we'll find them."

"Them?"

"Nobody builds a camp just for himself, and we aced two of their guards already."

"Wish we had gotten a look at the uniforms on those two bodies Harrison threw overboard," Manning said, shifting the huge Barrett slung across his back. He was down to six rounds for the sniper rifle, and who knew what was coming? Swinging up his MP-5 submachine gun, he checked the clip and worked the arming bolt.

"Those sure as hell weren't Russian or Japanese armed forces," Hawkins added.

"Think those men might have been working for the buyers and Harrison did another double cross?" Encizo asked. "Same as he did with Cascade."

"Could be. I'm glad he's dead."

"Traitorous little prick," McCarter growled, unconsciously rubbing his upper arm where his SAS tattoo was located.

The hovercraft dipped low as they flew over a stream, and now a jagged wall of rock formations appeared ahead. The lava ridge rose too high to go over, so James swung the hovercraft onto the beach once more to get around the obstruction.

"Well, their base isn't going to be in the volcano," James said, switching hands on the laboring joystick. "Heck, that's half the island covered already…." His voice trailed away, and the man started swinging the hovercraft back around.

"Trouble?" McCarter demanded, raising his AK-105.

Appearing pensive, James didn't answer at first, then he snarled a virulent oath and drew his MP-5.

"Ambush!" he shouted, firing at the beach.

At first, the rest of Phoenix Force saw nothing but vague outlines in the sand disturbed by their wake. Then the outlines stared to rise and shoot back at the hovercraft with cloth-wrapped rifles.

"Camouflaged!" McCarter snarled, cutting loose with the Kalashnikov in a figure-eight pattern.

But both of the men on the beach dived away from each other. They came out of a roll into firing positions to unleash a burst, then dived away again, pulling out grenades.

Shit! Aiming his AK-105 ahead of one man, Hawkins cut the fellow down with a short controlled burst as he stepped into the stream of lead, then the Kalashnikov jammed. As Hawkins savagely worked the bolt to clear the ejector, he staggered and almost fell when an incoming round from the other gunner hit him the chest, his jumpsuit ripping to expose the molded NATO body armor underneath.

"Etta kuri!" the man snarled in Japanese, throwing the grenade.

McCarter held his breath and shot the grenade out of the air. The glancing blow sent it tumbling yards away before the deadly egg exploded harmlessly.

As the cursing gunner on the beach dropped a clip to frantically reload, James accelerated the hovercraft and went directly over the fellow, only to cut their height in a sharp drop. There was a hard impact, a horrible grinding noise combining with a brief, high-pitched shriek and then red fluids splashed out from under the vehicle in every direction.

Circling about a few times to check for other buried

enemies, James finally landed the hovercraft near the water and killed the motors to save their dwindling supply of fuel. As the struggling motors died away, the sound was replaced by the pervasive noise of the gentle surf.

"So much for covert," Hawkins said, tucking the torn flap of his commando suit into his web harness. "After that grenade, half the island knows we've arrived."

"Good. Saves us the trouble of flushing them out." McCarter hopped out of the craft and started for the dead men.

"Cal, are you sure we can get this thing airborne again?" Encizo asked in real concern, as the machine settled into the beach.

"Hell, no, I'm not," James replied honestly.

"Yeah, thought so," the Cuban said, touching his throat mike. "Stone House, this is Firebird Two. We need an evac ASAP."

Leaving the others to stand guard, McCarter and Hawkins went to check the bloody corpses. The man near the lava ridge was only a mess of tattered clothing, bones and gore. Even his weapon was reduced to splintered wood and seared metal. But thankfully the first man was relatively intact. He lay face upward, his dead eyes staring directly at the sun. One hand still gripped his T-89 assault rifle, a pouch at his side filled with antipersonnel rifle grenades, their stubby shafts sticking up like arrow shafts.

"Good thing he didn't have time to use one of those babies on me," Hawkins commented, nudging the Japanese rifle out of the dead man's fingers. As the T-89 fell away, the left hand turned over, displaying a blue tattoo of three interconnected blue rings.

"I know that design," McCarter said, nudging the hand with the stubby barrel of his compact MP-5. "So Fukoka is the buyer, eh?"

"Nucleus," Hawkins said, as if something foul were in his mouth. "Barb had received a message from Mack that these lunatics were doing something big near Japan. We just naturally assumed it had to with North Korea."

"Nucleus has the Chameleon," McCarter said. "Okay, now we know who."

"Just have to discover where," Hawkins added. "These guys were planted to guard something, probably the entrance."

"Agreed," McCarter said, then touched his throat. "Okay, I want everybody on a recon sweep of the area. We do it by quarters in a five-meter spread, man-on-man coverage. Let's get moving."

Moving fast, the men split into teams and spread across the irregular ground. Watching for more traps, Phoenix Force spiraled out from the hole in the sandy beach used by the gunners, probing everything with EM scanners. But aside from some old Soviet coins and a few recent shell casings, they found nothing important.

Climbing to the top of the lava ridge, Manning looked down into a volcanic caldera, the unnaturally clear water of the sunken crater full of colorful fish, and...

"Get hard, people," Manning said into his throat mike. "We found the bastards."

Spreading out along the ridge to not offer an enemy sniper a group target, the others studied the calm bay and its black rock shoreline. Long cooled, the lava tunnel extended from the direction of the volcano to end in the bay, the waters lapping inside the dark entrance. Shimmering on the surface was the rainbow effect of a gasoline spill.

Grunting in satisfaction at the sight, McCarter started forward at a careful run, with the rest of his team close behind.

Moving off the ridge, the men found a trip wire that was easily circumvented, along with a set of land mines in the loose sand near the shoals. It would waste time to try to disarm them, so Encizo and Manning simply marked the spots by jabbing cold-chemical light sticks into the beach directly alongside the deadly mines and kept going. Glistening with dried salt, the wet rocks were slippery along the shoreline near the tunnel, but the team traversed the area without incident.

Positioning themselves on both sides of the mouth of the tunnel, the men of Phoenix Force used their pocket mirrors to carefully check the interior. Out of the direct sun, the tunnel was dimly illuminated by the light reflected off the dancing waters, but they could still see a wooden dock with two speedboats moored in place, both of them identical to the one used by Davis Harrison. Deeper in the crude dock was a stack of fuel drums set alongside a brick wall painted to resemble the cooled lava. In the middle of the wall were two large steel doors draped with netting.

Using sign language, McCarter directed the men forward. But as the team started to ease into the tunnel along a narrow ledge, the steel doors parted with a sigh and out came several men wearing uniforms like the guards in the speedboat. Only these terrorists were armed with T-89 assault rifles, grenades already tucked into the barrels of the weapons.

Phoenix Force cut loose with their 40 mm grenade launchers, but not at the men. The shells hit the drums of fuel, and the stockpile erupted sending out a blast of flame to race along the tunnel. Diving out of the way, the Stony Man operatives got clear just in the nick of time as the hellish explosion rushed out across the bay like a demonic shotgun blast.

"So much for them using the front door for a while," McCarter said, reloading, as pieces of the smashed dock and burning bodies fell into the clear blue water. "Anybody know how extensive this network of caves might be?"

"I used to do some mountain climbing as a kid and also know a lot about volcanoes," Hawkins said, keeping a watch on the grasslands that rose to meet the steep sides of the volcano. If anybody came toward them from that direction, they'd be spotted.

"Yeah?" McCarter prompted impatiently.

"So if this is a typical volcano," Hawkins continued, "there could be hundreds of underground caves and lava tubes, some of the tunnels extending for miles into the ground."

"A natural maze, eh?"

"Exactly."

McCarter gave a hard smile. "Excellent. That means there's going to be a lot steam vents around. Fukoka will have most of them sealed off, or rigged with explosives."

"Except for a few reserved as emergency exits." Encizo grinned. "Come on, there's a footpath over here that looks pretty well used."

"Good. T.J. is on point," McCarter said as another blast shook the tunnel, sending loose pieces of debris into the turbulent bay. "Gary plays God."

"Got you covered," Manning replied, bringing up the massive Barrett. "Let's move."

CHAPTER TWENTY-TWO

Cascade Headquarters

Limping out of the shadows, Lyons blew away a rushing Cascade guard who was trying to insert a clip into his M-16 rifle. The man died under the maelstrom of lead pellets, the useless weapon still clutched in his fumbling hands.

Reloading, Lyons tried his best to ignore his aching leg. The numbness had changed to a throbbing pain. But the bandage was holding and only a small trickle of blood was coming out from under the adhesive. It hurt, but he would live.

Moving past an array of conveyor belts, the Able Team leader slashed at a coaxial cable on the wall with his knife. It could be for receiving cable TV, but he recognized it as the type used for video cameras, so better safe than sorry.

Starting down a corridor edged with trash from takeout restaurants, he grimaced as he stood tall and held a butane lighter to the fire sensor on the ceiling. But when nothing happened, he abandoned the effort and continued looking for the corpse under the skylight. Apparently, Woods had killed the fire alarm system.

His combat instincts wire sharp, Lyons froze at the sound of a slamming door, closely followed by running boots. Licking dry lips, he stood with a tense finger on the trigger of his heavy weapon and waited until the sound receded into the distance.

Proceeding past a set of swing doors that hung badly off center, Lyons went swiftly down the middle of the hallway where the trash was sparse and stepping on the crunching containers wouldn't reveal his presence. The old building reverberated with echoes from all of the men rushing about searching for him, and that only served to heighten the confusion. Woods was smart and his lieutenant, Mannix, was ruthless, but apparently neither had seriously considered one lone man blitzing through their headquarters. All of the defenses were designed around an invasion of police. Police and the FBI had to follow rules; Lyons worked on the law of the jungle. Kill or be killed.

Suddenly, there was a motion in a shadowy doorway, and Lyons blasted the man before he could bring up the boxy weapon in his hands. Starting past the body, he paused at the startling sight of the Atchisson autoshotgun lying in the bloody arms of the Cascade terrorist. It was a much older model than his, and clearly not augmented by the technical geniuses of the Farm, but it was still one powerful piece of man-stopping artillery.

Kneeling on the filthy floor, Lyons checked the weapon, then slowly stood with an Atchisson clenched in each fist. The balance felt good. Oh, yeah, time to bring a little downtown justice to Peter Woods and his gang of madmen.

The bright red dot of a laser spotter moved across the wall toward Lyons, and he dived to the left, firing both of the autoshotguns behind him. Their combined roar felt like the wrath of God and he heard shattering glass mixed with the wails of dying men.

Rolling to his feet, Lyons spotted two men lying on the floor, one of them holding a Glock 17 equipped with a laser spotter. The red beam was still on and pointed upward at a niche in the wall.

"There he is!" a voice shouted. "Get him!"

Dashing into what seemed to be an old secretarial pool for the factory, Lyons ducked behind the splintery furniture as fiery flowers flashed in the darkness. The incoming rounds hit the floor and walls around him, kicking up puffs of plaster dust. Then the shooters found his distance and savagely pounded the desk he was crouched behind. Listening to the weapons, Lyons could tell the terrorists were firing in unison. A classic beginner's mistake.

Putting as much of his weight as possible on his good leg, Lyons waited for a break in the firing as the group paused to reload together, then he stood and swept the two Atchissons back and forth.

Down the hallway, screaming men disintegrated under the twin onslaught, several of them wearing flak jackets falling to their knees as their lower legs were blown away. Gushing blood, the thrashing men randomly stitched the bare ceiling and then one another with machine-gun rounds. The noise of the two Atchissons was almost beyond endurance, but Lyons gritted his teeth and fought to control the bucking monsters. More terrorists fell away, then one large man exploded into flames as the pressurized fuel tanks of the flame-thrower on his back were ruptured. The expanding fire-ball engulfed all of the terrorists in its chemical inferno, their screams of pain changing to animal-like squeals of agony.

Dropping the spare Atchisson, Lyons started to reload when he noticed a corpse dressed in rags stuffed into a corner. Could this be it, the spot he was searching for? Looking upward, he saw a skylight, but then spun as there came a soft, almost unnoticeable hiss from behind.

Crouching behind the battered desk once more, Lyons grabbed the spare Atchisson and attempted to slide in a magazine of shells as a large section of the graffiti-covered wall broke apart and started to swing away. The massive portal resembled something from an old bank, when the institutions used tons of solid metal to protect their money instead of advanced electronics. The armored door was actually bigger than the one used to protect the War Room at Stony Man Farm. There could be no doubt that was it, the entrance to Cascade!

As the yard of layered steel moved aside, blinding lights flooded the death room, and an army of shadowy men holding automatic weapons started squeezing out of the widening crack.

Instantly, the skylight violently exploded, showering the secretarial pool with glistening shards, and the first men out of the vault died on the spot, the sharp slivers of glass sticking out of their faces and necks. Even be-

fore the concussion of the blast faded, Blancanales and
Schwarz rapelled down from the opening in the roof,
their M-16/M-203 assault rifle combos laying down a
fusillade of mixed ordnance. The 5.56 mm tumblers,
HEAT and armor-piercing rounds cut through the living flesh of Cascade with the expected results.

Favoring his throbbing leg, Lyons stood, but with
only one Atchisson in his grip. Aiming carefully, he
fired off a full clip of fléchettes, the autoshotgun emptying in seconds. But he didn't aim at the other terrorists. With the vault door open, the hydraulic lines were
fully exposed, and the reinforced hoses vanished under
the hellish song of the Atchisson.

Spurting red fluid like a severed artery, the pressurized hoses for the vault came loose to lash about, soaking the terrorists with the slippery liquid.

Dropping to the floor, Blancanales and Schwarz immediately launched 40 mm grenades directly into the
disorganized mob of killers. The blinded men flew
backward out of the doorway under the concussive force
of the antipersonnel rounds.

Blancanales slapped a fresh clip into his M-16/M-203.
"You okay?" he demanded, glancing at Lyons's bloody
leg.

Shifting his weight, the Able Team leader raised the
two smoking Atchissons. "Ask me later," he growled,
starting forward with a slight limp.

Closing the breech of his grenade launcher, Schwarz
moved close to the left side of the former L.A. cop.
Lyons said nothing, but what might have been a smile
flashed on his face for a brief moment.

Taking the point, Blancanales swept into the well-lit room, firing short bursts with every step. The place was full of humming computers, and several people in lab coats fumbled to draw pistols. One of them was firing over a shoulder as he raced for a small door in the nearby wall. Blancanales and Schwarz fired in a figure-eight pattern, cutting down the technicians while Lyons triggered his double shotguns. The fleeing tech was cut in two, and the door was hammered off its hinges. As it crashed onto the floor, Tommy Mannix stepped into sight wearing a flak jacket and cradling a big M-60 in both hands.

"Long live America, you fuckers!" he yelled, triggering the weapon. The belt of ammo shrank fast as the M-60 threw out a stuttering rod of tracer rounds across the computer room. Dropping to the floor, the Able Team commando rolled into shooting positions and returned volley fire. Hit a dozen times, Mannix staggered backward, the M-60 continuing to chatter away, the heavy-duty rounds spewing destruction along the ceiling. Incredibly, the dying terrorist tried to bring the weapon to bear on Able Team once more, and Lyons hit him with both barrels. Mannix was torn asunder, gobbets of flesh flying backward into the office.

Guarding the open vault door, Schwarz stayed with Lyons as Blancanales took the point again and checked the office. There was nobody else in sight, only an open weapons cabinet and a gore-streaked desk with a fancy intercom, a few telephones and a small metal box. Its lid was thrown back to show a single button without any markings.

Even as Blancanales started to warily approach the desk, the box gave an audible click.

Firebase One

ALARMS WERE HOWLING all over the base as Major Fukoka scowled at the video monitors showing the fiery interior of the access tunnel. He couldn't see who the attackers were, but the professional soldier knew the sound of an AK-105 when he heard it. So the Russian army was attacking, eh? That was bad, very bad indeed, but not fatal.

"Sergeant, send all reserve troops to the access tunnel," he commanded. "Have them form a barricade with furniture and prepare to hold off hostile forces."

"At once, sir!" the terrorist replied with a shaky salute. Walking over to a vacant control console, Major Fukoka adjusted the dials until the monitor was filled with a picture of Dr. Tetsuto and several of his people working inside one of the missiles. There was a crude box lying on the catwalk near their shoes, wires dangling from its unpainted sides. One of the new Chameleons. Excellent.

"Dr. Tetsuto," the major said loudly into a microphone, "report on your status immediately!"

"Why? What's going on?" Tetsuto answered, both hands buried in the complicated wiring of the missiles. "Is this some sort of drill you're holding? Most inappropriate, I must state."

Such insolence! "This is no drill, Doctor," Fukoka said, barely controlling himself. "The base is under attack, and we need to launch the missiles immediately."

"Attack, you say?" Tetsuto repeated, pulling out of the

missile to look directly at the video camera. "Launch immediately? But that's impossible!"

"You must—" Fukoka bit his tongue and set his face into a neutral expression. "Why can't we launch? What is wrong with the units?"

"Nothing is wrong with them," the doctor replied, waving a hand at the ICBM. "But I have only a single Chameleon fully installed!"

"Incompetent fool, I'll have your head for this!" Fukoka roared in anger, starting to draw his pistol.

The doctor contemptuously waved the implied threat away as if it were meaningless. "Bah, this is not my fault. They were simply harder to duplicate than estimated. My people only need a few more minutes to finish the job."

"How long?"

"Ten, maybe fifteen minutes."

Fukoka inhaled sharply, then gave a nod of acceptance as if they were old friends discussing a minor matter.

"Accepted, Doctor," the major said. "Report when you are ready."

Hitting the controls, Fukoka killed the circuits and turned to the row of technicians sitting at the other consoles.

"The failure of Dr. Tetsuto must be rewarded," he said in a flat voice. "Prepare to fire all four of the missiles."

"All of them, sir?" a man asked, glancing at the blank screen where the old physicist and his team had just been shown.

"The other three ICBMs will act as protective cover for the one," Fukoka explained curtly.

Most of the technicians exchanged nervous glances, but the one at the fire-control board merely bobbed his head in formal acceptance.

"As you command, sir," he replied, throwing switches. "Beginning countdown in one minute."

"We have no time for that now!" the major barked, placing a hand on the grip of his weapon. "Blow the doors and launch the missiles. Launch them immediately!"

CHAPTER TWENTY-THREE

Cascade Headquarters

"Get hard, guys," Blancanales ordered, stepping from the office, holding a fistful of dangling wires. "Something just went live, and it doesn't seem to have an off switch."

Muttering a curse, Lyons swung about to glance over the row of control consoles, but saw nothing unusual happening. No red lights were flashing, nor were any of the meters showing power spikes.

Standing near the open vault door, Schwarz frowned. "You sure, Rosario?" he demanded.

Stepping over a dead man sprawled on the floor, Lyons joined Blancanales. "Definitely," he stated, shaking the wires. "These were attached to a protected switch inside a locked box on Woods's desk."

"Could be a radio call for help," Blancanales said. "With Bear blocking the airwaves, there's no way of telling."

"Maybe," Lyons agreed, casting the loose wires aside. "But just to be safe, keep the com link open."

Opening his mouth to offer a suggestion, Schwarz unexpectedly started to gag. There was a terrible stink coming from the room outside that cut through the pungent reek of the corpses like a thermite lance. Sweet Jesus, what was that? It was sort of like vinegar, he noted, trying not to breathe. Some sort of industrial solvent perhaps?

Glancing at the ruptured hydraulic lines, Schwarz discounted them as the source when he heard a soft hiss coming from the next room. Peeking carefully around the burnished jamb, Schwarz felt his stomach tighten at the sight of the yellowish mist rising from hidden vents along the old baseboards.

"Mustard gas!" the Stony Man commando cried out, raising an arm to cover his face as he backed into the control room.

Wasting no time, the rest of Able Team moved quickly away from the wide-open door, seeking refuge among the humming computers and slapping handkerchiefs over their noses and mouths as crude protection. Mustard gas was one of the few deadly military gases outlawed by the United Nations as too inhumane for warfare. One good whiff, and the victims writhed in agony, coughing out chunks of their dissolving lungs until merciful death came. There was no cure, or antidote.

The killer gas was also not going to be stopped by a damp piece of cloth like the sleep gas used in Alaska. As the tendrils of yellow gas started wafting past the vault door, the Stony Man commandos frantically looked around for any sort of gas mask, but there was nothing in sight on the walls.

"The arms cabinet!" Lyons said, from behind the cloth. But rushing back into the office, he returned a few seconds later to grimly shake his head in the negative.

Grabbing an empty chair, Schwarz moved it into the middle of the room and climbed on top. Pulling out a butane lighter, he held the flame to a water sprinkler set into the ceiling, but there was no result.

"Son of a bitch Woods knew that water dissolves mustard gas," he muttered, "rendering it nonlethal."

"There must be another way out!" Lyons growled, feeling sweat trickle down his back. "Woods is too smart to let himself be trapped like this! Start searching!"

"There's no time!" Blancanales shouted, patting his chest.

Finding nothing there, the man stepped over and yanked a hand grenade off Schwarz's web harness. Pulling the pin, he whipped the bomb hard and low into the next room. The grenade went out the door and through the swirling yellow fumes to hit the far wall and bounce back to roll behind the heavy steel door.

"Fire in the hole!" he shouted in warning, covering his ears.

Still moving away from the vault, Lyons and Schwarz did the same just as the grenade detonated. The force of the blast shoved the multiton steel door forward to slam shut with a deafening metallic clang. The men of Able team were still reeling from the concussion when they saw tiny snakes of yellow rising from around the vault. The door was closed, but without any pressure from the hydraulic lines, it wasn't sealed. All the grenade had done was buy them a few minutes of life, nothing more.

"Start searching for the exit!" Lyons commanded, grabbing a corpse off the floor and starting to heave it toward the door. But he released the body and backed away. The dead man would help to slow the gas, but only if Lyons could get near enough to place it carefully in position. If he risked a throw, he might hit the door and only jar it farther open and hasten their deaths. Damned if they do, and damned if they don't. Was this it? After a hundred battles, his team was going to snuff it trapped in a computer room?

"Like hell we will," Lyons growled, moving away from the misty yellow door.

Leaving the area, he found the others already busy, throwing open cabinets and kicking over supply boxes. A wealth of illegal weaponry was unearthed, but no disguised exits or gas masks. Working their way along the walls of humming servers that composed the million-dollar Cray, the three men pounded the brick walls and stomped on the terrazzo floor, soon discovering that the computer room took a sharp turn to the left, and then a left again after a short distance. As the men started to take the third left, they slowed to a halt as it was now painfully obvious that the refrigerator-sized units of the Cray went completely around the central office. There was no back room, or even a supply closet.

Retreating to the farthest corner, the men of Able Team caught their breath.

"This is not how I wanted to die," Blancanales snarled, "gassed like a bug in a kid's collection jar!"

Lyons's reply was to rake the ceiling with a long burst from the Atchisson. The foam panels were blown to pieces, revealing only the battered framework sectioning the seamless concrete roof. The former cop said nothing as he reloaded, possibly for the last time.

"Hey, wait a goddamn second," Schwarz said, slinging his assault rifle and walking over to a server different from the others. The unit was the same size and color was the rest, but this one had a glass window in the front that showed a set of spinning reels inside, feeding a strip of magnetic tape past an I/O header.

As a tiny streamer of yellow started snaking around the corner, Schwarz tapped the glass with a knuckle.

"This is a mag reel," he said suspiciously. "What in the world would Cascade want with an antique piece of junk like this when they own a freaking Cray?"

"Only one reason I can think of," Lyons growled, slinging his bulky weapon over a shoulder.

Ignoring the rising chemical stink in the air, the two men took opposite sides of the server and expertly ran their hands over the whirring and clicking machine. Blancanales sharply inhaled as he removed a small blob of C-4 from behind the latch of the window, and Lyons found another rigged to the back access hatch. Then Schwarz slid back a service panel to reveal a simple lever. Grasping the lever, he paused for a moment. This could be another trap, but the mustard gas was almost upon them, so what did the men have to lose?

He yanked the lever.

There was a hard click, and then a ratcheting sound as of protesting gears as the entire refrigerator-sized computer rolled aside on greased tracks to reveal concrete stairs leading into a dark tunnel. Without hesitation, Able Team raced into the blackness as the computer room began to fill with the billowing yellow cloud of toxic death.

Matua Island

STAYING OFF THE FOOTPATH to avoid traps, Phoenix Force raced quickly through the bushy undergrowth and colorful wildflowers. Once away from the beach, the ground became covered with thick grass that stretched ahead of the group for hundreds of yards going up a hillock and heading for the sleeping Sarychev. Checking his Kalashnikov, McCarter frowned slightly as the volcano rumbled, sending up a brief plume of dark smoke to mingle with the white steam.

"What do you think?" Encizo asked, scrutinizing the jagged peak.

"I think if she blows, we die."

"Can the chatter," McCarter subvocalized over his radio, slowing down as he studied the ground. What was this? For no apparent reason, the path across the smooth grass abruptly shifted direction and swung widely around to go through a grove of tall bamboo. A break had been cut through the bamboo, but bare dirt was stubbly with green bamboo shoots as the plants fought to reclaim the missing swatch.

"This makes no sense," James said, scowling. "Bamboo can grow an inch an hour in this kind of climate. They must trim it every day to keep this path clear."

"Which means they have a good reason not to walk

on the grass," Hawkins said, checking a compact EM scanner. "Son of a bitch, the meter is going off the scale!"

"More land mines?" Manning asked, instinctively bringing up his weapon.

"Bigger than that," Hawkins said, putting the scanner away. "A hell of a lot bigger. I think we just found their back door."

"Good," McCarter said. "Remember, we want the Chameleon back, so watch for Fukoka…" McCarter's voice trailed away, as he realized that nobody seemed to be listening. They were all frowning and adjusting their radios transponders.

"Check. One, two, check," McCarter said loud and clear into his mike, a hand touching his earplug. But there was only silence; he didn't even hear the soft hiss of static caused by the solar winds of the sun.

"It must be the jamming field," James stated, checking the power supply on his radio. "They turned it on full force."

"Then it's happening," Encizo growled, twisting his hands on the Kalashnikov as he glanced about the tropical island. "Whatever Fukoka is planning is happening right goddamn now!"

And that grassy field ahead of them had something to do with it.

"Calvin, keep trying to get through," McCarter directed as he stepped off the path and onto the green field. "If they turn the field off, we might get a message through to the Farm."

"Air strike?" Hawkins asked, frowning, staying

abreast of the man. "I think the *Kitty Hawk* aircraft carrier is at Tokyo Harbor."

"A recon at the very least," McCarter agreed, narrowing his eyes as he listened hard to the world around them. "Something is very wrong, and I do not like it one little bit." Everything had gone unnaturally still around them. There were no more birds singing in the nearby trees, no insects chirping, just dead silence.

"Got you covered, D-D-David," James replied, his face registering surprise as the ground started to shake with growing violence directly under their boots. "What the hell is going on here?" the man demanded, clutching his weapon.

Fighting to stay standing, Encizo cast a fast appraisal at the volcano. But the peak of Sarychev was still misty white, with no telltale displays of ash or smoke.

"Is this an earthquake? No, look there!" Manning declared, watching the grass ahead of them start to swell upward into a low dome.

Suddenly, the swell broke part into sections, triangular pieces flipping backward on thick metal hinges and throwing out a spray of loose soil. Now a large circular hole was exposed in the ground, its sides lined with ferruled sheets of unpainted metal and brick support columns. Streamers of white clouds rose out of the pit and vanished instantly in the sunlight.

Harboring a horrible suspicion as to what was happening, McCarter rushed to the edge of the opening and boldly looked down with his Kalashnikov at the ready. The swirling mists were thick, but not dense enough to hide some flashing red lights far below. Then the mists parted to reveal the all too familiar nose cone of a huge missile. It was a North Korean ICBM!

As a breath of arctic cold rose from the hole, McCarter realized that the white stuff wasn't mist or smoke, but evaporating fuel from the titanic engines of the missile! A combination of liquid oxygen and liquid hydrogen, the same as NASA used for the space shuttle. He started to shout a warning to the others when he spotted some Japanese pictographs neatly painted across the tip, along with a single crude word in English—Washington.

"They're launching at D.C.!" Encizo snarled, craning his neck to see into the frigid pit. "Sons of bitches painted a hello on it."

Bringing up his AK-105, Encizo aimed, but withheld firing. ICBMs were built to withstand the awful pressures of flying at Mach speed, two, maybe three times the speed of sound. Could the rounds from the Kalashnikov even dent this Korean colossus?

"Heads up!" Hawkins shouted as three more ground swells formed, and broke apart across the grassy field. "A goddamn flight of birds is being launched!"

James reached for his radio, then stopped. The transmission couldn't be heard ten feet away by the other members of Phoenix Force, so what was the chance it might reach halfway around the world? Whirling, James took off at a full sprint. Then again, the Chameleon had to have some sort of a range limitation. If he could just get far enough away from the jamming unit…

"Come in, Stone House!" James shouted into his silent radio, boosting the power to maximum. "Birds are flying for D.C.! Repeat, birds aimed at D.C.!" Then on gut instinct, he changed the settings to the international channel. "CQ calling CX!" he yelled into the throat mike, using the code to demand a response from anybody who could hear. "CQ calling CX! Mayday! Mayday! This is an emergency!"

"Grenades and C-4!" McCarter ordered, yanking two grenades off his web harness. The fuel lines would stay attached to the rockets until the very last second, constantly pumping in fuel to keep their tanks absolutely full. There were safety valves and automatic cutoffs, but those wouldn't do a thing if they got enough thermite and willy peter down those launch tubes.

Deep in his heart, the Phoenix Force leader didn't think the plan would work, but he refused to just stand still and do nothing as millions of people were murdered. North Korean missiles hitting Washington, D.C.? Christ almighty, that could be the start of World War III!

Just then, a low rumble sounded from below, the sound repeating from every silo as the entire field began to tremble slightly. A blast-furnace rush of hot air dispelled the icy mists, leaving the missiles in stark clarity.

"They've gone to prelaunch!" Manning cursed, casting away the Kalashnikov. "These babies are going to fly at any second!" Which meant there was no time to even try to disable the colossal ICBM! Manning ignored the powerful Barrett and ripped open the flap on a satchel charge of C-4, rushing to set the detonator for impact instead of time delayed.

Pulling out their own grenades, Claymore mines and another satchel charge, the other Phoenix Force commandos joined the two men at the edge of the silo. Then, tilting his head, McCarter raised a closed fist. The team went motionless at the silent command, and the Briton strained to hear the new noise over the building rumble of the missiles. For a second, he thought maybe it had just been a trick of wind, but then it came again, screaming Japanese voices from another silo. Civilians?

Debating for a full second, McCarter rushed over to the next hole and looked down inside to just barely see a small group of people in lab coats pounding on a closed door at the end of a catwalk. Far below them, writhing fire washed around the base of the ICBM as the engines rapidly increased the tempo of its fuel pumps to avoid deadly pooling as it built to full thrust.

McCarter frowned at the plight of the trapped missile technicians. Fukoka was killing some of his own people to do a fast and dirty launch. The bastard! It had to be because Phoenix Force was there. Uncaring about the fate of the trapped terrorists, McCarter started to turn away when he caught sight of the side of the missile. His entire universe seemed to focus in on the single brief glimpse. Open. The service panel was still wide open, the vulnerable internal machinery and circuits of the North Korean missile fully exposed!

"This one!" McCarter bellowed over a shoulder, preparing to throw the two grenades. "Aim for the catwalk!"

The noise and heat were steadily increasing from the silo as the screams of the technicians rose to raw-throated shrieks of blind panic.

As the others rushed to join their commander at the second silo, Hawkins cast a furtive glance at the missile marked for D.C. before joining them. As he arrived, he gave McCarter a hard stare that demanded an explanation. Still holding his grenades, McCarter jerked his chin downward. Hawkins followed the gesture and broke into a feral grin. Hell, yes!

A rush of billowing smoke and searing fumes started rushing from the underground silos.

"Now!" McCarter roared as he threw the grenades, even though he knew nobody could possibly hear him.

Their faces grimly intent, the rest of the team cast down their explosives. Then they did it again with the rest of the grenades.

Grabbing Hawkins and Manning by the shoulders, McCarter pulled them away from the silo and started running for the bay in the caldera. Wasting precious seconds, Encizo threw down a belt of 40 mm shells before joining the others. He knew that if the warheads were nuclear, they were all dead men from the fallout, if not from the initial thermonuclear reaction. But if the payloads in the warheads were conventional ordnance, then the team still had to make sure these death machines never reached American soil. There would be no second chance at this. It was all or nothing the first time.

Sprinting at full speed down the footpath, the men of Phoenix Force could only guess when the grenades went off, the explosions lost in the earthshaking power of the lifting North Korean missiles.

Then twin thunder announced the detonation of the satchel charges, the double load of C-4 sharply punching through the strident rumblings. The fiery noise of one missile took on a new and different aspect, deeper in tone, less controlled. There came the gut-wrenching scream of tortured metal, closely followed by a blinding flash of hellish light that seemed to fill the sky and turned the landscape black and white.

Knowing what to expect next, the running men dropped their rifles and covered their ears. A split second later, the shock wave arrived with triphammer force, the monstrous concussion slamming the men off the ground and sending them airborne.

Horrible searing heat hit the tumbling Stony Man warriors just before they splashed into the blessed relief of the cool saltwater bay. Instantly, years of training took hold and the members of Phoenix Force knifed away from the surface, diving fast for the imagined safety of the sandy bottom. They were halfway there when the entire bay shook to a massive detonation even more powerful than the first. Churning sand blinded them as there came worse heat and brighter flashes. Savage concussions pummeled them as they fought to ride out the underwater maelstrom, and retain their precious single breath of air amid total and absolute chaos.

CHAPTER TWENTY-FOUR

Gary, Illinois

Racing along the brick-lined tunnel, Peter Woods reached a sheet of plywood blocking the end. He kicked out hard, and the wood broke free with the sound of splintering wood.

Shoving his way through the splintery material, Woods entered a vast warehouse. The floor was empty aside from a thick coat of dust, and the air was dry and tasted stale. Good. This close to the river, the reek of the polluted water would have clung on for weeks before dissipating. Nobody had been in here for quite a while.

This warehouse was his private domain. The loading dock was the logical place for people to breech the factory defenses, which meant his beloved Rolls-Royce was now in the hands of the police. So be it. Just another sacrifice in the name of America. But that was why he had a second escape tunnel built without informing the rest of Cascade. What they didn't know couldn't be forced from them by any amount of torture.

Tucking the pouch tighter under his arm, Woods stood for a moment listening for any sounds coming down the tunnel. There had only been silence so far, but he expected to hear the sounds of the self-destruct charges going off at any moment. He had told Mannix only a piece of the truth. The charges would go off once set, but only after sixty seconds, not fifteen minutes. Just enough time for Mannix to close the vault door before everything was obliterated by the blast. Two tons of TNT was no atomic explosion, but it would certainly blow the entire factory to hell and back.

Crossing the room, Woods went past the plastic trunk filled with spare clothing, weapons and money and broke a wax seal on a bolt to throw open the one door. All of the others had been bricked shut by his own hands. Just a little added insurance in case of federal intervention.

Shoving the heavy door open, Woods blinked as he stepped into bright sunlight. He was in a small courtyard enclosed with tall fencing that was topped with concertina wire. There were a few scraps of stained cloth fluttering from the military razor wire showing that some fool had tried to get over and failed in the attempt. Briskly crossing the yard, Woods kicked open a locked metal box marked High Voltage and then smashed a glass insulator knob. Removing a small key from inside, he went to the only gate in the fencing, undid all three of the locks with the same key and threw open the gate.

Proceeding down the alley, Woods ignored the looks he got from the homeless people and exited onto the city sidewalk. There were some teenagers lounging by a liquor store, and a pair of old men playing checkers on a stone bench near what once had been a city park. Nobody paid the millionaire terrorist any attention at all as he started toward the nearby highway, the folder of schematics still safely tucked under his arm.

Firebase One

STAGGERING OUT of the choppy bay, the gasping men of Phoenix Force walked onto the war-torn beach.

Pausing to catch their breath, the team found unidentifiable wreckage strewed everywhere, bits of charred machinery and general debris mixing with chunks of smoking turf and the occasional human remains. Looking inland, McCarter saw with some satisfaction that plumes of black smoke were rising from the ruins of the grassy field, tongues of wild orange flame licking upward from the charred remains of the four silos.

"Mess with the best," McCarter muttered, lurching forward.

"Die like the rest," Hawkins agreed under his breath, reclaiming his dropped assault rifle.

Brushing off the damp sand, Hawkins grimaced at the sight of a bend in the barrel. Tossing the broken weapon aside, he drew a 9 mm Beretta from his hip holster and racked the slide. One of the benefits of the 9 mm weapon was that a brief soak in the ocean wouldn't bother it in the least. Searching along the path, McCarter and Encizo found their own assault rifles in similar unusable condition, so each pulled out his per-

sonal side arm. Manning discovered his Barrett undamaged, although the barrel and breech were choked
solid with wet sand.

"Hey," James spoke over the radio, "I'm glad to see
you all alive."

"Calvin?" McCarter said, touching his throat mike as
he looked about. "Where the hell are you?"

"Behind the lava ridge," James said, rising into view
down the shoreline. He waved and said something else,
but the words were garbled by a brief crackle of static
precisely as something exploded below the grassy field,
throwing fresh material skyward.

"And there go the diesel generators," Manning said,
trying to work the bolt. The action was stiff, and there
was a nasty grinding sound of sand in the works. Slinging the weapon across his back, he drew a .357 Magnum Desert Eagle and dropped the clip to check the
load, before slapping it back into the grip once more.

"Firebird Three, this is Firebird One. Repeat, please,"
McCarter ordered.

"Roger," James replied. "I said I went behind the
ridge hoping it might help with the jamming field." There
was another underground explosion. "Well, it didn't," he
continued. "But the lava served as a pretty good buffer
from the shock wave when the missiles blew."

"Glad to hear it. Get the backup weapons from the
hovercraft."

James turned, showing a cluster of Heckler & Koch
MP-5 submachine guns hanging over his back.

"Spare ammo, too," he said, smiling widely.

Rendezvousing with James near the lava cave, the

Stony Man commandos rearmed with their standard weaponry, and distributed the extra ammunition.

"Grenades?" Hawkins asked, stuffing magazines into a pouch on his web harness.

"Sure," James replied, tossing him one. "But do you really think we're going to need any more?"

Just then, a fiery detonation ripped open a section of the bamboo grove, throwing a shotgun blast of bodies and machinery into the smoky air.

"Not a chance," Manning answered honestly, shouldering the weapon as he brushed back his soaked hair.

"Now comes the fun part," McCarter said, eyeing the lava cave. "We confirm the Chameleon is destroyed."

"In there?" Encizo asked incredulously, jerking a thumb at the burning field. "David, do you really think there's a chance in hell that device is still recoverable?"

"Only one way to find out," McCarter answered resolutely, reaching into a pocket for a cigarette. He found the sodden pack, crumpled it into a wad and threw it away. Maybe it was time to quit smoking.

The other men looked hard at the mouth of the cave as if it were the barrel of a loaded cannon. In the background, explosions racked the distant field.

"Bring the Chameleon back intact, or confirm it has been destroyed," James said grimly, shifting his boots on the sand. "Those were the orders."

"Well, shoot," Hawkins drawled in a pronounced Texas accent, working the arming bolt on his MP-5, "who wants to live forever?"

Brief smiles appeared at the ancient battlefield joke,

and readying their weapons, Phoenix Force started forward together.

Splashing along the shoals, the warriors walked into the dim cave, the cracked walls of the interior dancing with reflected sunlight off the choppy water. The earlier fire was out, the barrels only blackened metal by now, but the steel doors were still closed tight.

Even as Encizo pulled out a block of C-4, the doors parted with a screeching noise, and volumes of thick smoke poured out, heralding the advance of a score of coughing people. Many of them were badly burned or dripping blood. Several were limping badly, Japanese assault rifles being used in lieu of crutches.

One of the terrorists shouted something in Japanese, and in spite of their serious wounds, the surviving members of Nucleus fumbled to pull out weapons. In unison, Phoenix Force knelt and returned fire, the barrage of incoming rounds tearing the Japanese criminals apart.

"You speak Japanese," Encizo said to Manning, climbing onto the dock. "What did he say?"

"He thought we were Russian special forces," Manning answered, covering the doorway until it was his turn to climb out of the water. "And that it was better to die in battle than under the questioning knife."

Questioning knife…military torture? Encizo arched an eyebrow at that in disgust, but said nothing.

Now with nobody living to block their way, the Stony Man commandos walked through the tilting doorway and into the enemy base. The belly of the beast.

Waves of hot air were rushing outward, carrying the reek of chemicals and hot metal. The ceiling crawled with smoke, and alarms sounded constantly. After only a few yards, Hawkins started blowing away the speakers with well-placed shots from his sidearm just to kill the annoying noise.

Broken and smoldering bodies lay scattered about, the floor itself sagging in spots as it partially melted from the tremendous heat below. Most of the doors lining the corridor were wide open, showing only death and destruction. A few of the rooms were dark, and the team broke cold-light sticks and tossed them in to ascertain the condition. Apparently very few of the members of Nucleus had survived the backblast of the underground missiles, in spite of the fact that launch silos were supposed to be able to contain just this sort an explosion, and for obvious reasons.

"Must have been short on funds," Manning said, aiming his MP-5 at the chest of a gurgling terrorist slumped over in a corner.

The man's shirt was slashed to ribbons, his belly yawning wide and trembling hands tried to hold in his ropy intestines. A long crimson trail stretched behind the vivisected man, showing his pitiful struggle to escape the depths of the destroyed base. But even if a medevac unit were on-site it would have made no difference; the terrorist was a dead man and nothing could save him.

In brutal mercy, Manning ripped a burst into the chest of the dying terrorist.

"Agreed," McCarter said, over the radio. "Anything near the launch bays will be destroyed, which means less for us to search. A liquid-oxygen–liquid-hydrogen fire burns as hot as thermite and doesn't leave much behind." He paused to fire at a movement in the murky shadows. A Japanese man cried out and fell into the light, dropping a pistol. "But we need to check the control room, offices and their repair bay, service dock, whatever," McCarter finished, moving onward.

"And blow the computers," Encizo added, sending a burst from his MP-5 into a room. There was an answering scream that abruptly stopped. "Just in case."

Suddenly, a terrorist rushed from an open doorway, holding an assault rifle with a bayonet. Hawkins killed him on sight.

"Fair enough," he growled, dropping the spent clip and reloading while walking.

Coming out a cloud of smoke, a coughing terrorist stumbled into the corridor clutching his bloody arm. McCarter was instantly alert. The man's face was badly blistered, but his uniform jacket was oddly clean, as if it came from somebody else.

James stepped in front of the terrorist and raised his MP-5.

"Eai! Eai!" the fellow cried out, crouching low as if bracing for a death blow. Tears started running down his cheeks.

Inhaling sharply, James stepped aside and waved the wounded man past.

But as the fellow hurried by, McCarter noticed that the usual tattoo of three blue circles was on the back of the man's right hand. His right, not the left like everybody else.

"It's Major Fukoka!" McCarter snarled, whirling and aiming from the hip.

At the sound of his name, the leader of Nucleus pulled a .40-caliber pistol from under his bleeding arm. McCarter and Fukoka fired at the exact same instant.

In an explosion of pain, white-hot light filled the universe and McCarter began to fall into a stygian blackness that seemed to stretch on forever.

Main Street, Gary

BURSTING OUT OF the dark tunnel, Able Team charged into the empty warehouse, weapons looking for danger. There was nobody in sight.

"Floor!" Blancanales said, pointing downward.

His teammates grunted in acknowledgment. In the thick dust there was a single set of footprints heading to an open door across the building.

Wary of traps and snipers, the team moved out of the building and into a small fenced courtyard with an open gate that led to an alley.

HURRYING DOWN Main Street, Woods saw that traffic was busy at the intersection as usual. Boldly walking into the middle of the street, the man suddenly staggered and clutched at his chest, then fell to his knees on the hard asphalt. Several cars just zoomed past the reeling man until a car with Ohio license plates braked to halt and a young woman rushed out.

"Oh, my God, are you all right?" she asked in concern. "Do you need an ambulance?"

Calmly, Peter Woods pulled the Colt from under his jacket and shot her in the throat. Bright red blood pumped out of her neck in long arcs from the ghastly wound. Gurgling horribly, the woman fell to the street, trying to block the flow of her life with both hands to no avail.

Whistling softly, Woods took her car keys from the street alongside her, got in her car and drove away. So far, his escape plan had worked perfectly. By now the factory was filled with poison gas, and there wasn't a living member of Cascade remaining to tell the FBI about him, or identify Woods in court. Had the Feds really thought that they could stop him with a surprise raid? Pitiful. It was just another example of how weak America had become. Nobody would go the distance anymore; nobody cared enough to do whatever was necessary to save their nation. All he needed now was a computer store so that he could get on-line and start sending the files out across the Internet.

At the corner, Woods started to drive through a red light, but then saw a police car idling at the curb near a coffee shop. Forcing his expression into neutral, Woods impatiently waited for the blasted light to change. He briefly looked at the assortment of stores lining Main Street, then dismissed them. A computer store in Gary? Not likely. Such luxuries weren't sold in this town, but they would be closer to Midway Airport. In just a few more minutes this would be all over, and then nothing could stop the long-awaited genesis of a new America. A strong, clean, white America. Oh, God, it would be so glorious when the rioting started in the streets.

In the distance, somebody was screaming for the police, and it took everything Woods had not to glance in the rearview mirror. Even in downtown Gary, eventually somebody would call for the cops after finding a body in the road. The police hurried out of the coffee shop holding steaming foam cups and jumped into their vehicle to race away with the lights flashing. The moment the police turned the corner and were out of sight, Woods drove through the intersection and headed for Interstate 55. He wondered if the fight between the Bloodhawks and the Comanches was over.

As the entrance ramp came into sight, Woods noticed three men running down the street. A big blonde with a bloody leg, a beefy guy and a stocky fellow with a mustache. All of them were wearing military web harness and carrying automatic weapons.

The Feds had found him! Stomping on the accelerator, Woods cut off another car and swerved around a pothole trying to reach the ramp.

BLANCANALES AND Schwarz fired rounds from their M-203 launchers. The 40 mm shells of willy peter hit the ramp and detonated into a sea of raging fire. Spitting obscenities, Woods cut hard to avoid the flames and crashed through a wooden safety barrier. The impact crumpled the fender of his stolen car, but barely slowed its speed.

Bracing himself with his good leg, Lyons cut loose with the Atchisson and blew the bottom off a telephone pole at the far corner. The base exploded into splinters, the spread of steel fléchettes peppering the brick wall behind. Trailing wires, the pole crashed into the street, and Woods wildly banked again to escape a collision.

Now the millionaire terrorist was directly facing the three men. As Able Team swiftly reloaded, Woods pulled out his Colt and pressed the gas pedal to the floor. As the car surged forward, he started firing out the window.

"Wait for it," Lyons ordered gruffly, his aching leg dripping blood.

The windshield of a parked car near Able Team shattered from the hot lead of the booming Colt, then the munitions bag hanging at Schwarz's side jerked as a .45 slug tore through the material. Gritting his teeth, he tightened his hands on the assault rifle, but did nothing else.

"Almost there…" Blancanales muttered.

The racing car was almost upon them when the scrambling civilians on the sidewalk behind the vehicle finally got out of the line of fire.

"Now!" Lyons shouted, triggering the Atchisson.

Together, Blancanales and Schwarz stepped away from each other and fired, unleashing a hellstorm of antipersonnel rounds. The fléchettes from the Atchisson ripped a path of destruction along the side of the car, tearing off the side panels and removing the hand holding the booming Colt. At the same moment, the barrage of lead buckshot from the grenade launchers blew out both of the left-side tires of the oncoming car.

Shrieking in agony, Woods tried to steer with the ragged stump, but the slippery blood got all over the steering wheel and he completely lost control. Veering wildly, he sat helpless as the stolen car went straight past Able Team to careen off an abandoned van and plow through the display window of a closed store. Glass went flying everywhere, and a burglar alarm started loudly clanging.

Softly in the distance, police sirens were starting to cut the air. Slapping in his last clip, Lyons limped toward the store and blew open the door to enter the establishment. His teammates stayed in the street, pulled back to give cover fire if necessary. They knew what had to be done to finish this dirty job.

Tilting slightly, the car was fully inside the store, its front end surrounded by the remains of a counter. The busted cash register lay on the floor, the open till empty. Everything was covered with twinkling shards of glass.

Struggling and cursing in the front seat of the vehicle, Woods was bleeding from a dozen small cuts as he fumbled to tighten a leather belt around the ragged end of his forearm. As Lyons approached, Woods cinched the belt tight and the rush of blood slowed to a mere trickle.

"Where are the plans?" Lyons demanded, loud and clear.

His face distorted with pain and rage, Woods spit, "Fuck you, pig! I want my lawyer!"

"Not this time, murderer," Lyons said in a voice from the grave, and sent the remaining few cartridges in the Atchisson into the front of the car. Under the roaring assault, the hood was torn away and the hot engine immediately woofed into flames as the fuel lines were completely shredded.

"What in hell are you doing?" Woods screamed in raw panic, fumbling at the door latch. "Get me out of here, you fool!"

But as the door came open, Lyons kicked it shut again.

"This is the last time I ask," he growled, dropping the shotgun and pulling out his .357 Colt Python. "Where are the plans for the Chameleon?"

Woods started in openmouthed shock at the grim warrior, then his eyes got hard. "You'll never find them without me," he panted, sweating dripping from his pale face. The shock of the injury was wearing off, and the real pain was starting to make itself known.

Lyons said nothing as he leveled the barrel of the Python. To Woods the black opening loomed like the end of the world.

"You can't do this to me!" the millionaire screamed, staring in horror at the rising flames.

With a grim expression, Lyons coldly clicked back the hammer.

"Okay, okay! I surrender! Name your price! I'm rich! You can have anything you want!" the terrorist yelled, raising his gore-streaked stump as if imploring sympathy. But there was none.

"Anything!" Woods begged, shifting his legs away from the increasing heat coming from the engine. "Please! Just get me the hell out of here!"

"The plans," Lyons said in a monotone. "And no more talk."

Licking his dry lips, Woods's eyes took on a wild look. Then he slumped his shoulders and nodded weakly. "Fine, here they are," he whispered, shoving the folder out the open window. "You win. Take it. The unit is yours now."

Lyons flicked a fast glance at the folder, then back at

Woods just as the man brought a small .44 derringer into view. Moving in a blur, Lyons slapped the weapon aside just as it discharged, the two rounds blowing gaping holes in the roof on the burning car.

With a snarled curse, Woods dropped the empty weapon. "You...you're no cop! What are you!" he demanded, all of the fight gone from his voice.

"Everything you're not," Lyons replied, and stroked the trigger of the Python once. As the dark hole appeared in his forehead, the rear of his head made a crimson geyser across the car, and Woods flopped backward onto the passenger seat, his anguished face relaxing into death.

Lyons lifted the folder off the floor, carefully checking the papers and computer disks inside. When he was satisfied, the Stony Man commando limped forward and tossed the folder onto the crackling flames. There was no way to know if any additional copies had been made, but there was nothing he could do about that right now.

"You! Drop that gun!" a new voice commanded. "This is the police!"

Lowering his piece, but not letting go, Lyons stood and watched the waterproof folder melt away, then the pages of schematics and blueprints started to turn brown and smolder.

"I said drop the gun, buddy!" the cop demanded, coming closer, his shoes cracking the loose glass on the floor.

Out of the corner of his vision, Lyons noted that the young cop was standing properly with his legs apart, two hands on the Glock 17, ready and fully prepared to blow him away.

"I want a lawyer," Lyons said, stalling for time. The sheets of paper burst into flames, the silvery finish of the disk peeling away, then suddenly flashing into smoke as it reached critical temperature.

"Look, drop the gun and back away from the car," the cop commanded. "It's gonna blow when that fire reaches the gas tank!"

Outside, there came the howl of another police siren, followed by the squeal of brakes and doors slamming. The backup had arrived. Time to surrender. But he still had to wait until the files were utterly destroyed, with no chance of a rescue and recovery.

Suddenly, there were flickering lights under the chassis. "She's going to blow!" the cop shouted, backing away, more glass cracking at every step. "Come on, buddy, this is no place to die!"

On that point, Lyons fully agreed, but he still delayed a few seconds until the last schematic crumbled into ash.

"I'm coming out!" he shouted, dropping the Python.

Turning, Lyons charged for the doorway as fast as possible with his bad leg. Several police were there with fire extinguishers and drawn pistols. Two of them rushed forward to grab Lyons and bodily haul him away from the crash site and throw him to the pavement.

"Freaking lunatic," a cop muttered, keeping Lyons covered while another officer snapped on the handcuffs. "Didn't you know that—"

The chastisement was interrupted when the store thunderously erupted into a fireball, the roiling blast throwing out a wave of glass and smoldering debris.

"Son of a bitch!" one cop yelled, rocking to the concussion.

As the rolling echo died away, several of the cops raced to the window to spray CO_2 onto the burning car wreck, but the carbon dioxide blanket seemed to have little effect on the gasoline-based inferno.

After reading Lyons the Miranda rights, the police carried the wounded Stony Man commando to a nearby squad car and locked his handcuffs to a thick ring firmly bolted to the floor. Then they left to divert traffic and handle the mob of gawking civilians.

In fairly short order, fire trucks arrived to handle the blaze, and a howling city ambulance parked alongside the squad car. However, considering the circumstances of his arrest, the police refused to relinquish their prisoner, but did allow an EMT do some quick repairs to the wound in their prisoner's thigh. When the cloth was cut away, the damage was a lot worse than he had thought, and Lyons had no objections when the paramedic gave him a shot of local anesthesia along with some antibiotics, tetanus and several other medicinal concoctions.

Even before the local took effect, the EMT started stitching the wound closed, and Lyons looked out the windows to take his mind off the needlework. Across the street, he saw Blancanales and Schwarz lounging near a garbage bin, and they didn't have a weapon in sight. Very good. That was fast work.

Touching a finger to his ear, Schwarz let him know that the Farm had been informed about the situation. Arching an eyebrow, Blancanales asked a silent question.

Turning away from them, Lyons nodded to show that the job was done. Then he settled back and tried to relax as the EMT started to wrap the freshly closed wound with clean bandages.

As the infusion of drugs began to take effect, Lyons felt himself starting to fall asleep and briefly wondered how David McCarter and Phoenix Force were doing.

EPILOGUE

Washington, D.C.

A roaring fire blazed in the eighteenth-century hearth, and an antique clock ticked loudly on a priceless Hoban drum table. Outside the widows, the rising green of the Jefferson Mounds could be seen framing the world-famous rose garden, and in the far distance rose the shimmering white needle of the Washington Monument.

"Six hours?" the President said, leaning forward to rest both arms on the desk. "You got him out in six hours?"

With its thick doors firmly shut, the Oval Office felt miles away from the daily hustle of the White House. Reclining in a wing-back chair older than the state of New York, Hal Brognola always felt as if the room had been freshly painted only hours earlier, even though he knew better. The filtered air was cool and clean, smelling faintly of flowers and furniture polish. The expensive rugs were freshly vacuumed just that morning, and every inch of the famous room had been electronically swept by the U.S. Secret Service for bugs and other spying devices every hour on the hour.

"Yes, sir."

"Purely for the sake of curiosity," the President asked, "how was it done so quickly?"

"Our cybernetic team simply had the Stony Man operative transferred to a federal jail, one that doesn't exist except on paper," Brognola explained with a smile. "We've done this sort of thing before, sir."

"Lord knows I wish the CIA was that effective," the President said with a tired sigh. It had been along day for the Man. "And what is the status of the device in question. Has it been recovered?"

Brognola shifted uncomfortably in his chair. Even here in the Oval Office, the Man refused to say certain things aloud. Paranoia or common sense? In politics, those were often the exact same thing.

"The Chameleon has been destroyed, sir," Brognola reported. "The one prototype and all of the files are gone."

"Destroyed? Damn it, Hal—"

"It was either that or lose it to the world," Brognola replied firmly. "My people made the choice in the field, and paid a high price to get it done."

The President leaned back in his chair and regarded Brognola sternly. Very few people were allowed to talk to him this way. It was a breath of fresh air and a pain in the ass at the same time.

"Accepted," the President finally said. "And how is David?"

"Thankfully, he'll live. Round bullets almost always

glance off a round skull. It's why we use hollowpoints and armor-piercing rounds for a sure kill."

Lacing his fingers, the President merely grunted at that.

"He'll be out on medical for a few weeks," Brognola went on, "then I'm sending him on a vacation for some R&R before putting him back on the duty roster."

"Please send him my best wishes for a speedy recovery."

"Thank you, sir. I will."

"However, during his absence, what will become of his team?" the President asked, gesturing with one hand.

"Somebody else will run the team until he returns," Brognola answered.

Sensing no further information was coming on the topic, the President glanced at a report on his desk marked with a red-stripped border showing it was a level-ten security document, for his eyes only. "I understand the damage to the Nucleus base on Matua Island was considerable," he asked slowly. "Were there any additional survivors aside from the rash Major Fukoka?"

"Not when my team left, no, sir," Brognola said bluntly.

The Man pursed his mouth at the statement as if it left a bad taste in his mouth.

"Accepted, Hal. And what was the breakage?" the President finally asked.

Brognola scowled deeply, and didn't reply.

The President scowled back. Brognola often hit him with the brutally logical argument, that if his field team could do the job, then at the very least the damn politicians could call the acts by their right name. His people didn't "relocate an unwilling witness"—they kidnapped the bastard. And they didn't "terminate with extreme prejudice"—they shot people dead. Calling these acts something different didn't wash away the blood any faster.

"Fine," the President relented. "How many people died, Hal?"

"Sir, it was a near thing, but we didn't lose a man," Brognola said. "On the other hand, you can scratch two terrorist organizations. Put together, Cascade and Nucleus don't have enough manpower to hold a poker game."

"Sounds like an excellent job, Hal," the President said with a weary grin. "Good work, as usual."

Lifting the security document off the blotter, the President fed it into a slot built into the desk. There came a brief series of whines as the government shredder annihilated the documents into dust.

"So much for portable stealth technology," the President said, reaching for a carafe to pour himself a cup of black coffee. Not his first for the day, and far from the last. "Thank God it's finally over."

"Amen to that," Brognola murmured.

James Axler
Outlanders®

EVIL ABYSS

An ancient kingdom harbors awesome secrets...

In the heart of Cambodia, a portal to the eternal mysteries of space and time lures both good and evil to its promise. Now, a deadly imbalance has not only brought havoc to the region, but it also threatens the efforts of the Cerberus warriors. To have control of the secrets locked deep within the sacred city is to possess the power to manipulate earth's vast energies…and in the wrong hands, to alter the past, present and future in unfathomable ways….

Available February 2005 at your favorite retail outlet.

Or order your copy now by sending your name, address, zip or postal code, along with a check or money order (please do not send cash) for $6.50 for each book ordered ($7.99 in Canada), plus 75¢ postage and handling ($1.00 in Canada), payable to Gold Eagle Books, to:

In the U.S.	**In Canada**
Gold Eagle Books	Gold Eagle Books
3010 Walden Avenue	P.O. Box 636
P.O. Box 9077	Fort Erie, Ontario
Buffalo, NY 14269-9077	L2A 5X3

Please specify book title with your order.
Canadian residents add applicable federal and provincial taxes.

GOLD EAGLE®

GOUT32

THE DESTROYER

NO CONTEST

The Extreme Sports Network is the cash cow feeding off America's lust for blood, guts and sex disguised as competitive athletics. From Extreme Rail Surfing to Extreme Nude Luge to the excruciatingly gory Extreme Outback Crocodile Habitat Marathon, it's ESN's life-or-death thrill ride to high ratings. But why—an outraged international community demands—do Americans always win and Europeans…die?

The answer, Remo suspects, lies in Battle Creek, Michigan….

Available January 2005 at your favorite retail outlet.